"SPARKS?"

"If you and I aren't destined to get back together, you'd think we'd stop generating sparks." John focused his gaze back on hers. "All you have to do is walk in a room, and I'm lost. I want you. Just you."

At the intensity in his voice, Spring slipped away.

John caught up to her and took her hand. "I wish you would stop running from me."

He kissed her before she could raise a protest. After an initial startled groan, she didn't resist at all. Her arms looped around his shoulders. Her body pressed against his. Willingly. Tantalizingly. He curved one hand over her breast. How right it was to feel her, hold her, lose himself in her scent.

"Let's go back down in the cellar," he whispered when they drew apart. "Make love among the pumpkins."

"What about snakes?"

"They can watch if they want."

INTO THE
MORNING

Celeste Hamilton

AVON BOOKS  NEW YORK

This is a work of fiction. Names, characters, places and incidents either are the product of the author's imagination or are used fictitiously. Any resemblance to actual events, locales, organizations, or persons, living or dead, is entirely coincidental and beyond the intent of either the author or the publisher.

AVON BOOKS
A division of
The Hearst Corporation
1350 Avenue of the Americas
New York, New York 10019

Copyright © 1997 by Celeste Hamilton
Inside cover author photo by T. Fred Miller
Published by arrangement with the author
Visit our website at http://AvonBooks.com
Library of Congress Catalog Card Number: 96-95494
ISBN: 0-380-79219-2

First Avon Books Printing: July 1997

AVON TRADEMARK REG. U.S. PAT. OFF. AND IN OTHER COUNTRIES, MARCA REGISTRADA, HECHO EN U.S.A.

Printed in the U.S.A.

WCD   10 9 8 7 6 5 4 3 2 1

moment, there was just Spring
erfect child.
ed with children every day. She
moved by their energy, strength,
n. But the emotions aroused by this
ifferent. Watching her, Spring ached.
r belly. In her arms. In her heart.
ted this child to be hers.
ing acknowledged that yearning, the
e light dissolved. The toddler ran to her
, squealing with laughter. The normal
sounds, and scents of a Saturday in the
ssailed Spring once more.
nerved, she hurried away.
t she couldn't forget that moment of en-
tment. A strange longing began to eat away
her. Her habitual optimism drooped like
uash blossoms beneath a hot, summer sun
ack home. She found herself daydreaming, often about the north Georgia mountains where
she had been born and where her parents still
lived. Since the encounter in the park, her life felt
off-kilter, profoundly changed. Spring knew that
the little girl had been sent to tell her something.
Yet fully a month passed before she could accept
that message.

When the revelation hit, Spring was alone in
the bed her husband seldom shared with her
these days. John was working, and she knew he
wouldn't welcome an interruption. But she had
to talk to him, tell him what she had realized.

She found him at the computer in a corner of

I am lucky enough to have many wonderful friends.
Some of you became even more special to me
during the writing of this book.

Beverly Beaver Barton
Vickie Hackney Bobitt
Faith Garner
Beverly Hise
Emilie Richards McGee
Leigh Neely
Susan Sawyer
Erica Spindler
Tawnee Kirby Stimson

Each of you are exceptional women.
Each of you play a unique role in my life.

This book is for you,
with my love and appreciation.

receded. For a
and this one, p
Spring wor
was frequent
and optimis
child were
Deep in h
She wa
As Sp
crystalli
parents
colors
par
Un
By
cha
at
so
b

∽ A Saturday mo
A Chicago park drench
A toddler in a ruffled pin
These were not the ingredi
Nelson would have picked to
Oh, she trusted in miracles. S
love at first sight, in flashes of
and in signs from on high. Raised b
who was full of magic, Spring resp
mystical currents flowing beneath
face of life. Yet as she strolled throu
neighborhood park, Spring didn't exp
child's simple, bright laughter to touch
soul.

The toddler was showing off for a couple seated on the grass. The man and woman clapped and sang as the child spun and danced her way toward Spring. Her dress's lacy hem swirled around chubby legs. Dark curls bounced. Blue eyes shone.

While Spring froze in mid-stride, sudden, pure light bathed the little girl. The crowded park their darkened living room. John was a crime reporter for the *Chicago Tribune.* People assumed it was a high-paying, rather glamorous job. Nothing could be farther from the truth. Basically, he got an up-close view of the city's underbelly for about the same salary as an elementary-school teacher. The only perk was that he loved telling people's stories. He relished digging for the details that lifted a run-of-the-mill news item into something more.

Several years ago, he did a series about a drug dealer who was trying to turn his life around. He won an award, and the columns were compiled in a nonfiction book. Though it sold poorly, a Hollywood producer took notice and optioned the work. Again, not much money.

The only difference that minor success had made in John and Spring's lives was to pay off a student loan. But soon after, the editor he had worked with on the book asked him to try a novel. The money allowed them to cut their credit-card debt and take a small vacation. The novel was in stores now, selling briskly, creating a "buzz" as his agent liked to say. John's editor was waiting on the first half of a new book. That's why every moment he had away from his regular job was spent in front of his computer. Spinning fictional stories fascinated him every bit as much as reporting. He was consumed by his work, by his ambitions.

And Spring's nights had grown long. For most of their marriage, one or the other of them had worked evening jobs. But she had never felt as alone as she did now, with John working right there in their apartment.

Tonight, when she reached his side, he flinched in surprise. But he didn't look away from his computer screen. "I'll come to bed soon, honey."

She laughed. "Liar."

He spared her a quick glance, a sheepish grin, as he raked a hand through his dark hair. "I think I've almost got this scene right."

His weariness and pallor only accénted his brooding good looks. Which was not fair, Spring thought. She just looked like a hag when she was tired. With a grin, she bent and pressed her cheek to his beard-stubbled jaw. "Fix the scene tomorrow. I need to talk to you."

"At three in the morning?"

"Yes." To get his attention, Spring rolled his desk chair backward and dropped into his lap. When John protested, she silenced him with a kiss.

After a decade of marriage, after several months of his distracted neglect, she was relieved he could still lose himself in her kiss. She had begun to fear he didn't want her, and that his work was a convenient excuse.

But he kissed her, and his hands moved with familiar ease over her. Cupping one of her breasts, he chuckled. "I guess I could take a break."

"First listen to me."

He drew back with a husband's long-suffering sigh. Spring told him about the park and the child and the bubble of white light. John listened, long ago having accepted Spring's trust in the metaphysical.

"That little girl was a messenger," Spring told him.

"What did she tell you?"

"We're going to have a child."

John went very still.

"I'm not pregnant," Spring hastened to add.

His relief was palpable. "Damn it, you scared me to death."

"But would it be so awful if I were pregnant?" When John didn't reply, Spring spoke straight from her heart, as she used to do before this awful distance had crept into their marriage. "I've decided I want a child."

He set her away from him. Slowly. The carefulness of his motions told her he was angry. John had learned at a young age to fear the loss of control that can accompany anger. He was adept at holding himself in check.

Lately, she resented that adeptness, that control.

He drew his chair back to the desk. "I need to work."

Her temper flared, as fiery as his was cool. "I want to talk to you about this."

"I don't have time."

She was incredulous. "I'm telling you I want a child, and you don't have time to listen?"

"Because it's not what you want." The words were flinty, like his gaze. "You've never wanted a baby before."

"I've changed my mind."

"No, you haven't." John stood, casting a long and lean shadow in the glow from his lamp. "It's the middle of the night, you're pissed because I'm working, and so you start this crap."

"At least I got your attention."

"That's a hell of a game to play."

"You know I don't play games."

"Then what's all this about?"

Spring forced a calmer note into her voice. "I want a baby. It's an understandable desire."

His gaze searched her face. "Where's this coming from? And don't say some pretty little girl in the park."

"That girl was a sign, pointing me toward what I need."

John's laughter was short as he gestured to the small, crowded room. "What you need is a nice apartment. New furniture. A second car. A vacation every year instead of every once in a while. Those are the things I want to give you."

She stepped forward. "I don't need any of that. I want—"

John silenced her with his fingers on her lips. His voice was deep, husky with fatigue and emotion. "Don't ask for the impossible, Spring. Please don't ask me for what I can never give you."

Her anger ebbed as quickly as it had risen. She

drew his hand away, pausing to brush a kiss across his knuckles. "If you could just let go of the past, John. Let go of your anger toward your parents."

"My past *is* gone. I was born the first time I met you."

If that were true, having a child wouldn't fill him with fear. Spring bit back that response; nothing she could say would make a difference. Once, she had hoped time would soften John's feelings toward his family. The years, however, had only hardened him more. To John, having a family represented the ultimate risk. Before, she had accepted that. But now . . .

Fear built to a roar inside her.

To quiet it, Spring slipped into John's arms. Here, she had always felt safe. Here, she had always been able to ease his pain.

John kissed her, drew her to their bedroom, to the bed that had always been their haven against frustrations, poverty, and disappointment. They made love. Combustible, sweetly fulfilling love.

But the distraction didn't chase her baby fantasies away.

A hunger was awake inside her. A primal need she had never anticipated. Working with children in crisis was her vocation, but Spring never thought having a child of her own was important. She had her career, her parents, brothers, and sister. Most of all, she had John. They used to share a dream for their future. Living well. Traveling. Just the two of them.

But they had been out of sync for a while. The
first glimmers of real success with his writing
had changed John. He was caught up in dreams
that seemed to have nothing to do with her. She
had tried not to worry, not to make too much of
her growing unease.

But now she had a dream he didn't share.

As John slept beside her, Spring closed her
eyes and again saw that beautiful little girl dancing in the sunshine in the park. It was a vision of
morning, in sharp contrast to the shadows falling
across her marriage.

Chapter One

Two years later . . .

∽ In the parking lot of a new fast-food eatery, Spring gazed at the distinctive sign framed against an early-morning sky. "Golden arches," she murmured. "Progress comes to White's Creek, Georgia."

"Ma'am?"

Spring turned and found a young man, pimply-faced and gangly in his restaurant uniform, studying her with a troubled frown. "The manager sent me out to see if you're okay."

She loved the soft roll of words off the youth's tongue. "You sound so good."

His stance grew wary. "Ma'am?"

Only then did Spring realize she must look a sight—feet bare, eyes bloodshot, her shorts and shirt rumpled after her marathon drive from Chicago. She could have broken the trip up, but having made the decision to come home, she had stopped only for essentials. Then, when she was

9

rolling into White's Creek, she had spotted this sign.

She'd been here for over an hour, watching the sun come up over the north Georgia mountains she loved. This spot, on a hill outside the town of White's Creek proper, afforded a wonderful view. Spring couldn't fathom why the town fathers had let this beautiful land go to a fast-food franchise.

There was no telling how long she had stood here under the famous arches. Small wonder the manager had sent someone out to check on her.

"I'm fine," she assured the youngster. She turned up the wattage of her smile, and he visibly relaxed. "I used to live here, and the last time I visited my folks this place wasn't built. How long have you been open?"

"'Bout four months now."

"So now the town's got Big Macs to go with the cable TV and the Internet." Spring chuckled, though remorse tightened her chest. "Everything changes."

The youngster again looked uncertain as he backed away. "We'll be open in a few minutes. Seven o'clock."

Spring glanced at his name tag. "Thanks, Larry." He started to turn, but she stopped him. "Have you always lived around here?" His expression, when he nodded, was hesitant. "Who're your folks?" He frowned again.

She couldn't blame him for his reticence. Caution with strangers had come to White's Creek along with other late-twentieth-century developments. Spring knew from personal experience that the worst always accompanies the best.

She apologized with a quick smile before she introduced herself, using her maiden name. "I don't mean to be acting so weird. But everything looks a lot different than when I was last in White's Creek."

The boy named Larry asked, "When was that?"

"Over two years ago."

"Not so much has changed since then."

"Oh, but then I wasn't looking at it with these eyes."

Larry's gaze narrowed once more.

Thinking he must truly believe her a kook, Spring laughed. "I sound like my mother. She always says we have different sets of eyes for looking at different things. I've come home to stay, so now I'm seeing the town with a whole new pair of eyes."

"Your mother sounds a lot like my grand-mama."

"So maybe not everything has changed around here after all." Spring nodded toward the town. "Does Willa Dean still live in that big white house at the corner of Maple and First?"

"Old Miss Busybody Dean?" Looking instantly contrite, Larry added, "What I mean is . . . Mrs. Dean—"

"Must still be sticking her nose in everybody's business."

He grinned. "Yes, ma'am."

"I bet she's faster than any fax machine when it comes to spreading the news." Spring directed a thoughtful glance toward the roof of the house in question. "I think I should pay Willa Dean a visit."

The smile she sent young Larry was so dazzling he blinked as she strode to the aging, dusty, red Corvette parked nearby. She got in her car and whipped it around toward the road, waving. Larry couldn't say exactly why he felt so thunderstruck. She was pretty, yes, but she was older, in her twenties.

Still, he waved back at her until he realized his boss was coming toward him, demanding to know what was going on.

Manager Ernie Fritz was round and soft and losing his hair. Few of the kids working here believed he led the high-school basketball team to a state championship only a dozen years ago. Larry had looked him up in an old yearbook, but could find little of the athletic boy pictured on those pages in the man who now puffed, red-faced and harried, across the parking lot.

Larry relayed the gist of the conversation and the name of the pretty lady in the Corvette and a strange look came into Mr. Fritz's eyes.

"Spring." The man laughed out loud. "Well, I'll be damned. Spring DeWitt *Nelson*. So she's moving home, huh?"

"Who is she?"

Mr. Fritz was staring off in the direction the Corvette had gone, looking dazed. His face was all tight, but loose, too. Happy and yet completely sad.

"You know her?" Larry prompted.

"We were in high school together."

Larry blinked, stunned to think the lady in the Corvette was the same age as his fat, balding boss. And yet, as Larry studied Mr. Fritz with widening eyes, he saw something new—an . . . energy of some sort. That was the only way Larry could think to describe the change in his boss. In his face and his posture. Mr. Fritz straightened, somehow. Grew taller. Shook off a load.

The growl of the Corvette's engine faded, and Mr. Fritz murmured, "I bet you know a girl like Spring, Larry. Pretty and wild and nice, all at once. The kind of girl who makes you think it's . . . possible. Not probable . . . but *possible*. You know?"

Larry, bad-complexioned, thin, and dateless, but still not without hope, knew. Only it had never occurred to him a grown man, especially someone like Mr. Fritz, knew that feeling, too.

"Spring was the one we all secretly loved. We weren't supposed to, but we did."

Mr. Fritz turned abruptly back to the restaurant before revealing any more surprises. Larry, however, stared down the road Spring had taken until Mr. Fritz shouted loud enough to get him moving again.

* * *

Spring stopped in front of a two-story, multi-gabled house. The white paint was as flawless as she remembered. Like the shady lawn, the porch and steps were a deep, glossy green. On the porch, Willa Dean, tall and spare with iron-gray hair, wielded her broom while she kept her eagle-sharp eyes on the main road into White's Creek. The broom stilled as Spring got out of her car and walked up a neat concrete walk bordered by rosebushes blooming in various combinations of pink and white, red and cream.

"Your flowers are as beautiful as ever, Mrs. Dean."

The older woman descended to the third step, squinting. Her mouth sagged open. "Well, Spring DeWitt. Look at you."

"Nice of you to recognize me."

"You haven't changed much, exceptin' you look even more like your mother than ever. You sure got her eyes." The stern set of Willa Dean's mouth revealed she hadn't meant the comparison as a compliment. Her critical gaze raked Spring from her bare feet to her untidy mass of thick, dark hair.

Spring laughed. "It looks like you're still doing all you can to battle filth."

"How's that?"

"Here you are, out in the heat at just past seven, sweeping your porch. How do you do it?"

Willa mumbled a reply.

Spring continued, "I bet you've been up since five, cleaning and polishing, weeding and watering. I guess that's why this house has always been one of the town's showplaces."

Willa's thin chest swelled. "It isn't easy to keep up an old house like this."

"I'm sure it isn't." Spring struggled not to laugh. "Yet with all you have to do, you still manage to keep up with everybody else's business."

The old woman flattened like a stepped-on tick. Scrawny fingers tightening on the broom, she glared at Spring. "What is it you want?"

"I just got back, and decided to say hello to you first. I figured it would save time in spreading the word."

A muscle in Willa's cheek twitched. Spring knew the woman would like to tell her to go to hell, but her avocation as a busybody would no doubt win out over such base impulses.

Sure enough, Willa asked, "Planning a long visit?"

"I'm home to stay."

Unasked questions brimmed in Willa's close-set, dark eyes.

"John's not with me."

"Oh?" The simple word masked a world of interest.

"He won't be coming."

"I see." Curiosity fairly oozed from Willa, but Spring had to give her credit for not giving in to it.

"I thought you should know, so you can tell everyone."

Willa's mouth pinched even tighter. "Can't imagine why I'd want to do that."

Spring's laughter was without bitterness, something she considered an accomplishment in light of the lies this old gossip had spread about her once upon a time. "I wanted to give you an exclusive, Mrs. Dean. You've got the scoop on my return. You can tell everyone Spring DeWitt is back in town."

"I don't know why you'd think I'd want to do that," the older woman retorted.

"Oh, but you do." Spring chuckled as she walked back to her car. "You do." She bent over a rosebush and neatly avoided pricking her finger while snapping off a large, pink bloom. She waved it at Willa Dean before she got in her car, gunned the engine, and pulled away in a squeal of tires.

Willa let her broom clatter to the steps.

If Spring DeWitt had been raised properly, she wouldn't have stopped to cast aspersions on a decent, God-fearing woman's character. She wouldn't have spent so many years doing who-knows-what with every boy who winked at her. And she wouldn't have run off with John Nelson nearly twelve years ago.

Willa could still remember the sight of them leaving town, laughing and yelling and honking the horn of the very car Spring was driving today. They had driven by her house and shouted something vile at her. All because Willa had tried to warn John's mother, Debra, about Spring.

Not that it did any good. The girl, truly her mother's daughter, had bewitched John. A fine thank-you his behavior had been for Debra and her husband. Sam had been owed more for adopting John and giving him the best of everything. Willa knew more than a little about ungrateful children, so she had pitied Sam Nelson, God rest his soul.

Trembling with outrage, Willa hurried into her cool, clean home, the house she worked her fingers to the bone to keep up. Spring had mocked her for that. But Willa would make no apologies for her housekeeping, thank you very much. She had pride in appearance, not like those DeWitts.

Spring's father, Ned DeWitt, could have done better. He could have married Willa's niece, Sharlene. Willa and her husband had taken Sharlene in and brought her up. Sharlene would have made Ned a decent wife, helped him do something with his life, kept him in church and on a straight-and-narrow path.

But Ned had come home from the service, jilted Sharlene, and married that witchy mountain girl—Spring's mama. Callie was content for Ned to eke out a living farming, letting his old family place junk up like a scrap heap. All Callie did was give Ned five children he couldn't afford.

Sharlene had run off with a Bible salesman. And while she had a right tidy life up in Asheville, she didn't call Willa, hadn't visited in over a decade, or brought her children around.

Righteously indignant over new and old slights, Willa barreled into her bright and clean kitchen. Her husband, Floyd, looked up from his breakfast of bran and fruit. "Land sakes. What's set you on fire?"

"Never you mind." Wishing, as she had for years, that Floyd had never retired and started meddling in her daily routine, Willa grabbed the telephone and dialed. Her call was answered on the first ring. "Ebbie? You won't believe who's moved back to town."

At the table, Floyd set aside the county newspaper and listened to the real news of the day.

Spring imagined she could hear the telephone wires singing. Word would spread quickly. Everyone, including John's mother, would soon know Spring had returned to White's Creek.

She frowned at that intrusive thought. Debra Nelson meant nothing to Spring. For years, Spring had blamed her for the demons John tried to outrun. But John was no longer Spring's concern, and now his family should be nothing to her, either.

Lifting her face to the wind and banishing thoughts of her husband, Spring drove down one familiar, sun-dappled street after another, passing all the big landmarks.

The high school, three-storied and square, boasted a tangle of new rooms hitched onto one side. The pharmacy, post office, and bank were unchanged. But the old five-and-dime was now divided into office space for a Realtor and an insurance agency, and the Palace Movie Theater housed a video rental store in what used to be the lobby.

The center of this business hub was the domed, redbrick courthouse. A statue of the town's World War I hero stood out front. Police cars were parked beside a side entrance that led to the sheriff's office and jail. On a bench nearby, elderly men had already gathered to whittle, talk politics, and watch the comings and goings downtown. Spring didn't doubt they were the same men who had occupied that bench when she left town.

A building across the square caught her attention. *City Diner* was spelled out in faded white script on a green awning. Spring guessed the lettering hadn't been freshened since a storm had ripped down signs all over town some fifteen summers back. She wasn't surprised to see the restaurant still open or the crowded tables lining the front windows. Progress be damned. Egg and cheese-filled English muffins couldn't beat the pancakes or biscuits and sawmill gravy at Ebbie Ruth Denison's diner.

The thought of an honest-to-God, arteryclogging Southern breakfast made Spring's stomach rumble. In front of the diner, she pulled to a stop behind a pickup loaded with produce. A short, round woman came out the restaurant's front door. It was the legendary Ebbie herself, her hair only a slightly deeper shade of red than Spring remembered. Ebbie was as big a gossip as Willa, with one difference. Ebbie had a heart.

Amused, Spring watched her haggle with the farmer who was selling produce. Nobody got the best of Ebbie. Eventually, money was exchanged, and the man carried two baskets of tomatoes into the diner. But Ebbie remained on the sidewalk, a hand shading her eyes as she gazed toward the sheriff's entrance to the courthouse. The farmer's pickup prevented Spring from seeing what held her interest.

Spring tooted her horn and the diner owner turned, frowning. Leaning toward the lowered passenger side window, Spring called out a greeting and identified herself.

Ebbie's mouth flew open, her second and third chins trembling like one of her famous Jell-O fruit salads. Grinning in delight, she cast another glance toward the courthouse before waddling to Spring's car. She crossed pudgy arms on the open window and leaned in. "Lordy, lordy. I heard you were in town."

"So Mrs. Dean already called you."

"Honey, I'm first on her list." The redhead laughed the rusty croak of a dedicated smoker. "Goodness, you don't look half-naked to me."

"Mrs. Dean said I was?"

"She claims you tore up one of her rosebushes, too."

Touching the blossom she had tucked behind one ear, Spring laughed.

"Why don't you come in for a chat? Otherwise, I'll have to rely on Willa's wild tales for my information."

While in high school, Spring had waitressed for Ebbie. She had affection for the woman, but right now she would sooner face a stampede of runaway hogs than one of Ebbie's third degrees. "Some other time. I'm in kind of a hurry to see my family."

Slyly, Ebbie arched a penciled-in eyebrow. "Just your mama and daddy, or John's family, too?"

Spring didn't rise to the bait. Willa had surely told Ebbie that Spring was back to stay without John. And she knew very well the relationship between Debra, John, and Spring.

Ebbie drawled, "The reason I'm asking is because John's mother and brother are over at the sheriff's office now."

Stunned, Spring's gaze swung to the courthouse. The pickup was just pulling from in front of her car, so she now had a clear view of the Sheriff's Department entrance. But she didn't see Debra or John's half brother, Logan.

"That's Debra's Mercedes." Ebbie nodded toward the big, gold sedan parked behind a squad car. "And I heard Logan was picked up early this morning."

"Logan?" Spring turned back to Ebbie, gaping in disbelief. "Sweet little Logan?"

"Sweet little Logan is seventeen, and he turned into hell on wheels about the time Sam Nelson died."

The small boy who had once followed John around like a puppy was seventeen and in trouble with the law. Spring had a hard time taking that in. But proof of that reality appeared quickly when Debra stalked out of the sheriff's office with a young man trailing behind.

Unmistakably Logan, Spring thought. Even all grown-up and even from this distance, she would recognize him. Not because he resembled John. Logan was taller, bigger. And he looked incredibly like the father the two brothers didn't share.

Debra was in the car before Spring had a chance to take in more than the woman's perfectly coiffed blond hair and her smart, tailored pantsuit. No obvious changes there. She didn't even glance Spring's way.

Logan did. Across the twenty-five or thirty feet that separated them, Spring felt his gaze boring into hers. He couldn't recognize the Corvette, could he? Or her? It had been twelve years since she had seen him. Logan had been barely five years old then, and there had been zero contact between them since.

But he stared long and hard at Spring. Without thinking, she raised her hand. He swung into his mother's car without responding. They drove away, leaving Spring to stare after the expensive car with a frown.

Ebbie sighed. "Logan keeps the deputies busy."

"Doing what?"

"Fighting, mainly. I hear he's got a mean streak. Comes by it honest, I'd say."

Spring and the older woman exchanged a long look. Spring had always suspected Ebbie knew a lot about the Nelson family secrets. But Spring wasn't about to enlarge upon that knowledge now.

After promising Ebbie she would stop in soon, Spring pulled away from the curb. Distracted, still thinking of Logan and Debra, she followed First Street around the courthouse square. She noted the furniture store that had expanded into two storefronts, the dress shop that advertised a sale in orange-on-black-lettered signs. Down Elm Street was the elementary school where Spring's sister, Rainy, now taught. And finally, at the edge of the business district, was the city park.

As the white gazebo in the park's center came into view, memories of John overwhelmed Spring.

She cursed herself for coming this way. Almost against her will she slowed the car. She couldn't help remembering a Fourth of July thirteen years ago in this park. The holiday fireworks over, she and John had lain on a blanket, sweet green grass beneath them, a carpet of stars overhead. . . .

* * *

They necked for a while. Nothing too hot and heavy. Spring was sure John had heard the lies other boys had told about her, but he hadn't pushed for more than she was ready to give. That was only one of the reasons she wanted to give him everything.

They hadn't been going out long. White's Creek was a small town, but their families came from two different worlds—rich and poor. John had attended private boarding schools and summer camps all his life, so they hadn't known each other until his stepfather decreed he was to spend the summer and his senior year in White's Creek.

Against John's sinfully full and skilled mouth, Spring whispered, "I know you may not feel this way, but I'm glad you got expelled from that fancy school."

"I wasn't too happy about it at first." He touched her cheek. "Not until I met you."

"You said your stepfather was awful mad."

Pulling away abruptly, John sat up. "Let's not ruin what's left of the night by talking about Sam Nelson."

John always used his stepfather's given name. He never had a kind word for the man, or for his mother. About the only person he spoke of with any affection was Logan, who had just turned four. Spring, whose own family was a happy one, was sorry about the trouble in the Nelson home. But she couldn't be sorry John's stepfather had kept him in White's Creek. Not when she had fallen in love with him on first sight.

Filled with that hot, secret knowledge, Spring sat up and hugged her knees to her chest. John was silent beside her, as he often was when she tried to talk to him about his family. Her mother was always telling her not to push people so hard, so Spring sought a safe subject. "I guess tonight was the last Independence Day celebration I'll see in this town."

She felt John turn toward her. "What about next year?"

"Wherever I get a scholarship, I'm going there early in the summer to find a place to live, to find a job, and get settled. Since I plan on going somewhere far away, I figure the sooner I move, the better off I'll be."

"You think you'll be happy far from your family?"

Spring already knew leaving her family and these mountains would be like carving her heart in two. But as long as she could remember, she had planned to leave. Her mother, who could see these things, knew she was going far away as well. Spring knew there was a world full of adventure, just waiting for her. She had never said that to anyone but her family, but she told John now.

Instantly fearing he was going to make fun of her, she went on the offensive. "Just because I don't have a fancy private-school education doesn't mean I can't hack it at some big university."

"All I meant was there are plenty of major colleges right here in Georgia."

"And that's where I'll go if I have to. But I'd rather go farther away, see something else, know other places. Isn't that what you want?"

In the strong midsummer moonlight, John's profile was outlined in stern relief. "You can bet I'm going away. The day I graduate, I hit the road. And I'll never be back. Never."

Spring shivered at his fierce tone. "My mother says

never is a dark place on the far side of someday; you can't get there from here."

John laughed. He seemed to like Spring's mother. *"She's something else, isn't she?"*

"You don't know the half of it." Spring's chuckle was rueful. When John found out just how different her mother was, he might not laugh. Some folks weren't amused by Callie DeWitt's powers.

John studied Spring. *"I bet you will get away from here."*

"I know I will."

"And I might just go with you."

Those husky words had barely sunk in before he kissed her. Spring didn't ask him what he meant. She didn't question how the two of them could pledge themselves to each other so simply or so quickly. Her parents had taught her to trust the guiding voice inside her. And the voice said John Nelson was her destiny, part of the adventure she had been waiting for. . . .

And now the adventure was over. Finished.

Weary beyond measure, Spring drove away from the place where she and John had first shared their dreams. She had come home to forget him, and forget him she would.

She headed into the countryside. Impatient to see her parents, Spring set her foot hard on the accelerator. Miles out of town, she turned down a narrow, graveled drive. Honeysuckle vines and overgrown boxwoods pressed in on either side of the lane. Fat cattle looked up from their grazing to watch Spring's car pass.

Mountains rolled behind the rise, where a rambling farmhouse sat. Yellow paint, her mother's years-old attempt at beautification, peeled in the summer sun. Here and there a sage green shutter hung askew. Unfinished mechanical projects dotted the side yard and the lane leading to a weathered gray barn. In defiance of unmown grass, flowers grew in a whirling patchwork of color. Petunias, mostly. Pink and white. Deep purple, bright yellow, and dusty rose. Bees and butterflies danced among the blooms. The morning air carried the sounds and scents straight to Spring's welcoming senses.

Three dogs, a beagle and two mongrel companions, came running and barked in excitement as Spring got out. She knelt to receive the anointing lathes of their rough tongues, then laughed at a gray tabby who paraded three tumbling offspring through suddenly cowering canines.

Spring's arms were full of kittens when she heard her name called. Her father was hurrying up from the barn. Spring had time only to note the new silver in his hair and the new lines on his thin face before she met him. He hugged her tight, kittens and all.

When the meowing reached a fevered pitch, her father drew back, grinning. "Your mama saw you coming in her dreams."

Spring wasn't surprised at her mother's ability to divine the future. "And here I wanted to surprise you."

With a work-roughened hand, Ned DeWitt

stroked his youngest daughter's cheek. "When one of you kids is in trouble, your mama knows. She can't always see exactly what the trouble is, but she feels it."

"I left trouble behind, Daddy."

Ned gave her a level look from his dark brown eyes. Spring straightened her shoulders, intending to deny once more the presence of problems, but the slam of a screen door stopped her.

"Spring! Spring, darlin', I've been waiting for you." Her mother's voice, raised in excitement, sent Spring speeding toward the porch. She met her mother on the front steps.

"Put these cats down," Callie admonished, plucking kittens from Spring's arms. "I want to hold my daughter, not all of Miss Priscilla's brood."

"Oh, Mama." Spring went into her mother's slender, strong arms. Against the worn cotton of Callie's pink blouse, she buried her face. Her mother smelled of bacon and a pungent mix of the herbs she gathered each summer morning from her garden. She was so dear, so familiar, so completely accepting, that Spring let loose of the tears she had been holding in for the last few hundred miles.

Callie stroked a hand down Spring's back, murmuring her name. "That's right, baby. Cry it out."

Spring allowed her mother to rock her gently back and forth, whispering words of comfort while she cried.

But when the storm had passed, Callie drew back, her regard suddenly fierce, her voice now stinging like a whip. "Dry your eyes, Missy."

"Mama?" Dazed by the change, Spring blinked tears away.

Anger flared in her mother's silver-blue eyes. More gray than blue, the color of a stone rubbed smooth by a rushing mountain stream, her husband called them "angel eyes," both for their otherworldly radiance and for the way she managed to see into souls. No matter what Willa Dean said, Spring knew she didn't have her mother's eyes. More than one person had looked into Callie's eyes and retreated, fearful that their closely held secrets and hidden shortcomings had been divined. Instead of angel, some called her witch.

Right now, Spring understood that feeling.

"You've run away from your marriage," Callie pronounced. "Don't expect me to be condoning that."

"But Mama—"

Callie shushed her with an upraised hand. "You come inside and eat some breakfast. Then you can try to explain this mess you and John are in." She marched up the porch steps, the banging screen door barely missing the kittens who followed her.

Spring turned to her father.

Ned shrugged. "Best to do what she says, Daughter."

As if to underscore his words, Miss Priscilla turned around on the top step and hissed.

Chastened, Spring scrambled into the house.

Chapter Two

Early in the evening of Spring's homecoming, Callie came into the kitchen from the garden. Spring was already in bed, worn out from her trip, and Callie's heart was heavy. To her husband, she said, "Our girl's in trouble."

Her husband looked up from the coffee he poured. "That's why she's home. We can help her."

"Maybe."

He cocked an eyebrow. "It's not like you to sound so pessimistic."

"She's not going to give John much of a chance."

"Maybe he don't deserve her chances." As Callie would have expected, Ned came down squarely on his daughter's side.

He was always tender with the children. Too tender, sometimes. He had never wanted to deny them anything, even some foolishness he could ill afford. Callie knew strength grew more from wanting than having. Same as she knew children needed a push now and then,

31

some vinegar to go with the sweetness of love.

Just like now. If Ned had his way, they would fold Spring to their bosoms and stroke her hair and rain curses on John Nelson's head. But Callie could see that wouldn't do.

"Trouble has two sides," Callie chided him. "You know that. Hasn't trouble partnered with us enough?"

Ned sighed, and admitted she was right as he came around the table to give her a hug. "Spring'll find her own road. Same as she always has."

The cold February night her youngest was born, Callie had known the tiny, black-haired girl with the stubborn cry would travel rough through life. So Callie gave her a happy name, a name that called to mind the sweetest of seasons. Callie still hoped her daughter's life would live up to that promise. But Spring's immediate future was veiled from Callie's view. Oh, last night she had sensed her coming home, but that was all.

It had been this way since the day Spring had seen the little girl bathed in white light in a Chicago park. Spring had been right to call the girl a messenger. Callie knew it had been a fork in her daughter's life road. But was it the right way to go?

Chilled suddenly by worry, Callie whispered to her life's love, "Hold me, Ned. I'm worried about Spring."

He complied, crooning, "Stop your frettin', now. Just enjoy having our baby back with us for a time."

Callie held tight to him. But for only a moment. While Spring was asleep, she had to call John.

Standing in the middle of the spacious Chicago apartment he had shared with Spring for over a year and a half, John mouthed a silent prayer into the telephone receiver. His mother-in-law said Spring had reached Georgia safely. That, however, was the only encouraging news.

"Her heart is set up hard against you," Callie said.

"What about my heart? She's the one who left." His voice came out rough around the thickness in his throat.

"You could come after her."

"That's probably just what she wants. She can't control me here. She thinks getting me to run after her will give her an edge. You know how she is. Spring always wants her way."

No matter what she thought, Callie didn't criticize her daughter. "John, is it pride keeping you from following her?"

"Hell, yes. Pride and a deep aversion to coming anywhere near White's Creek, Georgia."

Still in a calm and reasonable tone, Callie said, "There's nothing here that can hurt you anymore."

Ignoring that gentle rebuke, John continued in

a harsh tone. "I just don't get it. Spring has become a different person. Before now, she never wanted children. She never wanted to move back home. She understood why I wouldn't live there, either. Why has she changed her mind about everything? What's she doing there?"

"She feels you don't love her any longer. She's hurt and wanted to come home."

"Not love her?" The very idea sent a pain through his chest. "Everything I've ever done has been for her. There's only one thing I won't do. I don't see why that should be the end of us."

"Spring sees it differently."

"She thinks I'm selfish and shortsighted. She's furious with me. But we can work this out. I am still her husband, and this is her home."

"No, this is her home."

He couldn't believe what he was hearing. "Callie, how can you say that? You always saw that she would move away. You've told me yourself that you always saw her leaving you, moving away young. You encouraged her to follow that destiny."

"But I never said she wouldn't come back to the mountains."

He snorted in disbelief. "Convenient of you to leave out that part of your prophecy. Now it can fit the situation."

Static crackled across the line.

Callie's voice, when it returned, was less gentle than before. "You listen here, John Nelson. If I didn't love you, my patience would just about be worn in two. You've refused to visit, and we've had to come to you. You've made our girl mighty unhappy lately. But this family loves you because Spring chose you. And I love you for yourself."

Few people had ever done that. But right now John didn't care. "I never asked for anyone's love but Spring's."

"Oh, no?" Callie laughed. "I've seen you prance like a new-groomed horse with the love from this family."

He didn't bother arguing what was a simple, plain truth. That wasn't important. Getting Spring home was. "Talk to her, Callie. Convince her she's making a mistake."

"I've already let her know I don't approve of her running away from her problems. But what about you? Aren't you doing much the same?" Before he could protest, she added, "You can talk night and day about it being the changes in Spring that's driven the two of you apart. I'll grant you she's developed some longings you never planned on. But what about the changes in you?"

"Me?"

"The coldness you've let claim your soul."

His laugh was acid-edged. "Just cut the mystical, mumbo-jumbo bullshit, Callie."

"You can't be pretending to me about what you feel deep in your heart. I've always been able to see exactly what you've tried to hide."

He closed his eyes, knowing she was right.

From the moment thirteen summers ago when Spring took him to meet her parents and Callie laid her hand on his shoulder, he knew she divined his most painful secrets. And without words, she had soothed him. Like Spring, Callie always made John feel he was something more than the nobody Sam and Debra claimed him to be.

Now, Callie's special warmth reached across the miles that separated them. "Come to Spring, John. Come rest in the shade of the mountains. I want you and my girl to work this out. This is where the two of you can figure out how to do that."

He was tempted. More tempted than he wanted to admit. But his chasing Spring to Georgia played right into her hands. She probably thought he wanted her back bad enough to give in to her wishes about having a family. Hell, she might even be thinking he would return to White's Creek for good.

The note she left him had said that godforsaken place was the "home of her heart." That was more bullshit, in his opinion.

She'd also written that he no longer needed her. And maybe that wasn't bullshit.

Maybe this marriage was broken. Maybe he didn't need her. If so, this was the time to find out. While she cooled her heels hundreds of miles away.

"I have to go," he told Callie abruptly.

"What are you going to do?"

"Drink a toast to my wife's sojourn in Georgia."

She made a disgusted sound. "You're being a fool. Only a fool throws away what's most precious to them. Didn't you learn anything from your mother's mistakes, John?"

Mention of Debra send anger thundering through him. He didn't talk about his family. Not even with Callie. Impatiently flipping off the phone, he sent the cordless receiver slamming against the apartment's exposed brick wall. It bounced off, beeping but not shattered.

The pointless gesture felt damn good. If he were the sort of man who busted up furniture, he would do that as well.

But the violent impulse ended in a hurry. John had worked a lifetime to keep a tight rein on his temper. The few times he had slipped, he regretted deeply. So, in the place of anger, he soon felt only emptiness. Much like the empty spaces that stared back at him from around this apartment.

Gone from the mantel was the lopsided but oddly charming blue-and-gold pottery Spring had made in a class last summer.

Gone from the sofa was the crocheted comforter her mother gave them the first Christmas John and Spring were married.

Gone from the top of the antique dresser in one corner were Spring's family pictures. As he had told Callie, he hadn't wanted to be part of their family. He had done all he could to hold himself back from the DeWitts' warmth and all-encompassing interest in each other. But, *hellfire*, after years of living with those pictures, it felt wrong for their faces not to smile out at him from Spring's mix-and-match collection of frames.

Cursing under his breath, John crossed to the kitchen. He seemed to remember a bottle of Scotch someone had given them last year. Locating the unopened bottle in the back of a cabinet, he poured half a glass and gulped it down.

He only wished the warmth could fill this dark, yawning crater of hurt inside him.

But when the glass was empty, Spring was still gone, and John's ache was still acute. He supposed he could drink the rest of it, get good and goddamned drunk. But he hated the taste, and knew he would hate it more when he woke up tomorrow alone.

He wandered restlessly to the living room and sank down on the deep-cushioned sofa he and Spring had bought together before moving into this apartment. With a wistful look on her face, she had pronounced the green to be the color of the moss that grew in the deepest shadows of the woods back home. John had simply found the hue soothing, and the design suited to the ambience he wanted to achieve in their new home.

Ambience. John laughed at his choice of words. Until a couple of years ago, the only ambience they had been able to afford was early garage sale.

He and Spring came to Chicago right after high-school graduation. As they were both in college, they had lived in a series of dreadful apartments, making do on her scholarships, student loans, and several part-time jobs. They did everything short of selling his expensive, rich-boy's car to survive. For some damn reason, Spring had a thing about the car that had carried them off on what she called their grand adventure.

While John went to work at the *Tribune*, Spring finished graduate studies in psychology and social work and took a job counseling children from high-risk environments. Not much money, but for her giving heart, a world of satisfaction.

With two paltry but regular paychecks coming in, they splurged by buying a bed frame for their mattress and moved to an apartment with fewer roaches and more windows. They felt wealthy until the car needed major repairs and the rent went up.

John became frustrated. His stepfather had once delighted in calling him a no-good dreamer who would never amount to anything. Spring's love and trust had helped him believe in himself. Reporting, for which he had a natural affinity, had shown him he had valuable talents. But John knew the world, like Sam Nelson, judged most people by the money they made. He wanted to be judged a success.

Money wasn't something Spring gave much

thought to. Their disagreements over finances had been the first breach in their marriage. In hindsight, John saw that was only the beginning. They started growing apart about the time his first nonfiction book was published and optioned for a movie.

Admittedly, he got stars in his eyes about that movie. He was crushed when nothing came of the deal. To this day, the movie was still in "turn-around," a synonym for "dead" as far as John could tell.

Then his first novel about a bad guy turned snitch became a sudden, unexpected best-seller.

They didn't get rich, but his next two-book contract got him and Spring out of the near-slums and into a condo. They bought an original oil for the spot over the mantel. A brass bed for their loft. This winter, John had left the *Tribune* to write fiction full-time.

He had imagined he and Spring had it made. He had wanted to spoil her. Buy her a big diamond. Take her to Europe.

All she wanted was a child.

Children.

She wanted a baby of their own and to adopt a troubled little girl with whom she had been working.

At the start, her obsession with having a family was so stunning, John ignored her. When she began trying to convince him, their arguments began. The breaking point came last month.

She had asked him to meet her downtown for a reception connected with her job. John had been happy to go. There had been so much tension between them that he welcomed a chance for a night out.

But the reception was in reality an "Adoption Fair." Photographs of children with descriptions of their backgrounds were posted throughout a large convention center ballroom. Couples interested in adoption were wandering among the displays, studying children as John might artwork. One of Spring's colleagues assured him events like this were held all over the country. He could appreciate the benefits of a large, open-invitation meeting, but he felt ambushed.

He looked for Spring and found her talking with a couple who were interested in a child she had counseled. While John waited, her supervisor approached him and started discussing "Chrissy, the girl you and Spring are considering adopting."

Alarmed, he tried being noncommittal, but her boss insisted on leading him over to Chrissy's photo. He felt so sick, he barely glanced at the little girl's innocent, trusting face.

Rudely, he walked away. Halfway across the room, he passed Spring, still talking with prospective parents, but with her gaze centered on him. She knew exactly what had happened. He was tempted to make a scene, call her on this dirty little trick.

He settled for walking out the door.

She arrived at home hours later. John had been seated right where he was now, on their sofa. Spring said nothing, rare behavior for the woman he knew to be volatile and emotional. So he did something unusual. He started the argument.

"What was getting me down there at that circus supposed to prove?"

Spring's jaw clenched. John saw her trying to control her anger. But she couldn't. Her silver earrings gleamed as she tossed her head. "It was not a circus."

"What else can you call it?" He shuddered. "All those people down there, pawing through pictures of those poor little kids. It was a sideshow."

"Some of those kids will get a chance because of 'those' people. Tonight was a good thing. I thought you might see that, might even see yourself in the photographs of those children. Just imagine what your life would have been like if you had been raised by someone who wanted you, who knew how to parent."

"But I wasn't," John sneered, pushing himself to his feet. "I was raised by Debra and Sam Nelson and a bunch of teachers at a succession of pricey schools. So what makes you think I can parent, either?"

"You're a good person, the kind of person a kid like Chrissy needs. With what she's been through, you should be able to identify with her."

"But I don't want to identify with her. I don't want to draw upon my unfortunate childhood to help anyone."

"But if you could make a difference—"

"But I can't." Those words came from a painful place in John's heart.

Spring stubbornly ignored them. "You have it within yourself to be a wonderful father."

He took hold of her shoulders. "Look at me, Spring. Look at me and listen. I don't want to adopt that little girl. I feel sorry for her, but I'm not what she needs. I'm not what any child needs. I know too much about how wrong families can go. I just can't do it."

Spring was silent, her gaze on his. "How can you close yourself to the possibility that it could be good?"

"Because there's just as strong a chance that it won't be good, that I'd let a child down, disappoint them. And that's not a risk I'm willing to take."

"You would never hurt a child."

"That's not the point. I don't want a child."

She searched his face, frowning. As if she couldn't find what she wanted to see. "After all these years, why are you suddenly a stranger to me?"

"I'm not the one who has changed."

"This isn't about mere change, John. We've fallen apart, disintegrated."

The coldness of her expression aroused real fear in him. "You're overreacting." He caught her elbow, but she pulled away and walked toward the stairs that led to their sleeping loft.

He followed. "We can get back to normal, Spring. You can set things right. Give up this baby thing. Now. I'm not changing my mind."

She faced him again. "What about what I want?"

Panicking, his fingers fastened once more on the smooth skin of her arm. "Aren't you listening to me? Don't you hear me anymore?"

"Why can't you hear me? I want children to nurture and to love. I know I once said I didn't, but now my feelings are different. Maybe it's because I'm older. Maybe it's just nature taking over. But I want a family." She pressed a hand to her stomach. "It's more than want. It's something I have to have."

Moments passed while John studied his wife's lovely, vibrant features. Maybe she was right. Maybe he hadn't been listening to her. For it was only now that he heard the aching desperation in her voice.

He released a deep breath. "If a child is something you can't live without, maybe we're just wasting our time."

John wasn't certain if he expected Spring to protest, to fling her arms around him and beg his forgiveness for changing the rules of their marriage. But she did nothing of the sort. She just looked profoundly sad. "You're right, John. We are wasting our time."

He took a step backward, startled.

Her demeanor was dangerously cool. Her beautiful gray-blue eyes—usually so expressive—were devoid of all emotion. "You checked out of this marriage a while ago. I guess I'm just now admitting it to myself."

"What are you saying?"

"I'm saying that everything in your life is more important than I am."

"You're angry because I work so much. You resent the writing—"

Her icy facade slipped a notch. "Of course I resent it. It's like you're on a holy quest instead of writing about cops and robbers."

Her disparagement of his work stung, mostly because it had become a familiar refrain this past year. It seemed the only way he might please her these days was to donate his sperm or sign his consent on some adoption papers. When had it changed? When had she decided the two of them weren't enough for her happiness?

"Sorry if my job's no longer noble enough for you. I could go back to chasing police sirens and earning a pittance."

"At least then you acted like yourself."

"And how do I act now?"

"Like . . ." She stopped, obviously trying to regain control.

"Just say what you feel. Let me have it."

"All right. You're full of yourself, John Nelson. You've become selfish and self-centered and I . . ." The muscles in her throat worked as she swallowed. "I don't like you very much anymore. I don't . . ." Her words didn't come out easily. "I'm not sure if I want to be with you any longer."

He couldn't believe his ears. "So you're going to bail? You're going to throw everything we have away?"

Uncertainty clouded her features.

Sensing that weakness, John lifted his hand to her cheek, threaded his fingers through her hair. "When we left home it was just going to be me and you. And we've been happy. Tell me you've been happy."

She bit her lip. "Not lately. Not for a—"

He didn't let her finish, couldn't bear to let her say he had let her down. That was his biggest fear. "We've been a family, all the family I want. I don't want kids, and you know why."

Several beats passed before Spring whispered, "You wouldn't be like _him_."

Knowing just who she meant, John closed his eyes. "We are not discussing Sam Nelson."

"But your stepfather's the reason you feel this way about having a family."

Swinging away from her, John muttered, "Of course he is. So is my mother, and so is my poor, dead soldier of a father. They all let me down. I'm a poster child for the modern dysfunctional family. A walking cliché. You should bless me for breaking the vicious cycle and remaining childless."

"It doesn't have to be that way."

"Stop it!" The words were a minor roar. John wheeled back to Spring. "Don't start in with that crap about me facing my personal demons. I'm not some kid you're trying to reach."

She recoiled, blotchy color suffusing her cheeks.

"Don't tell me to go home, Spring. Don't tell me to forgive Mother or bury Sam. Damnation, why are you doing this?"

"Because I'm sick of pretending your past doesn't matter. It does, and you need to face it."

He blinked. "What are you talking about?"

"I'm sick of it." She swung her arms wide. "Sick of all of this."

"Of what? Our lives? Our home?" Fury shook through him. "We've worked like dogs to achieve this. I've done everything I can to give you this. I'd give you the world on a platter if I could."

"None of this was for me, and you know it. Everything you've done has been for Sam Nelson and for your mother."

"Stop it," John muttered, jaw tightening.

But Spring squared her shoulders, challenging him. "You got through college so fast in order to show them you could. I think you wrote that first book for them. You would probably stay married to me forever just because Debra said we'd only last six months."

"That's crap. She probably doesn't even know where we are, what we're doing."

She snorted. "Every dean's list you made was sent home to be published in the county paper. When your first book came out, it was front page news in White's Creek. Mama has all the clippings in her scrapbook. And even if Sam or Debra somehow missed those notices, my parents tell everyone who will listen that we've done good."

An emotion more dangerous than anger was licking through him. "If I'd wanted Sam or Debra to know about me, about our lives, I wouldn't have waited on the county newspaper or your parents. I would have gone back to White's Creek and rubbed their noses in my success."

"Maybe you should. You'd feel a hell of a lot better if you'd just admit that it mattered what Sam thought of you, that it still matters what Debra thinks."

"It doesn't," John shouted, his face close to hers. "Sam has his other son. His real son. I'm nothing. Nothing I ever do will be good enough for him."

Spring's voice rose to match his. "Will you listen to yourself? You talk about him in the present tense, like he's still here, like he can hurt you."

John stepped away, hands balling into fists.

And Spring kept shouting. "Of course you can't please him, John. He's been dead for over four years. And Debra's not ever going to care about anyone but herself. I think you've faced all that. All that's left is to admit it still hurts."

"Shut up."

"No, you're going to listen."

"Just stop it." John grabbed her arm, wanting to slap her. So strong was the impulse that he actually raised his hand.

Eyes widening, Spring fell back a step.

Shock and remorse punched his gut in quick succession. He would never strike Spring. Never.

Or would he?

That doubt, like a serpent's bite, spread poison through him. The room spun. John's world tilted.

Spring stepped close, hanging on when he flinched and tried to get away. "Don't go there, John."

Voice roughening, he turned. "I wanted to hit you."

"But you didn't. You wouldn't." She got in front of him, put her arms around him, pressing her face against his chest, whispering, "This is me, John. I know everything you've tried to forget. I know everything about you."

Before he could give in to the familiar feel of her in

his arms, John set her away. "You obviously don't know everything."

She just stared at him.

"If you really knew me, really understood me, you wouldn't be wanting a child with me."

He left her standing there, staring after him. He went to the police precinct headquarters where he had hung out when he was a reporter. He roamed the streets, forcing himself to think about his work, his book. Instead of staring down the dark alleys of his past, he focused on his dreams. Dreams for himself. For Spring. For the life they had pledged they would build when they had stormed out of White's Creek, Georgia. The life they had been living before she started wanting a child.

He had never promised her a child.

In the end, that was unimportant. No matter what they had shared in the past, no matter what their promises to each other, it was what he couldn't give her that mattered most.

Over three weeks of silence and festering hurt had passed. Yesterday, John had come in from a day of research at the county coroner's office and found Spring gone. Even after reading her note, John couldn't believe what had happened. He had checked with her work and friends and found she had been making plans to leave since the day after that last blowup.

John lifted his feet to the coffee table in front of the moss green sofa. He stared at the painting across the room, at the intense swirls of colors and textures that reminded him sharply of his complex and mysterious wife. After loving her all these years, she still had levels he hadn't explored. He knew every inch of her body, and still she could take him by surprise. As she had done by leaving.

He would surprise her by not following.

He sat for a long time, alone in the apartment they had furnished together.

Finally, he went to bed.

He worked the next day, escaping into a fictional world he could control. That became even easier as the days wore on.

But a part of him was always waiting for Spring.

By God, he could wait her out.

Chapter Three

∿ Before coming home to White's Creek, Spring couldn't imagine a situation where she would need Debra Nelson's help. But if she wanted to remain here, she needed a job. And that might require Debra's intervention on her behalf.

In the middle of July, Spring learned the county school system had a position opening, an "at-large" counselor who would work with students at a variety of schools, from kindergarten to the high school. Spring had the credentials. She had the references. She had the experience.

But this was White's Creek.

Spring had left here in a cloud of dust with the son of the family who owned half the town. Even before that, she was a rebel. In high school, she campaigned against dress codes and locker searches and other assorted imagined and real injustices. Once, she had scandalized everyone by attending a dance with a friend who was black. In their town, fifteen years ago, that was just not done. Maybe that's why she had delighted in doing it. Spring did so love to surprise people.

Not that she hadn't been an excellent student. She made straight A's, graduating third in her high-school class. Perhaps academics came too easily to her, didn't occupy her enough. With time on her hands, she flirted a lot and dated widely but not always wisely. Her reputation had been smudged by a couple of spurned suitors, then tarred by the likes of gossips like Willa Dean.

Small towns have long memories. So maybe it wasn't too surprising that the school board now hesitated over hiring Spring.

One hot Saturday afternoon out at the farm, her sister, Rainy, who taught third grade and had always been as straitlaced as Spring wasn't, tried to put things in perspective. "Spring, there may be some new blood moving into this town, but it hasn't taken over yet."

Spring had interviewed for the job on Monday, and she knew the position had to be filled soon. School started the third week of August. "What can I do?"

Rainy placed her hands on her plump hips. "Well, you're not helping matters by flirting with Ernie Fritz out at McDonald's."

"Ernie is an old friend," Spring protested. "He and his wife had me over to dinner just last night."

"But Ernie can't hire you. You need to be thinking about who can."

Her sister was right, Spring realized.

The next afternoon, she wound up in her most conservative dress in the sunroom at John's mother's house. As the town's richest citizen, Debra was sure to hold plenty of influence over everything, including the hiring of school-system personnel. "Mrs. Nelson," the maid had informed her, "will be down in a moment."

Spring settled back in a floral-upholstered chair and tried to tell herself she hadn't lost her mind. Unease wouldn't allow her to get comfortable.

She didn't like Debra Nelson. No, that was too mild. The woman was everything Spring despised in a mother. Spring shouldn't be asking for her help, no matter how much she wanted that counselor's position. Coming to Debra was a betrayal of John.

Spring didn't pause to think of the irony in remaining loyal to an estranged spouse who hadn't bothered to call her since she arrived home. Most of the time, she could avoid thinking of how piqued she was over John's not trying to contact her. Here in this house, however, Sam Nelson's house, all she could think of was what John had endured from his parents.

"I've got to get out of here," she muttered, pulling herself from the chair.

"So soon?"

The voice behind Spring made her whirl around. She found John's brother lounging in the doorway that led to the hall. She had no idea how long he had been standing there since she hadn't heard him come up.

"Logan," she breathed, putting a hand to the pulse that pounded in her throat. "You scared me to death."

He didn't reply. He just stood there, blond and tan in the sunlight that poured in the glassed-in room, something between a smirk and a smile on his lips.

Ever since that first day Spring had been back in town, she had been looking for Logan. Ebbie said he drove a fast little silver car. Once or twice, Spring imagined she glimpsed it out on the road near her parents' farm. But if Logan was lurking about, he was adept at avoiding detection.

Once her pulse returned to normal, Spring put out her hand. "How are you, Logan? I suppose you remember me."

He ignored her gesture and shoved his hands into the pockets of his baggy denim shorts. "I remember the Corvette that's parked outside. My father bought that car for John."

"Right. Your father and mother gave John the Corvette for his eighteenth birthday." Spring tried, but couldn't stop the sarcasm that crept into her voice. "It was quite a showy gesture on their part." In truth, they had been playing one-upmanship with friends who had brought their own son a less expensive car for his birthday.

Logan's blue eyes hardened. "Dad almost reported that car stolen when John took off with you."

She wasn't surprised. "I guess that would have been his right, even though it was a gift."

"I think Mother talked him out of it."

Spring was surprised. Debra wasn't known for forgiveness or charity. "So you remember when John and I left?"

Logan shrugged. "I know what my dad told me." There was something distinctly proprietary in his references to Sam. Did he think Spring cared that he was Sam's biological son and John wasn't? She couldn't imagine why.

"Why do you have the car?" Logan asked. "You get it in the divorce or something?"

"John and I aren't divorced."

That raised an eyebrow. "But he gave you the car?"

"I always liked the Corvette better than he did."

"They're great cars. I had one until I wrapped it around a telephone pole." Something akin to pride flickered in his expression.

Spring barely took that in. Her work had taught her to dismiss most teenage boasts. She was more interested in studying Logan's face. There was some faint resemblance to John. Around the lips, she thought. But Logan was much more handsome. Where John's features were uneven, the nose a little big, the chin a little long, Logan's features were model-perfect. That, combined with his height and athletic build, made him quite something. His father had been equally handsome. And very evil.

Was Logan like Sam on the inside as well?

Ebbie had told Spring that Logan was known as

a bully and a troublemaker. He had been arrested for DUI. He had been in several fights. He had been bounced out of all the private schools to which Debra had sent him. The public schools here didn't want him, but his mother's influence smoothed the way and kept him out of a juvenile correction facility. Word was, however, that the schools and Sheriff Kane were about fed up.

Spring didn't want to believe all the bad press on Logan. Not when she could remember the boy he had been. In particular, she recalled him as the mischievous little four-year-old who had caught her and John out in the pool cabana behind this house one cold December night. She remembered a door creaking open, a scramble in the dark as she tried to button her blouse and John tried to zip his pants.

Then the lights had beamed on, and Logan had stood there, grinning at them. "You're it!" he had called, giggling in delight.

John had made a dive for the light switch. The last thing he and Spring wanted was to be discovered by Debra or Sam. And if Spring remembered correctly, Logan had to be bribed to keep his mouth shut.

The memory, the only good one Spring had of this house, made her smile. "Tell me," she asked Logan. "Are you still into chocolate-covered peanuts in a big way?"

He started. A slow, genuine smile replaced his smirk. "How'd you remember that?"

"Keeping you quiet about the pool-house incident cost me and John a fortune in peanut clusters."

He crossed his arms, looking more relaxed and less belligerent by the minute. "Just what was it the two of you were doing out there?"

She laughed. He joined in. That's the way Debra found them when she swept into the room. And the laughter ceased. Abruptly.

Debra White Nelson had that effect on people, Spring thought, even as she politely extended her hand to her mother-in-law.

Debra was a beautiful woman. Blond hair done in a fashionable short bob. Flawless complexion, unlined, even around the dark eyes that reminded Spring so much of John's. A tiny nose and firm chin. A figure set off to stunning effect in a sky-blue cotton dress. Looking at Debra, no one would believe she had a son nearly thirty-one years old.

"You and Logan seem to be having a good laugh," Debra said as she briefly pressed Spring's hand. "What were you talking about?"

From someone else, the question might have been seen as a casual inquiry. From Debra, it was a command.

Logan answered it that way, "It was nothing, ma'am." His polite tone belied his look of disrespect.

Tightening her expertly lined lips, Debra said, "You may run along now, son. I'm sure Spring came to speak with me."

The young man turned to go without saying

anything more, but Spring stopped him. "It was really good to see you, Logan. Maybe we can get together again."

He darted a look from Spring to his mother, then shrugged as he turned away. "Whatever."

When he was gone, Debra sighed. "I apologize for my son's manners. But then, I assume you're not surprised. I'm sure you've heard all sorts of tales about Logan since you got back in town."

"I've heard a lot of gossip," she admitted. "I try not to put much stock in that."

If Debra heard the mocking censure in Spring's tone, she gave no sign. She simply gestured for her to sit down. Spring hesitated.

Debra frowned. "My maid said you wanted to talk to me."

"I guess . . ." Spring cleared her throat. "I guess I do. But not about what I intended."

"Oh?" Debra placed her hand on the back of a nearby chair and impatiently tapped one rosy-tipped nail against the wicker back.

Spring cleared her throat. "I think what I came to say to you is that John is doing well."

If the woman felt any emotion at all about her eldest son, she didn't show it. "Yes. I see his books in the stores."

"Ever read one?"

Debra didn't answer. Her gaze met Spring's. "I'm glad John is doing fine."

"Is that all? You don't want to know anything else about him?"

Only a slight squaring of her jaw revealed

Debra might be growing irritated. "John made it clear long ago that he didn't welcome my interest."

Spring blinked. "Did you ever try to contact him after we moved to Chicago?"

"He made his feelings known before you left."

"So it really has been twelve years since you spoke to him?" Spring was startled and didn't know why. John had never told her anything about any contact from his mother. Yet, somewhere deep inside, she had been unable to imagine a mother, even one as bad as this one, who wouldn't at least try to check up on her son. It would have been difficult for her to have tried to reach John without Spring's knowledge, but he would have hidden it from her, anyway.

Debra lifted her chin. Her voice was carefully modulated, but with an edge of steel. "Really, Spring, I don't know what you're trying to ask me."

There was a list of questions Spring would like to put to this woman. But for asking them, Spring would no doubt be thrown out on her ear.

So she forced herself to back off. "I shouldn't have come here," she murmured. "I don't know what I was thinking." With a last nod, she started toward the door. "I can find my way out."

In the broad, handsome hallway, Spring was reaching for the handle of the front door when Debra's voice sounded behind her. "Is John coming here to see you?"

Slowly, Spring turned around. The other

woman's face was as composed as ever. Perhaps Spring imagined that hint of trepidation.

"I don't think John wants to come anywhere near this place," she told Debra.

His mother clasped her hands together. Was it relief Spring saw in her posture? "So the two of you . . ." Debra cleared her throat. "I take it that you're divorcing."

"It's a possibility."

"I'm sorry."

That made Spring chuckle. "Considering you and Mr. Nelson were dead set against our marriage, that's kind of an empty sentiment."

"You were married quite a while. Obviously, Sam and I didn't understand how much you cared for each other. We thought it was a simple high-school crush, best discouraged before it got out of hand. That's the reason we intervened."

What a joke. And the woman actually seemed to believe it. Spring chuckled again. "If it's any consolation, you and Sam managed to play quite a role in our breakup, even after all these years."

Debra's brow wrinkled. "What do you mean?"

"Sometimes it takes a long time for the damage parents inflict to heal. Sometimes the wounds never close." Spring didn't bother to stick around to see if Debra understood she was being brought to task for her lack of parenting.

Spring opened the door and walked out into the July heat, glad to be free of this mansion that had so often been a house of terror for John. What a fool she had been for coming here.

Logan stepped out from behind one of the broad columns on the front porch. "Did you get what you wanted?"

"My goodness, you like to sneak up on people, don't you?" Spring tried to brush past him.

However, he stepped in her path and repeated his question.

She gave him an annoyed glance. "Listen, I'm not someone who is going to be intimidated by you, so you might as well let me get to my car."

"You don't look too happy. Debra must not have been in a generous mood."

Only then did Spring realize the young man thought she had come begging for money from his mother. That made her hoot with laughter. He was so surprised, she neatly sidestepped him and headed down the shallow brick steps to the car she had parked in the circular drive.

"I know you asked her for something," Logan insisted, following her.

"Even if I did, it's none of your business." Spring slipped her keys from her purse and swung open her car door.

Logan just wouldn't give up. "You look mad. What did she say to you?"

"Oh, for heaven's sake." Spring rolled her eyes. "You know, Logan, if you want to talk to me, I can think of lots better places to do it than out here in the blistering hot sun. And I know of plenty of things I'd rather talk about than your mother." Impulsively, she tossed him the car key. "You want to drive the Corvette?"

For a moment, his eyes shone. The eagerness was masked in a hurry, however. He walked over and held out the keys. "Maybe some other time."

When she took her key chain, Spring also took hold of his hand. He didn't draw away as she expected. She didn't want to feel a connection to this young man. There was no real reason she should. His own brother had rarely even mentioned him. But she felt this pull toward Logan. He did remind her of John, especially John as she had first met him. Beneath Logan's swagger and his studied indifference, there was the same vulnerability and need she had once sensed in John. And if that were so, then perhaps Logan had endured much of the same childhood as John.

John claimed that couldn't be true. Logan was Sam's real son, he had said. Sam had loved Logan, treated him like a little god. He had chosen John to hate.

But in Spring's work, she had found that monsters weren't always so selective about their victims.

"Call me," she told Logan, looking him straight in the eyes. "I'd like to get to know you again."

She had surprised him so completely that he forgot to pretend not to care. "Why?"

She decided on honesty. "You're John's brother."

"And you're almost his ex-wife."

Strange how deeply those words cut. She released Logan's hand. "Whatever's happened between me and John, he's in Chicago and I'm here.

So are you. I think it would be nice if we were friends."

He didn't make any promises. Spring drove away from the big house set behind the iron-and-brick wall. She ached all over, as bruised as she might have been after a physical struggle. And she hadn't even asked Debra to help her get that job she wanted. She could only imagine how she would be feeling if she had sunk to that depraved level.

Damn, but she missed John.

Once she gave into that feeling, she hurt more than ever. She had been trying so hard not to think of him. She jumped every time the phone rang. She flew to the mailbox when the postman's truck came rumbling up the road. But there had been nothing. No contact. John had simply let her go.

The pain of acknowledging that ate at her insides. She wasn't about to go home and let her mother see what kind of shape she was in. Callie had eased up about Spring's running away from her problems, but the woman could read her daughter's moods and feelings without even trying.

So Spring drove out to Silver Lake. An ill-advised choice, perhaps. Too many hot summer afternoons had once been spent here with John. Too many cool nights under a harvest moon. Too many discoveries, both sweet and sad, had been made within sight of the smooth water.

* * *

A brisk, early November breeze whispered through the open windows as John drew his mother's car to a stop on an offshoot of Silver Lake Road. He and Spring had been to the movies and out to get a hamburger, but he had been quiet all night. Much quieter than usual.

"What's wrong?" Spring asked, scooting close to him in the broad, front seat of the Cadillac.

"Nothing."

She knew what that meant. "It's your stepfather, isn't it?"

He sighed. "He's always on me about something."

"What is it this time?"

"I don't want to go to the country club with him and my mother tomorrow."

Spring knew the Nelsons regularly went to the club in the nearby, larger town of Gainesville, Georgia. She would have loved to have gone, just for the experience. But no invitation had been forthcoming. She doubted one would. "You always go there for lunch on Sunday. What's the big deal?"

He paused for only a moment before explaining, "My mother's trying to set me up with the daughter of one of her friends."

"Oh." Spring tried not to panic. She was confident John really cared for her, but his parents weren't too happy about it. A girl from their world would be more appropriate. John did most everything he could to keep from rocking the boat at home. Spring was his only defiance. She knew he sometimes had to lie about seeing her. His life would be easier if he dated someone else, especially someone Debra and Sam had chosen.

He seemed to sense her rising dismay.

"Don't worry." He took hold of her hands and gripped them hard. "I'm not interested in that girl."

"I know, but—"

"I'm not interested in any girl but you." He hesitated, and though the interior of the car was dim, Spring could feel the intensity of his gaze. His voice deepened. "You know how I feel about you."

Breathless anticipation squeezed her lungs. An eternity seemed to pass before John said what she had yearned to hear. "I love you, Spring."

"Me too," she whispered, and slipped into his arms.

The magic of the moment was marred by his wince. Spring drew away. "What's wrong?"

"Nothing." He pulled her back toward him. "Come here." But again he groaned.

Concerned, Spring held him off. "What's wrong with you?" She flipped on the overhead light so she could see. He was bent forward, holding his right side. "You're hurt," she said, alarmed.

"I'm all right." Impatiently, he cut the light. "It's nothing but a bruise."

"From what?"

"Just an accident."

"But what did you do?"

His voice rose. "It's nothing, I tell you. Nothing. Jeez, is this what you want to talk about after I tell you I love you?"

It wasn't what Spring wanted to talk about at all. But a horrible suspicion was growing in her mind. Though she and John hadn't yet gone all the way, they knew one another's bodies. So she knew just how many bruises he'd had since they started going out. He didn't play football. She knew he wasn't clumsy. So . . .

Spring turned the light back on. "Pull up your shirt, John. Show me this bruise."

"Shit, Spring, this is—"

"Show me."

Realizing resistance was futile, John jerked his shirt-tail out of his jeans and pulled it up. From the ribs to the waist of his well-defined, muscular torso were a series of large, purpling bruises. They were so bad Spring gasped.

"Me and Logan were goofing around, wrestling," he tried to explain.

Spring knew better. Horrified, she raised her gaze to John's. "Logan didn't do this."

"He didn't mean to."

"It was your stepfather."

All the confirmation she needed came in the way John couldn't meet her eyes. Defiance tilted his chin upward. "It's not a big deal, Spring."

"We have to tell somebody. He can't get away with this."

"No," John said, emphatically. "Who would we tell? Who's going to believe Sam Nelson, upstanding citizen and employer of half the city, smacks his stepson around for kicks?"

"My parents will believe," Spring insisted. "They'll help you."

"Sam will crush them first." John's laugh was bitter. "My God, Spring, he owns a majority interest in the bank. I bet your parents have a loan or two there. Sam

could make it hard on them if they tried to make accusations."

"What about the sheriff?"

"How's he going to get elected without Sam's support?"

What he said made sense, but it went against her nature to just sit back, to let this wrong go unpunished.

"Listen to me," John said, and caught her hands in his once more. *"You don't tell anyone about this. Not your sister or your parents. No one."*

"But surely if you told your mother—"

"That's no help." John's face hardened. *"And if you love me, Spring, you'll keep quiet. It would only get worse if he thought someone knew."*

A sob caught in her throat. *"He could really hurt you."*

"I can handle it. I know how to handle it." In John's eyes was sad evidence of long experience in dealing with his stepfather's punches.

Gently, Spring moved back into his arms, where she gave in to her tears.

"It will be okay," John murmured against her hair. *"In just six more months, we graduate. I can hold on until then. As long as I have you, I can hold on."*

Looking back, Spring knew how foolish she had been to say nothing. She should have shouted the truth from the rooftops until someone stepped forward to help John. At the time, however, she had been young and frightened.

But she had been smart enough to realize sharing this with her was hard on John. He had his pride. He didn't want her to think him weak because he didn't fight back.

She had never thought him anything but brave. Even before she learned about the psychology of abuse, Spring had understood John's need not be ashamed. If he had fought back, Sam might have hurt him more. Or sent him away again.

She had been most terrified of John leaving. She had even suggested they break up, so that Sam couldn't use John dating her as an excuse to hit him or send him off to another school. John wouldn't hear of that, of course. He said she was his escape, the only good thing in his life. Sometimes, Spring thought the secret they shared about his family was as strong a bond as their love.

The mistake they had made later on, when they were older, was in not talking about it openly. Spring hadn't asked him to discuss it very much, because she knew how painful it was for him. He wouldn't go for counseling, and even with her education, she let him get away with that. He had sealed his pain away. And it had festered. She wished she had been a little more pushy. She wished she had discovered sooner just how profoundly his parents had damaged him.

Yes, his *parents*. Not just Sam.

The one thing Spring had forced John to reveal was that Debra had known all along that Sam beat her son. She had known, and she hadn't intervened.

"And I was going to ask that woman to help me get this job." Groaning, Spring buried her face in her hands. She was ashamed of herself for even considering Debra's help. She would get a job from Ernie down at McDonald's before she let John's mother do a thing for her.

As it turned out, however, flipping burgers was not Spring's destiny. She got the counselor's job. The school superintendent said her qualifications had been so much higher than any of the other candidates' that they felt she had to be hired. Spring was suspicious. She almost asked if Debra was behind the hiring. Then she blew it off. If the woman had indeed spoken up on Spring's behalf, it was one of the few charitable things she had ever done.

Spring went to work in early August, studying files, setting up schedules and plans. Her office was a small cubbyhole on the ground floor of the elementary school where Rainy taught. Spring, who genuinely enjoyed her sister's company, looked forward to the chance to see her as often as possible. But she didn't expect to be in the office that much. As a counselor-at-large, she would be visiting all the county schools.

It was good to be busy. It kept her mind off John. Callie said she was just plain sticking her head in the mud, avoiding making tough decisions about her future.

Spring did her best to ignore her mother's

advice. With her first paycheck, she rented a small house in town. She missed the farm, but the privacy was wonderful.

It was fun putting the furnishings together using cast-offs from Rainy, her parents, neighbors, and friends. She called the decor "eclectic chic." Rainy, who liked her furniture in matching sets, said it was "early junk." The sisters, so different in looks, temperament, and taste, argued good-naturedly over paint and curtains. Spring began to wonder how she had ever lived so far from Rainy or her parents.

Callie, who called Spring's move into town foolishness, still came around to stock the kitchen pantry with spices and herbs. For luck, she hung a four-leaf clover pressed between glass in the kitchen window.

Ned and Spring's three older brothers, who lived in Atlanta and Nashville, supervised the moving of the furniture and went over every window and door, making a great show of worrying about Spring's safety. She loved their concern, but was relieved when they left her alone to the peace and quiet of her very own place.

By far the most intriguing visitor Spring had was Logan. Actually, he started seeking her out before she moved. First he surprised her while she was eating alone at Ebbie's. Then he came to her office at the school. She let him drive the Corvette. They shared an ice-cream cone. When he started dropping by her house, she took to keeping a supply of chocolate-covered peanuts on hand.

If Spring hadn't read Logan's school records or heard her colleagues talk about him, she might never have believed he was the same boy they privately referred to as "The Royal Terror." With Spring, Logan was just a teenager. He talked to her about music and movies and girls. He was not unlike the boy she had met at McDonald's on her first day back in White's Creek. A very normal boy. But every teacher at the high school seemed to be praying they could get Logan through his senior year without some major incident of violence or defiance.

September eased toward October. Spring's life fell into a routine. Work, family, friends. One day she even found herself responding to the warm interest of the young high-school principal. She supposed she was moving on.

Away from John.

Half of her looked at that as a death.

The other chose to see it as a rebirth. Life after John.

Brave thoughts. But they didn't keep her warm on the first night the temperatures turned chilly.

In the lonely apartment in Chicago, it was downright cold. John hardly noticed. He no longer jumped when the phone rang or went eagerly to the mailbox, thinking he would hear from Spring.

He concentrated on his work. And every day, when he woke up alone, he told himself this was all for the best. Spring had clearly made her choice.

Over a couple of beers with some buddies, he had been advised to file for divorce. "The world is full of babes," one friend told him. "Get free and get busy meeting them."

John laughed, though he felt like throwing up. He had been married since he was eighteen. Like most normal men, he didn't mind looking. But straying from Spring had never entered his mind. It didn't now, even though she was gone.

He wasn't filing for divorce. In his opinion, this whole operation belonged to Spring. She had to make the first move.

Chapter Four

〜 "You should file for divorce."

Spring looked up from her desk at her sister. "Good Lord, Rainy, what brought that on?"

Her older sister, who was perched on the corner of Spring's desk, said, "You haven't spoken to John since you left him in June. You're acting like a single woman. Seems to me you ought to make your situation fit your actions."

"That sounds just like something Mama would say."

"Mama's a smart woman."

"And if she wants to disapprove of me and something I do, she should do it herself instead of siccing you on me."

That tart comment brought fire to Rainy's normally placid brown eyes. "This is my opinion, not hers. Mama never shies away from passing opinions on whatever we do." She hesitated, then added, "Mama worries about you a lot, Spring. Especially since you moved to town."

"Rainy, surely you're not going to suggest that I shouldn't have found my own place."

"Of course not. God knows, I couldn't move back in with Mama and Daddy." Rainy shuddered. "Sometimes I want to back a truck up to the door and start shoveling the junk out of their house."

"Better not let Mama hear such blasphemy. She does love her mess."

"Since when does Mama have to hear what we're saying to know what we're thinking?" Rainy giggled. "There are times when I understand why some folks think Mama's a witch. She can be a little bit spooky."

"You're shaking in your shoes because she's predicted there's another baby in your future. Maybe a girl, after all those grandsons."

The color drained from Rainy's cheeks. "You hush up, now. That's not funny. I'm thirty-five years old and thirty pounds overweight, and Jess and I are perfectly content with Randy and Colter."

Spring clucked in dismay. "It's a darn shame Mama is so rarely wrong with her predictions."

"I wish she'd keep some of what she sees to herself."

"Don't look so nervous, Rainy. You and Jess know what causes babies. You can take the proper precautions."

"You're full of sassy talk, Spring DeWitt Nelson."

"Just DeWitt, remember?"

"Does using your maiden name mean you're at least considering a divorce?"

"I've always used my maiden name at work."

"And John was all right with that?"

"He never said if he wasn't."

"I wonder what he'd think now."

Spring didn't answer. As determined as her sister was to talk about her husband, she was just as determined to avoid the subject.

From the doorway, a male voice said, "Miss DeWitt, here's that box you sent me for."

Spring looked up and into the rapt, adoring gaze of Larry Stevens, the young keeper of the golden arches from her first morning back in White's Creek. Spring stopped by the fast-food restaurant often, and in the process the young man had become an ardent admirer.

This afternoon, Larry and his sister, Mollie, had run over to Spring's house to pick up some Halloween decorations she had forgotten at home that morning.

"Thanks." Spring stood, smiling at Larry as she directed him to put the box on a nearby table.

"No problem at all," he croaked.

Over his shoulder, his sister gave Spring a grin. She knew all about her brother's crush.

Two afternoons a week, Mollie's work-study program brought her to the suite of administrative offices where Spring's cubbyhole was located. Larry often found a reason to stop in.

These two kids had become special to Spring. They were perfect candidates for trouble, but they were managing—so far—to beat the odds. Mollie and Larry shared the same father, who had disappeared a long time ago. Another marriage and three children later, their mother had died with her second husband in a car accident. Now they all lived with the maternal grandmother. They weren't poor, as the grandfather had been a successful attorney. But raising five children was still expensive and draining for a woman the age of Mollie's grandmother.

At seventeen, Mollie was a year older than Larry, but to Spring she seemed decades beyond him. Family responsibilities had given her a seriousness that often dismayed Spring. Her grades were good, even with the hours she worked at her part-time cashier's job at Wal-Mart. Because she had so little time to herself, she had few friends. No boyfriend, either. She had little fun at all from what Spring could tell.

Beneath her outwardly calm, red-haired exterior, Spring feared there was a volcano waiting to erupt.

Larry left for his job at McDonald's while Mollie retreated to the outer office to finish her work. The siblings shared a car, but on the afternoons she worked here, Spring gave her a ride home.

They were barely out the door before Rainy gave a disapproving snort.

"What was that for?" Spring asked.

"Do you have to flirt with every male who comes within range of your batting eyelashes?"

"Oh, please." Ignoring her, Spring took her seat and sipped from the mug of water she kept on her desk. "Larry is a perfectly harmless and sweet boy. He needs someone to talk to, and he has a little crush on me."

"I know, I know." Sighing, Rainy plopped down in a chair in front of Spring's desk. "I guess it's not really Larry Stevens I'm worried about." She hesitated, then added, "It's Dan Strickland."

Spring's gaze fell. Dan was the high school's young and very handsome principal.

Rainy leaned forward, keeping her voice low. "Spring, you've been seen with Dan a lot lately. But you're still a married woman, so of course there's talk."

"If I painted my toenails blue, there'd be talk in this town," Spring responded sarcastically.

"Well, the gossips are out in force, all right. I heard today at lunch that you and Dan were snuggled together under an umbrella at last Friday night's football game."

"It started raining like the dickens. Was I supposed to just sit in the downpour?"

"Wasn't there someone else to share an umbrella with?"

"I came with Dan."

Rainy said nothing, though her expression was troubled.

Spring glared at her in defiance. "If you must know, I've seen Dan more than a few times. I didn't tell you because I knew you would give me a lecture."

"But if you're seeing Dan, don't you think you should be thinking about divorce?"

"Maybe." *Divorce.* Spring hated the very word.

"Oh, Lord," Rainy murmured. "What is it that you're waiting for from John?"

"Nothing."

"Then what are you doing with Dan?"

He keeps the emptiness from eating me up inside. Spring ignored that bleak thought and kept her tone carefully flip. "Dan makes good conversation."

"That all?"

Spring gave a wicked laugh. "We like to leave the curtains open at my house while we dance naked from room to room. Then we move out to the porch swing and indulge in all sorts of depravities. Swings can be a lot of fun. I'm sure that's what the neighbors are really talking about."

Closing her eyes as if praying for strength, Rainy sighed. "I didn't bring this up because of the gossip. I'm beginning to think Mama is right about you trying to avoid making a decision about your marriage."

Spring found the whole subject distasteful. So she was grateful when Assistant School Superintendent Nita Grant stuck her head in the doorway. "Can I talk to you, Spring?"

Rainy took the hint, though she gave Spring a last, reproving look before she left.

Grim-faced, Nita pulled the door shut behind her. "I thought you might want to know that Logan is in the hallway. He's been suspended."

Spring groaned. "What'd he do?"

"There were two incidents, actually." Nita cleared her throat. "First, some inappropriate behavior with a young lady."

"Inappropriate?"

"The football coach caught Logan and a companion very close to *doing it* in a classroom near the gym."

Sighing, Spring pushed a hand through her hair. "My God, it looks like they could wait until the final bell, at least."

Nita didn't laugh.

"Sorry," Spring said quickly. "I wasn't trying to make light of it."

"Well, while the coach was confronting that situation, the girl's steady boyfriend came in."

"A steady and Logan Nelson. My, my, what a busy girl."

"There was quite a scene, I understand," Nita continued. "Logan broke the boyfriend's nose. He got a few punches in on the coach, too."

This, at last, was the behavior everyone had told Spring to expect from Logan. What had he been thinking? She straightened her shoulders. "What can I do, Nita?" The woman knew Spring was developing a relationship with her young brother-in-law.

"I thought perhaps you could impress the seriousness of the situation on him and his mother. So far this year, Logan's been on better behavior than anyone expected. There's been some minor trouble. Cutting classes, that sort of thing. But what happened this morning is unacceptable.

Dan Strickland, the superintendent, and I are fed up. Other parents are asking questions. If anything else this serious happens, Logan will be expelled."

"Debra Nelson probably won't like that."

Nita looked weary. "I know. But we've got to draw the line. She may be descended from the town founding Whites, and Logan's father may have left her a fortune, but he has to behave. We expect it of all other kids. Why not him?"

"I agree. But don't think Debra or Logan will take this news any better coming from me. I do like Logan, and I think he's beginning to like me. But we're not close."

"Just talk to him, will you? His mother is supposed to come by. I'll send her in."

Logan soon appeared in the doorway. The only signs of his altercation was a small cut over one eye and a bruise on his jaw. Predictably, his expression was defiant, though he couldn't quite meet Spring's gaze as he took the seat she offered.

She faced him with arms folded. "Well, you've done it up royally."

He shrugged. "The guy shouldn't have punched me."

"And maybe you should have waited until after school to try to make it with his girlfriend."

Hands braced on his denim-clad thighs, he focused on a point above Spring's shoulder. "It was just an impulse."

She groaned. "That's kind of a lame excuse,

isn't it? You had to know you were going to get caught."

He looked down at the floor. "I am sorry I punched the coach. He just got in the way."

"An apology might be a good move."

"Sure."

Spring reached out and touched his arm, virtually forcing him to look up at her. "Logan, do you understand this is the last thing they're going to take from you at school?"

"Sure it was," he scoffed. "They've told me that a dozen times. My mother always fixes things up."

"Not this time."

He clearly didn't believe Spring. And why should he? A lifetime of having excuses made for his behavior had taught him to expect a free ride.

Spring was casting about for a way to convince him he was really in deep trouble when Debra came in.

Debra's navy blue suit trimmed in gold braid matched her heavy gold jewelry. She looked chic, confident, and in a very big hurry. She glanced at her watch when Spring invited her to sit down. Logan didn't even look at her.

"I'm late for a meeting as it is," Debra explained.

Spring moved behind her desk. "I'm sorry about that. But Logan is in trouble, and Nita wants me to talk with you both about it."

"I know what happened. I spent an hour with

the superintendent just after lunch." Mouth tightening, Debra glared at Logan. "I know he's suspended for two weeks. What else is there to say?"

Spring repeated what Nita had told her about this being Logan's last chance.

Debra didn't look any more convinced of that than had her son, but she did turn to him and say, "I hope you're listening."

"Yeah, right." He pushed himself lazily to his feet. "I'm just going to go outside and wait while you two make the arrangements."

Spring started to stop him. But it would do no good, of course. Nothing she was going to say would convince him he had used up his last bit of leeway at school. So she let him go, but stopped Debra. "We still need to talk."

A flicker of annoyance crossed her features, but she sat down while Spring closed the door behind Logan.

"This is it," she told Debra. "The end. I know you don't believe it, but it's the truth."

Bracelets jangling, Debra folded her hands together on her lap. "That's what the superintendent already told me."

"How are we going to get through to Logan?"

"He seems to like you. Maybe you can make some kind of impression on him."

Spring was surprised to hear the woman encouraging her relationship with Logan. "You don't mind that he and I have become friends?"

"Of course not."

"Strange, considering how much you dislike me."

"I don't dislike you."

Spring couldn't stop her laughter. "Excuse me, but that was a joke, wasn't it?"

"No, it wasn't," Debra retorted. "I think it's admirable the way you've always tried to better yourself. It's something you and I have in common."

Of course, Debra would understand ambition. She had sold her son for Sam Nelson's money.

But Spring bristled at being compared to this woman. "Falling in love with John was not a calculated move to better myself."

"But it ended up getting you away from here. You got an education, made something of yourself."

"I would have done that without John. In my family, we were raised to be achievers."

"I know your parents are proud," Debra murmured.

Something in the way she said that made Spring want to challenge her. "How about you? Are you proud of your sons? Of the way you've raised them?"

John's mother looked down and toyed with her bracelets yet again. Only the color heightening her cheeks betrayed that Spring's last question might have struck a nerve. Her voice was steady and clear when she glanced up again. "Aren't we supposed to be discussing what to do about

Logan? As an *expert*, what are you advising me to do?"

Spring ignored the slight sarcasm in reference to her credentials. Because Debra was right. This was about Logan. "He's full of anger. He needs counseling to learn how to deal with it."

"I've done that," Debra replied. "Nothing's helped so far, obviously, else we wouldn't be having this discussion. Frankly, I'm at a loss."

"Logan needs someone to talk to. Even if counseling doesn't seem to do any good, he has to stick with it."

"You can work with him, can't you?"

Shrugging, Spring said, "I could, but—"

"I would pay you, naturally."

That offer almost pushed Spring over the edge. She hated that the slight tremor in her voice revealed Debra had made her angry. "This is not about money. Of course I'll make myself available to Logan, as I've already done. But I don't think I'm the best choice. I think Logan might open up more to a man."

"If you make the arrangements, I'll try to make sure he keeps the appointments." Debra stood, draping the strap of her expensive leather purse over one shoulder as she turned toward the door.

Spring got up, as well, fumbling for a good-bye, but Debra turned back before she could get it out. "Spring, please understand me. I do want someone to help Logan. Since his father died, he's been . . ." She bit her lip. "Impossible. I hope you can recommend something that will turn him around."

The genuine concern in her voice surprised Spring. She didn't want to believe Debra really cared. Spring wanted to paint her as the cold and heartless bitch who had let both of her children down. It was far easier to think of people in terms of black and white than in the shades of gray which was usually much more the norm.

Debra left without another word. Spring sat quietly at her desk thinking that perhaps it was her training. Or perhaps it was just her way. She couldn't help wondering what forces had gone into shaping Debra. Spring knew little about her besides the obvious facts.

What could John tell her?

She thrust that thought aside almost as quickly as it appeared. John would say nothing about his mother but the very worst. And anyway, it wasn't Debra's emotional makeup or John's opinions that mattered right now. Logan was the member of the Nelson family of primary concern.

With a laugh, Spring realized she was actually thinking of the Nelsons as a family. And herself as part of it. The problems of Debra and Logan and the strained relations between Spring and her husband were all bound up together. In some weird cosmic sense, they had been rocking along in the same boat for a long, long time.

And because of that, John would be the best person to help Logan.

The thought was discarded almost before it was formed. The only way John would ever get involved with Logan would be if Spring called him. Something she wasn't going to do.

Laughter sounded in the outer office, and when she went to investigate, Spring found Logan hadn't left. He was leaning against a wall, talking with Mollie, who was working at a tall filing cabinet. They both stared guiltily at Spring, laughter dying. Her gaze flashed from Mollie's flushed features to Logan's face and back again.

"You can go," Spring told him.

"Okay." His smile reminded her of how charming he could be. It was focused on Mollie.

Frowning slightly, Spring watched him leave, then turned to Mollie. She had to say the girl's name twice before getting her attention. "You okay?"

"Sure."

Spring took a step closer, keeping her tone casual. "Do you know Logan?"

Mollie shrugged. "Everybody knows Logan."

"Are you friends?"

"He's in my French class. We talk sometimes."

"Was he bothering you out here?"

Now Mollie glanced up. "Bothering me?"

"You know, being a smart aleck, or something."

"We were just talking."

Still Spring frowned. She couldn't imagine quiet, serious Mollie Stevens and troublemaking Logan Nelson running in the same circles.

"Can I ask you something?" Mollie asked as she closed the cabinet drawer.

"Of course."

The girl hesitated, her green eyes troubled. "Is it true you're married to Logan's brother?"

Spring assumed everyone knew about her marital status, but she supposed there were some people in White's Creek who didn't spend their time gossiping. She explained the situation to Mollie.

"Logan says he doesn't really know his brother."

"That's true."

"How come?"

Now Spring paused. She was all for being open and honest with the kids she worked with, but there were limits when it came to her personal life. "It's a long story."

The girl looked instantly contrite, her cheeks flaming red. "I'm sorry. I shouldn't have—"

"No, no," Spring hastened to reassure her. "It's no big secret. We'll talk about it another time."

"Sure." Mollie turned away, nodding toward the clock over the door. "Are we about through here for the day?"

"Just a few more minutes." Spring returned to her office, closing the door behind her before crossing to the window. With a sigh, she leaned her forehead against the glass, just in time to catch Logan's little silver car pulling out of the parking lot.

Spring didn't want to be drawn into this family

drama. She didn't want to care about Logan's hell-bent-for-leather race toward self-destruction. But she did.

It would frost that night.

October had brought color to the trees around White's Creek. The mercury plunged when the sun burned past the horizon. Spring loved being out on these cool autumn nights, loved the almost weightless feel of the clear air, the way the stars seemed closer, the moon bigger.

Tonight as she drove through the dark with the window down on the Corvette, she could smell the coming frost. She welcomed the coolness. She needed the fresh air to blow through her hair, to clear away the problem beating at her brain.

After dropping Mollie at her house, Spring couldn't stop thinking about Logan. Finally, she had gone over to the high-school counseling department. She had looked up Logan's files once before, just after she took this job. This evening, however, she made a closer review of his records. The files told a story of rebelliousness and disruptive behavior dating from grade school. Conversely, test scores showed him to be highly intelligent. And if a subject or teacher engaged his interest, he was capable of performing well.

This latest violent outburst was far from Logan's first. In this respect, his conduct had deteriorated since the death of his father over four years ago. Little provocation was necessary for him to explode with his fists. He had been banned from high-school athletics following a series of vicious incidents on the football field. In at least one case, Spring was shocked that criminal charges hadn't been filed. Terri Tate, the counselor who had tried to work with Logan for the past few years, suspected substance abuse might be compounding the problems.

Every time Logan had been around Spring, he had been straight and sober. Was her judgment clouded because he was John's brother? Or, like his father, was he a very good actor?

The records also showed a pattern of behavior in Logan's parents. Instead of helping him face his problems, they had used their influence and money to get him out of trouble.

The records portrayed him as a hopeless mess. Spring thought otherwise.

But just how had the bright-eyed boy he had been become the troubled young man he was?

Spring was afraid she knew the answer. She had special knowledge of what might motivate a young man who had grown-up under Sam Nelson's rule. John might have turned his anger in more productive directions than Logan's current path, but both brothers were on the run.

Perhaps her impulse had been right. Perhaps John could help Logan. And in the process, there was a chance that Logan would help John.

The rush of Spring's car tires over the asphalt seemed to sing a cautionary tune. *Don't care, Spring. Don't get involved. Stay away. Away and safe.*

Spring had started tonight's drive with no

particular destination in mind. Funny how her car just seemed to find its way to an untidy house set well back from the road, the home where chrysanthemums had replaced the flowers of summer. They bloomed in the moonlight, their broad heads of bronze and yellow left bare to face the dew that would surely freeze by dawn.

The dogs barked as Spring stepped out of her car, quieting when she spoke to them. On the screened front porch a shadow moved, and the kitchen door opened as Spring approached the steps. She wasn't surprised when her mother's slim frame appeared in the darkness. Of course her mother had seen her coming. Seen her long before the lights from her car swept along the long front drive.

"Mind the spider's web by the door," Callie said by way of greeting.

"Hello to you, too, Mama." Spring took care in opening the screened door, avoiding the web that glistened in a stream of the light from the kitchen windows.

Callie bent to study the insect's lair closely. "Small web. Means fair weather's going to hold." She sniffed the air. "Probably a few days."

Spring had no reason to dispute Callie's claim. Her mother's weather forecasts, based on the sounds, scents, and sights of the natural world, were seldom wrong. "I'll make sure I tell the high-school football coach tomorrow. After that mud bath the team played in last week, he'll welcome the news."

The swing creaked as Callie sat. "Come over here by me, Daughter. Tell me what's wrong."

Spring obliged, tucking her arm through her mother's and placing her head on her shoulder.

"You've been thinking about John," Callie observed.

"Of course." Spring raised her head. "Mama, please talk me out of calling him."

The question didn't shock Callie. Through the darkness her gaze was bright and direct. "Spring, my darlin', why would I try to talk you out of what your heart knows is right?"

Releasing a long sigh, Spring snuggled closer. "Oh, Mama, why in the hell can't you ever be wrong?"

Chapter Five

❧ For nearly forty years, Ebbie Ruth Denison's City Diner had been a gathering place for the meek and the mighty of White's Creek, Georgia. She was proud of her success.

The food was simply Southern—fried chicken, country ham, and flaky biscuits dripping with honey. All prepared as if Ebbie might be serving her family. Which she had been, most nights, when her five young ones had been coming on.

Ebbie's husband had taken up with a fancy woman from Atlanta, leaving her the diner, but cleaning out all their cash. After he was gone, Ebbie moved her brood into the rooms over the diner.

They took their meals in the restaurant. They waited tables, cooked, and cleaned. Ebbie accepted no excuses for shirking duties. She gave no apologies for the smells of onions and grease that filtered up the stairs and into their clothes and hair. She made do and, in the end, did well enough to offer an education or other start to each of her children.

Two sons and a daughter had taken her example of hard work and gone on to lead happy, productive lives with families of their own. Another daughter, not seen in a decade and a half, had run wild through every willing man in town and was probably still running wild somewhere else. Another son, her baby, was buried in the Methodist cemetery next to John Nelson's real father. No hero, Ebbie's son had been shot while holding up a gas station twenty-five years ago.

Most nights, Ebbie was content in the apartment that used to be so crowded. Other times, she imagined her two lost lambs showing up at the door. She imagined welcoming them home.

Some folks would be shocked to learn of such tenderness. Ebbie enjoyed her reputation for flattening or inflating folks with a look or a word. Only those closest to her knew she was a marshmallow inside.

She reigned supreme amid her scarred wooden booths and Formica-topped tables with a forty-year collection of advertising art crowding the walls. When changes were sometimes suggested to the diner, Ebbie resisted.

"No need to be getting fancy-schmancy around here. Folks in White's Creek are used to keeping things familiar-like."

The City Diner and Ebbie were a part of the town, nearly as integral as the phone and electric lines. Everybody knew Ebbie.

She, in turn, never forgot a face or a name.

Which was why she smiled in recognition on the raw November afternoon when John Nelson sauntered into the diner.

Hands on her broad hips, Ebbie paused at the end of the counter and took a good look at the tall, lean man who stood just inside the door. And she understood why the two other women in the place gave him a second look, as well. He wasn't really handsome. Never had been. But he had something.

He wore black jeans, a gray sweater, black leather jacket. Expensive clothes, Ebbie judged. His dark hair was wet from the cold rain that had been falling since early morning. As he wiped his feet on the doormat, he darted a quick look around the nearly deserted diner.

Despite the twelve years since he had last been here, Ebbie would have known John anywhere. Those deep-set dark eyes, his long, chiseled face, and generous, almost sinful lips marked him as his father's son. Son of his real father, not of Sam Nelson.

As John continued to hesitate on the threshold, Ebbie let loose with a belly laugh. He looked at her and started to smile.

"Look what the rain drove into town," she drawled. "Are you slumming or looking for work?"

"Slumming, obviously." He strolled toward her, still smiling. "You got anything worth eating in here?"

"Some people say so."

"People in this town? They just don't have anything to compare you to."

Her laughter was hoarse and dissolved into a cough.

John's expression turned to concern as he patted her on the back. "Damn, Ebbie. Are you still smoking?"

She went behind the counter and poured herself a glass of water. Once it was down, she glared at him. "Don't tell me you've turned into one of those healthy-living sermonizers."

"Not really. But I don't smoke."

"Something else'll just kill you."

He doffed his jacket and settled onto a stool, laughing. "Spring always says—" He stopped abruptly, smile fading.

"Yes, *Spring*." A glint appeared in Ebbie's eyes as she poured him a cup of coffee. "I reckon that's why you're in town."

"She called me," John admitted.

"Did she now?"

The dubious note in the older woman's voice put John on the defensive. "We are married, you know. Have been for a while."

"So I've heard." The bell jangled over the door, signaling another customer, and Ebbie shrugged and handed John a menu. "You let me know what you want."

John stared at the pink, typewritten insert of daily specials without really seeing them. He

knew he should ignore Ebbie's insinuating tone
and be patient. Just as she served her food only at
the peak of freshness, she didn't let loose of any
information until she was ready.

So John ordered the meat-loaf platter and
looked around the diner. Unlike the other
changes he had seen driving into town, this place
was almost the same as it had been on a late June
day thirteen years ago. He had just been expelled
from prep school. Well, not just. First, he had
spent three long weeks as a virtual prisoner in
Sam and Debra's house. The afternoon he had
come in here had been his first day out.

John remembered the date because it had been
his half brother's fourth birthday. Debra and Sam
were hosting a big party for Logan, and as usual,
Sam wanted John out of the way. He went gladly.

Since he had been away at school and camps
most of the time, John was a stranger in his own
hometown. He had no friends, no attachments of
any sort. The few times he had mingled with kids
his age on other visits, he had found himself an
outsider. Some boys scorned him for being a rich
kid. Even the children of people on the same
economic level kept their distance. John figured it
was because Sam had spread some kind of tale
about him. Something damaging that still
wouldn't reflect too badly on Saint Sam. He
wanted all his friends to admire him for being so
good to the son his wife had brought to their
marriage. That's why he had adopted John. Just
for the show.

Sam had figured out the worst punishment he could inflict on John was to make him stay for that summer and his senior year in high school. He was right. John had learned at three years old that living with Sam was hell. His vacations home had always been nightmares.

But John had known freedom was just a year away. That alone had put him in a cocky mood when he walked into Ebbie's diner that long-ago summer afternoon. He had sat down at the counter, just about where he was now. A group of young toughs in a back booth had eyed him with belligerence. John had studiously ignored their rumbles of adolescent challenge. And suddenly . . .

A beautiful girl appeared in front of him.

Ebony hair was caught up in a ponytail. Blue-gray eyes flashed. Red lips curved into a smile. Her enveloping white apron couldn't hide the curves beneath.

She blew him away, even before she set her elbows on the other side of the counter and leaned close. "Ignore those creeps in the back. They're children. Threatened anytime a real man walks in."

John couldn't remember his reply. He recalled only the way his world had shifted when Spring smiled at him. Went from gray outlines to vibrant colors.

"You look happy, at least."

Ebbie's gruff comment pulled John from the past. He cleared his head, and glanced down at the platter the diner owner had placed on the counter. "What man wouldn't be happy with food like this in front of him?"

"I don't think it's the meat loaf and mashed potatoes making you smile." Eyes narrowing, Ebbie picked up her glass of water again. "What's brought you back?"

"I told you. Spring called."

Ebbie laughed.

"You can ask her yourself."

"Oh, I don't doubt she called you. But did she ask you to come home?"

John realized he was defending himself to someone who had no business questioning him. It didn't matter that Ebbie obviously thought Spring hadn't called him here for her own benefit. It didn't matter that Spring had claimed she wanted him here for his spoiled half brother's sake.

John knew the truth. Spring wanted him back. She had been the one to bend, the one to call.

He had let some weeks go by before coming for her. After what she had put him through, she deserved to squirm. She never needed to know he had almost hopped a plane the minute she called. Or that he had nearly taken the rental-car agent's head off that morning because his reserved car wasn't ready and waiting at the Atlanta airport. It would do no good for Spring to find out how fast he had driven up State Highway 19 into the north Georgia mountains. He had stopped here at

Ebbie's deliberately, so he could say he took his time once he got to town. That was all Spring needed to know.

That, and how much he wanted her back.

Smiling now, John concentrated on the truly delicious gravy ladled over his potatoes.

His silence intensified Ebbie's interest. "Spring seems awful happy here at home."

"So you see her often?"

"She comes by a fair amount." There was a pause. "She and her *friends.*"

John resisted her bait and speared another forkful of meatloaf.

"She's fit right back into the community."

"That's funny, considering she never quite fit before."

"Not everybody judged her like your folks did," Ebbie retorted.

The food turned sour in John's mouth. He had to force himself to swallow. "The way I remember it, lots of folks judged Spring's whole family."

"Lots of small-minded gossips."

"Like your buddy Willa Dean."

Ebbie cackled. "Land sakes, John, you sure are bitter over old news."

Keeping his voice low, John leaned forward. "My mother and stepfather might not have been so hard on Spring if Willa Dean had kept her mouth shut instead of spreading lies."

"Do you honestly believe that?" Serious now, something akin to pity stirred in the older woman's expression. "You really think the tales of one unhappy old woman made that much difference to your family?"

Maybe she was right. But they couldn't turn back the clock to find out.

Ebbie looked tired all of a sudden. "I've got to get to work on my dinner specials. If you're looking for Spring, her office is up at the administrative offices in the elementary school on Locks Street."

John stood, leaving a half-eaten plate of food, not bothering to disguise his eagerness. "How much do I owe you?"

"No charge. Consider it a welcome-home meal."

Knowing the older woman rarely offered charity with such openness, John leaned across the counter and kissed her plump cheek. "You're a peach, Ebbie. You always were."

"Hush, now," she growled. "I've got a reputation to keep up."

John hurried away, sparing only a courteous, "Excuse me," to the two gray-haired matrons who came in the door as he was going out.

Both of them looked at each other with rounded eyes, then at Ebbie.

"Yep," she said, with an arch smile. "That's exactly who you thought it was." Laughter whooping out, she braced herself against the counter and met the deluge of questions that followed.

When they were gone, she settled into the kitchen, knowing that within thirty minutes, everyone in White's Creek would know that John Nelson was back in town.

The muscles in Spring's neck were tight and aching on the drive to her parents' house for dinner. The county school counselors held a planning meeting on the third Friday morning of each month. Today's gathering had been a doozy. Money for new existing programs was scarce, and the budget constraints always made Spring impatient. Didn't anyone understand how many special-needs children there were in this county?

She had vented her feelings a little too forcefully in today's meeting. Mild-mannered Terri Tate had regarded her with the sort of horror she might reserve for a tornado. It wasn't that Terri or the other counselors didn't agree with Spring. They, however, had given up trying to make the school board or the county government see how desperately their department needed a bigger allocation of money for working with children who came from neglectful or violent domestic situations. Social Services was doing all it could. The schools had to do more.

Today, Spring had challenged her colleagues to present a united front to the school board, which was already considering budget requests for next year. Everyone had agreed, but in their eyes, Spring saw they had little hope of succeeding.

Afterward, Spring blew out of the office in a real temper. Her mood darkened during her afternoon at one of the county's most rural schools, where increased funding was needed most. She had returned to a jammed desk, a dozen messages, including the secretary's note that a gorgeous man had stopped by to see her.

Probably some parent worried about his son's SAT scores. Those were the only parents who ever stopped by without an appointment. Those and people like Debra Nelson.

Someone you don't want to think about, Spring told herself as she turned down the drive to her parents' house. They were having a family dinner tonight. Her brother, Clay, was coming up from Atlanta. A real occasion, since Clay was unmarried and had quite a social life. Callie was always after him to settle down, so Clay didn't visit as often as he could.

Maybe he figures my marital troubles have Mama occupied.

Spring groaned as her mind turned automatically in the direction she wanted to avoid. Since calling John, she had worked extra hard at not thinking about him. He had made it clear he wanted nothing to do with his brother.

Logan was back in school after his suspension. He had kept his first appointment with the new counselor Spring had found, but didn't show for the next one. And when Spring tried to talk seriously with him, he got angry with her, calling her a "meddling bitch." He hadn't come around in a week.

Last night, she had seen him in the Wal-Mart parking lot, picking up Mollie Stevens after work.

Spring had been so shocked, she kept her head down rather than acknowledging the young couple. She couldn't imagine what the girl was doing with Logan. But Mollie wouldn't be the first to fall prey to the attention of a handsome guy, no matter how troubled he might be.

"I should know," Spring murmured wryly. She noted an unfamiliar blue Chevrolet parked alongside Rainy's minivan. Now why would Clay be driving a rental car instead of the BMW he was so proud of?

Spring rolled her shoulders as she left her car. Callie appeared at the screened door before she could get it open. "Be calm," she advised her daughter.

"I'm trying." Spring matched her mother's serious tone even as she stooped to greet the three dogs who had taken refuge on the porch from the rain.

Callie's brow knit. "Then you know."

"About what?"

"I think she's talking about me."

Over her mother's shoulder, Spring looked into John's dark gaze. Eyes as bruised as his soul, Callie used to say.

Spring didn't expect to be hit quite so hard by John's presence here in the open doorway to her parents' kitchen. She had been married to this man for twelve years, but staring at him twisted her insides. Her heartbeat went thin and reedy, then thundered like a gathering summer storm.

"Hang on," Callie murmured, taking her hand.

Blood pumping hard through her veins helped Spring frame the correct words. "What are you doing here?"

His smile disappeared. "You asked me to come."

"Not here. You're not welcome at my parents' house."

Callie protested.

John bristled. "Funny, they've made me feel right at home. And besides, you weren't in your office."

"You could have waited," Spring said.

"I didn't feel like cooling my heels in the hall like some kid waiting to see his teacher."

"You said you wouldn't come to White's Creek."

"But you knew I would."

"I haven't been able to predict what in the hell you might do for a couple of years now."

Color stained his cheeks. "Goddamn it, Spring, you called—"

"It's just like you to say no and then come running."

"Running?" His voice rose. "The only running that's been done was by you. You ran away from our marriage."

"Some marriage."

Her flippancy made him take a step toward her. "The least you could have done was tell me instead of leaving that note."

"You're a fine one to complain about our not talking to each other."

"But a note? A damn note?"

"Oh, stop it, John. You said all of this when I called you. It didn't make me regret leaving you then, and it doesn't now."

"Then why in the world—"

"That'll be enough." Spring's father appeared at John's side, cutting off his angry words with a hand on the younger man's shoulder. Ned sent a warning look toward Spring, as well. Quietly, he said, "Rainy's boys are inside, listening. Can't you two wait a bit before yelling at each other?"

Spring gulped in some much-needed air.

One of the dogs growled low in his throat, underscoring the tension in the atmosphere.

John started toward the door. "I'll leave."

Callie dropped Spring's hand and stepped in front of him. "Is that the only thing the two of you can do with each other these days? Walk away?"

John froze.

"Mama, just let him go."

Instead, her mother reached out and took John's arm. "Why can't you stay? Have dinner with us all. Clay'll be here soon."

"This is insane," Spring said. "I don't want him here."

John shot her an angry glance and took a breath before grinning at Callie. "One of your dinners does sound good."

Furious, Spring said, "Don't you dare. Mama, you tell him to go."

Her mother set her chin. "I reckon I can have anyone I want to my dinner table."

"I can see what you're trying to do," Spring told her. "You think if you can just get us to sit down and have a civil meal together, I'll cool off and you can talk some sense into me. I won't have it, Mama. I just won't have it."

Callie snorted. "You keep up that tone with me, Missy, and you'll be the one asked to leave."

Spring swore, and her father slipped his arm around her waist, as if he was afraid she would lunge at her husband and mother.

"I stopped to eat at Ebbie's," John continued, conversational as you please with Callie. "But you know how she talks. I left half a plate full."

"Then you come right in here." Callie led him toward her kitchen. "I've got a pork roast in the oven that's tender as butter."

John followed, sparing a look of challenge for Spring before he passed through the doorway.

Only when he had disappeared did Ned let go of Spring. He closed the door and blocked her way.

She couldn't believe she was being double-teamed this way. "How can you and Mama expect me to sit down to dinner with him?"

"You're an adult, that's how." Temper flashed in her normally mild-mannered father's expression.

"And being an adult should mean I don't have to see anyone I don't want to see."

"You really don't want to see John?"

"That's what I said."

"But how in the world are you two going to sort this business out if you don't talk to each other? You called him. Invited him here."

"Not because I wanted to see him. I called for his brother's sake."

Ned gave her a disbelieving look. "Didn't you figure he might think you were using his brother as an excuse?"

Those had been John's exact words on the subject when they talked, but Spring had believed him when he said nothing she could do would lure him to White's Creek.

"I think you knew he'd come," Ned said. "So you needn't be acting like this is such a surprise."

"Did you and Mama have to put out the welcome mat?"

"You wanted us to turn him away?"

"Not Mama, maybe. She's made it plain she thinks I've been too hard on him. But you, Daddy, I thought you understood."

"I do, Daughter." Ned's anger appeared to cool as he took her hand. "I know you're just as confused as you were when you came home last June and not doing much about it. I'm on your side, with whatever you decide about this marriage. But I also don't see what you gain by refusing to have anything to do with John."

"I'll refuse if I want to," Spring said, well aware she sounded like a petulant child.

Impatiently, her father said, "Good Lord, girl. Being confused is one thing, but acting like a damn fool is another."

He left her fuming on the porch. She stayed there perhaps half a minute before stalking out to her car. She might have left if she hadn't realized how absolutely right her father was.

John was here. She had called him. She couldn't avoid him or her marriage any longer.

But this whole setup made her want to scream.
So she did.

She called out John's name, same as she might have when they were two crazy teenagers.

He rushed out of the house and down the steps, sputtering, "What the hell?"

Spring faced him in the rain, hands on her hips. "I'll be damned if we'll sit down with my family like nothing has happened between us. If you want to talk, we'll do it somewhere else."

To her family, who had clustered on the porch behind him, she said, "Show's over. We're taking the encore to my place."

Chapter Six

∾ Driving through the cold, damp night, John found himself fuming over two simple words. *"My place,"* Spring had said.

For some insane reason, he had imagined she was still living with her parents, occupying her childhood bedroom until he came to get her or she decided to come back to him. It was a shock to realize that assumption was completely false. As false as every other expectation he'd had about this evening.

Just what had he envisioned? Spring flying into his arms?

"Yeah," he murmured to his empty car. "That was exactly what I wanted."

Spring in his arms was the image he had held on to since her phone call. The fantasy had featured her begging his forgiveness, promising never to leave him again, saying she wanted things to go back to the way they had once been: just the two of them.

His plans had not included their reunion being played out in front of half the DeWitt clan. That was his fault. He should have waited for her at school. Or he should have pleaded an emergency to the secretary at the administrative offices and had her call Spring.

Instead, he had driven over to her family's farm. Funny how happy he had felt when he saw their ramshackle house and felt Callie wrap him up in one of her warm hugs. Ned had hung back, a little less welcoming, though he had put out his big, callused hand. Both of them told John straight out that they didn't like the situation as it now stood between him and their daughter. John had promised to do something about that.

And now, he was driving down a vaguely familiar road, trying to keep up with the Corvette while Spring led him to *her* place. A place all to herself, separate from *their* place, which was waiting, silent and empty, back in Chicago.

By the time her—*his*—car pulled to a stop in the drive of a simple white cottage, he was ready to chew glass.

He was up on her porch before she could get there. "Nice to see you're taking care of the 'Vette."

"I always took care of it. You're the one who wanted to sell it."

"It's always cost a fortune to keep up."

"Maybe I think it's worth it."

"And maybe . . ." His words trailed away as John realized they were standing on the lit porch, arguing. If there were any nosy neighbors about, something he didn't doubt considering what he remembered of this town, those neighbors could hear every angry word he and Spring exchanged.

He held up his hands. "Let's go in. I don't like the idea of people standing around here, listening to us and taking notes."

Sending him a disgusted look, Spring inserted the key in the lock and flung open the door.

Familiar scents assaulted John the minute he crossed the threshold.

Spring.

Her name was the only description he had for the spicy-sweet fragrance that filled this cottage in much the same way it had filled every home he had shared with her.

He knew there were a dozen or so ingredients to the potpourri Spring's mother made especially for her. But to John, trying to explain this smell was like trying to analyze the ingredients of a morning in late April. When flowers were bursting to life. When the earth was damp and moist. When an evening rain had washed the air so clean it sparkled. The smell was rich, yet light enough to linger instead of overwhelm.

Too many nights, John had been alone in the apartment Spring had deserted, with only this scent to keep him company. By the time she called, her fragrance had started to fade.

By God, that wasn't right.

He stood just inside the arched doorway from the small front hall and took in the home she had made for herself without him. On the floor was an old rug, the jewel-colored pattern faded to a soft sheen. Mix-and-match sofa, chairs, and end tables. A scarred pine armoire filled with books. Everywhere were the touches he might expect from Spring. Dried flowers in the pottery. Framed photos on the desk by the front window. A collection of old hats on the coatrack by the arched doorway. The only real surprise was the half-grown cat, gray and fuzzy and intent on greeting Spring, who padded in from a room down the dimly lit hall.

The cat clinched it. Spring had made herself a home. Not a temporary dwelling. But a home. Away from him.

Chest aching, John demanded, "Why did you call me if you didn't really want to see me?"

She set her cat onto a nearby chair. "My God, John, could we at least sit down before you attack me?"

He cringed, remembering the night of their last argument, when his anger had taken over, and he was tempted to strike Spring. He was still ashamed of that moment of weakness. He would never do that again.

So he drew in a breath and took his emotions down a notch. "I'm not attacking you, Spring. I'm asking."

"Same difference, I think." She turned away, kicking off her shoes and gracefully shedding the emerald green sweater she wore over a black, knee-length turtleneck dress. With the same fluid movements, she crossed the room and switched on a lamp beside an old red velvet armchair.

The action was so simple. So infinitely familiar. Watching Spring move had always been a turn-on. He had missed this, missed the quiet moments and everyday actions that bound two people together.

John had to force his words past the tightening of his throat. "Why did you call me?"

Spring's sigh was weary. "I told you why I called."

"If you mean that story about Logan, surely you didn't really expect me to come home for his sake."

Her defiant expression said it all.

"You've got to be kidding."

"He's a very troubled young man."

"Well, too bad." Disgust cracked through John. "So the spoiled little brat has a few problems. Big deal."

"Is that how you remember him? As a brat?"

It wasn't, of course. Of all the troubles that had flowed through the big house Sam Nelson had ruled, Logan had been the least of them. He had been little more than a baby when John left. But Logan had also been the favored child, the real son. John didn't have to stretch too far to imagine Logan had grown up pampered and spoiled and indulged. He wasn't surprised to hear he was in trouble.

Spring's expression had turned thoughtful. "I remember Logan wanting to be with you a lot our senior year."

"What does that have to do with anything?"

"He wanted to be your brother."

"He was four years old," John scoffed.

Her eyes narrowed. "Does that mean he didn't have feelings?"

"Of course not. But I can't believe I meant anything to him. Not really. Not with Sam around to tell him what a loser I was."

"Sam is dead."

"Yeah, I noticed the town smelled better with the king of all skunks six feet under."

Flinching, Spring turned away. "I hate talking to you when you get sarcastic like this."

"Then do something about it."

"What?"

"Change the subject." He took another step into the room, pausing beside the brocade-covered sofa. "Tell me the brother I don't even know isn't the only reason you asked me to come here."

"But he is."

"I think he's an excuse."

She walked over and picked up the phone. "If you doubt your brother is a troubled kid, then let me call my supervisor. She can fill you in."

John came over and took the phone out of her hand, placing it carefully on the end table. "I didn't say I didn't believe Logan had problems. Any kid of Sam and Debra's would have to be screwed completely. What I want to know is why you think I can help?"

"Don't you think you and Logan might have something in common?"

This was the same preposterous notion she had advanced when she called him, the idea that Logan had also fallen prey to Sam's rages and fists. John couldn't believe that was the case. The hatred he had felt from Sam had been intense and personal, nothing like the love the man had always lavished on Logan.

"Logan and I have nothing in common," he muttered. "Nothing but a few stray genes."

"You're so blind," she said. "And here I thought there was still some hope of you coming back to the world of the living."

Not bothering to ask what she meant, John sneered, "White's Creek, Georgia, isn't the world. It's more like the edge of nowhere."

Spring raked a hand through dark hair still damp from the rain. "I like being back here. Close to the mountains. In a place where I can see the sky. I can breathe here."

"There are lots of places with fresh air." John paused a moment, for effect, before adding, "Places like California."

"Smog capital?"

"Not up north. Carmel. Monterey. There, it's beautiful."

She paused, looking puzzled. "When were you in Carmel?"

"I took a trip a month or so ago. Spent some

time in LA, then drove up the coast." He waited, but since she didn't ask, he explained his visit. "There's renewed interest in a movie based on my first book."

"Congratulations."

Her faint sarcasm cut deep. He answered in kind. "Thanks so much for your enthusiasm."

Spring clasped her hands together, raised them to her chest, as if praying for strength. "I'm sorry, John. I'm glad for you. Really, I am. I want you to have what you want."

He searched her somber face. "I wish I could believe you."

The muscles worked in her throat. John knew her well enough to see she was struggling to hold on to her composure.

With obvious effort, she said, "I never thought there'd be a time when you and I wouldn't want the same things."

John reached out, touching her face. "I never thought we'd be sleeping in different beds, much less different states."

Just as he started to move toward her, Spring pulled back. Her shoulders sloped with weariness, and for the first time John noticed the faint shadows beneath her eyes.

She looked so vulnerable, so in need of a strong arm to support her that John swayed toward her again.

Ducking away once more, she whispered, "You took me by surprise, coming here this way."

"I wish it had been a pleasant surprise."

"So do I."

Those short, blunt words snapped him back to reality. He gritted his teeth, trying not to lash out at her again.

"Can we talk tomorrow?" she said.

"So I came all this way, and you put me off?"

"I need some time to think."

"What have you been doing for the last few months?"

"Trying not to think about ending our marriage."

"Real productive," he observed, the words etched in acid.

Twin spots of color in her cheeks betrayed her returning anger. "I suppose all you've done is think about our situation?"

"I've been working. I finished my book."

"How nice you could work in between lunching with Hollywood executives on the West Coast. Did you fly to New York to have cocktails with your editors the same day?"

"Right now I wish to hell I had flown anywhere but here."

Spring jerked a thumb toward the street. "Your car's outside. Don't let me stop you."

"So you're throwing me out?"

"I hear the Pine Cone Lodge is a nice place to stay."

With those cold words ringing in his ears, John left in a hurry. He was shaking with fury, so tight

with anger he had a difficult time getting the key
to fit the ignition switch.

Why did she make him so angry?

When the car finally sprang to life, he drove off
in a fury, eager to put some distance between
them. Fueling his temper was weariness at a day
of travel and thwarted anticipation. At the same
time, he was still so wound up he couldn't face
the prospect of checking into the Pine Cone
Lodge in godforsaken White's Creek. He should
leave, he decided. Drive back to Atlanta. Get on a
plane to Chicago. He should admit this trip was a
complete failure.

How had he blown this? Only a few hours ago,
he had anticipated a sweet reunion. On the plane,
he had allowed himself to think he and Spring
might end this night by tumbling into bed together.

He was a fool.

That was the main reason Spring remained in
her snug little house, while he was driving alone
through the cool, rainy night.

The Pine Cone Lodge was located north of
downtown, just where John remembered.
Through the lingering rain, the vacancy sign
glowed neon orange. Only two cars were drawn
up to the rooms that ranged left from the office.
Neatly trimmed boxwoods grew out front, and
the red paint on the window shutters looked
fresh. Tired as he was, John dreaded walking in
and getting a room. He didn't want to be answer-

ing questions from people who might remember him.

But the desk clerk was an unfamiliar young man who didn't bat an eye at John's name when he presented his credit card and checked in.

His room, last one on the end, was surprisingly pleasant. Two double beds and a blue plaid sofa were arranged for television viewing. A table and two chairs were set up next to a tiny kitchenette, with the bathroom beyond. Framed photographs of mountain scenery decorated the walls, and the bathroom counters and tub gleamed like new. John had a feeling Old Man Harris, who used to run this place, had passed management on to someone else.

John set his laptop computer on the sofa and his duffel bag on the bed. He looked at those two plainly covered beds for a long while, remembering the first time he had stayed in a place like this.

With Spring, of course.

Prom night.

While most of their classmates were dancing in the gym, he and Spring had been in a Blue Ridge, Georgia, motel, making love.

They weren't supposed to be together. Debra and Sam had ordered them apart.

At first it had only been Debra who had objected to John dating Spring. One problem was Spring's undeserved reputation. The other was Ned DeWitt's modest means and Callie's fortune-telling and selling of herbal tonics.

Sam, on the other hand, had started out approving of Spring. Bedding a poor girl with questionable morals was, to Sam, the first manly thing John had ever done. While John objected to this vile characterization of his relationship with Spring, he held his counsel. John knew the truth about Spring and about them. He could live with Sam's lewd remarks if it meant he could be with her.

The problems really started when Sam realized John cared about Spring. Sam targeted anything John loved. Spring was no exception.

So John and Spring spent the last few months of school sneaking around, using her brother and his girlfriend as a shield. John had arrived at the prom with Clay DeWitt's date, but they swapped early. John and Spring then drove to Blue Ridge. Debra and Sam and Spring's parents weren't expecting any of them home until early morning, so they had the whole night. Spring thought Callie probably knew what they were up to, same as she seemed to know everything. But Callie didn't try to stop them.

The intensity of first love had driven them past petting months before prom night. But the hours in that motel room remained vivid in John's mind, even now.

The coarse textured sheets on that lumpy motel bed.
The musty smell.
The freedom of having time alone.

There was no reason to rush. No furtive glances out a car window. No slipping away to a hollow deep in the mountains, where winter's freeze and the April thaw had made their trysts nearly impossible.

For the first time, John really lingered over Spring's smooth skin. Her lush breasts. The honey-sweet valley between her thighs. He explored each and every one of her most feminine mysteries, his desires dictated only by love and the pleasure he wanted to give her.

He touched.

And tasted.

He made Spring come with his tongue and his lips, made her writhe and moan and beg to have him inside her. He complied, of course, gladly.

Before that night, John had known he could give Spring pleasure. He hadn't known he could make it last so long. He hadn't known she could be so inventive or adventurous. That night, for the first time, he truly understood why people called it "making love."

Dawn slipped her rosy fingers over the north Georgia mountains too soon the next morning. John and Spring lingered too long in their room. But it was hard to think about getting home when Spring slid her body over his one last time.

She lowered herself ever-so-slowly onto his erection.

She looked into his eyes and said, "I'll love you like this forever, John Nelson. You can count on me."

Heady words for a young man who had never counted on anything or anyone.

But he had believed in them. Because he believed in Spring.

*   *   *

But now he was back in Georgia, in a motel room alone, while Spring was in *her* place.

John felt he would to choke to death if he stayed one minute more in this room.

Spring let the phone ring for a long time, fearing it might be John. She was reeling from the mere fact of seeing him again. She didn't want to talk to him anymore.

But the phone kept ringing, and her cat, Basil, kept walking back and forth over her legs. Spring was finally forced to sit up in bed and grab the receiver.

"Are you all right?" her sister said.

Allowing her body to ease back against her pillows, Spring shook her head, not trusting her voice to remain steady.

Rainy seemed to know what she was feeling without hearing a word. "Want me to come over?"

"No. I want to be alone."

"So John's not there?"

"I don't know where he is."

"He's left town?"

"I don't know. Maybe . . ."

Rainy hesitated, obviously weighing Spring's right to privacy against her own curiosity. The latter won. "Did you two talk about anything? Reach any conclusions?"

Spring sighed.

"Oh, Lord," Rainy murmured. "I wish I could help you, honey."

"I wish you could, too."

"I could bring you some hot chocolate. We could get under the covers and talk, just like when we were kids."

Spring managed a smile. Briefly, she yearned to do just as Rainy suggested. But the break-up of Spring's marriage, something that seemed inevitable at this moment, wasn't something Rainy could solve.

So Spring said, "You stay at home with Jess. Curl up tight next to him, Rainy. You thank God and your lucky stars and Mama's sight that you've got him and your boys."

"Mama's sight?" Rainy asked.

"She said Jess was the one for you that first night he came to pick you up."

"In his uncle's awful old green pickup." Rainy chuckled. "There were signs on each side, advertising watermelons for sale. And we were going to the drive-in. I almost pretended to be sick, so I wouldn't have to go with him in that awful-looking contraption."

"Mama talked you out of that fast."

"Sometimes she's right."

"And sometimes she's just damned pushy."

"She meant well tonight," Rainy said, soothingly. "She's got a soft spot for John. Always has. She says you're the only one who can help him. If you'll remember, that's what she's always said."

Spring squeezed her eyes shut. "I haven't helped him at all. He's so cold and selfish, so preoccupied with what doesn't matter. I know him so well and yet not at all. I just want him to go away and leave me alone."

Rainy was silent.

"What is it?" Spring asked, knowing her sister had something more to say.

"I just want you to ask yourself something, and answer it honestly. Are you going to be able to live with yourself if you let John leave town before you talk out your problems? Are you that ready to give up your marriage?"

Spring's affirmative answer never got past her lips. No matter how close the end felt, she wasn't ready to say those words out loud.

"I didn't think so," Rainy said, her tone soft with understanding.

"I'll talk to you tomorrow." Quickly, Spring hung up the phone.

Basil nibbled at her hand, and Spring stroked the cat's long, soft fur as she stared at the ceiling of her bedroom. Lights moved across the uneven plaster, indicating a car on the street outside. For a moment, the lights didn't move.

Spring sat up, holding her breath, waiting for the lights to pass. When they didn't, her first thought was of John. He had come back.

She slipped from bed and hurried to the bedroom window overlooking the front porch. She was just in time to see a car pull away from the house across the street. Probably her neighbor's college-age daughter, returning from a date.

Spring shrank back from the window and returned to her bed. She spent a long time pretending she wasn't disappointed the car outside hadn't been John's.

Chapter Seven

～ John didn't plan to find his way to the house where he had once lived with Debra and Sam. The last place he ever dreamed of revisiting was that solid, redbrick mansion with the stately white columns.

But that's where he wound up after his motel-room walls closed around him.

The rain had stopped. The moisture remaining in the air took the form of a low, shifting fog. Through this screen, the lights of Sam Nelson's big house glowed with deceptive warmth. More fitting, John thought, were the sharp spires topping the iron fence surrounding the well-groomed estate. When he was a boy, he had imagined Sam had placed those razorlike spokes on the fence in order to keep him a prisoner.

The idea still had merit.

He shivered and looked around. The fog had closed in down here near the creek, isolating the house even more than usual. The old fear was suddenly on him. He hated that sensation. He was a grown man, and Sam was dead. But the longer he sat in his car, staring at that house, the stronger grew his certainty that at any moment, Sam could appear.

Later, John was never sure what made him drive through the ornate, open gate. Maybe it was an attempt to defy his fears. Maybe it was that fool idea Spring had suggested, that he might be able to help Logan. Whatever the reason, he soon found himself crossing the front veranda and ringing the doorbell. He steeled himself to see Debra again after all these years.

But he wasn't prepared for her to look just as he remembered. Or for her to stare at him like she couldn't imagine who he might be.

John was determined to stand there until she did.

"John . . . Johnny?" The nickname slipped out, stolen from a childhood he didn't know he could remember. A time when this elegant blonde standing in the doorway to her fine home had chased her son through a small, untidy house.

"Johnny. Johnny. Come to Mommy, Johnny-boy."

He blocked that tender memory as fast as he could. She didn't deserve even so minor a tribute.

She still had a hazy look in her eyes. Her voice was slurred, as if she might have been drinking. Yet John knew she could hold her liquor well. "I heard you were in town," she murmured.

"The old gossip mill still works, I see." He lifted his gaze to the stairway that curved gracefully behind her, the chandelier that rose in lit tiers over the carved rosewood paneling and the polished marble floor.

Echoes came rushing out. Like wind escaping a tunnel. Like the screams he had stopped allowing himself to scream when he was only a little boy.

John knew those sounds weren't real, but they pushed him back with a very real force.

Debra stepped out on the veranda. Shivering, she tightened the belt of her pink silk robe over matching pajamas. "Aren't you going to come in? It's cold out here."

He shook his head, stunned by the onslaught of painful memories being sucked out of this house.

"I suppose you're in town to see Spring."

"Well, I didn't come for a visit with you."

Some of the haze cleared from her eyes. "Are the two of you reconciling? Divorcing?"

"Do you really care?"

There was rebuke in her tone. "There's no need to be rude."

"Only you could worry about manners after not seeing me for over a dozen years."

"Maybe if you would come in and sit down, we could talk in a civilized manner."

"Maybe I don't want to be civilized with you."

Her chin stiffened. "Then what are you doing here at eleven-thirty at night? Obviously you want something. What is it?"

"I don't know, *Debra*." He'd be damned if he'd

ever call her mother again. "I have no idea what I'm doing here." He started to turn, intending to leave.

She stopped him with an outstretched hand. John thought she might touch him, and he realized he couldn't remember that sensation. He had no memory of his mother's touch.

"Logan's here," she said.

"I don't want to see him. Not now." John turned on his heel. He had to get out of here.

He was on the top step when Debra said, "Please, John . . . Johnny. Wait."

He didn't want to respond to the pleading note in her voice. He knew she was a great actress, able to play any role necessary to get her way. But knowing that and resisting her were different matters. Not giving in to her had been difficult for him most of his life. He hated admitting it still was. He turned to face her again.

While John hesitated, someone came through the doorway behind Debra. It had to be Logan. Who else could look so much like Sam? John was caught off guard, even though Spring had told him how much Logan resembled his father. For a moment it was if a ghost had come back to life.

John got hold of himself fast. This wasn't Sam. This was Logan. A seventeen-year-old kid. The little brother he hadn't exactly loved, but hadn't hated, either.

Logan paused, framed by the light from the hall. "Mother, what are you doing out here?"

"Talking to your brother."

Only then did Logan notice John at the edge of the veranda. He did a double take. His features hardened.

"Can't you say hello?" Debra prompted.

There was no reason not to. John stepped up and extended his hand.

His brother didn't make a move to touch him. "What do you want? Did you come to see what you lost when you got yourself disinherited?"

Obviously, Sam had given Logan his attitudes as well as his looks. John knew he should ignore the challenge in the boy's voice, but he wasn't going to lie down and roll over for anyone, least of all his family. "I know what I lost, Logan. It's not anything I cared about."

"I just bet." Logan's face flushed, his hands doubled into fists at his sides. He was trembling with rage, angry with John in the way Sam had always been.

John wanted to know why. "I don't want to argue, Logan. I don't want what was Sam's or what's going to be yours."

"Then what are you doing here?"

"Spring had this stupid idea that you and I should get to know each other."

"She's wrong."

"No joke."

"I guess she's allowed a few mistakes. After all, she did marry you."

Impatience edged past John's determination to

keep this civil. "She's certainly wrong about there being anything to commend you."

Logan sneered, "But she was right about cutting you loose. That's for sure."

The game they were playing was childish. John was actually glad Debra intervened. "Logan, just stop it. Now."

He ignored her in favor of taunting John. "What'd you do? Come back to town to try and get Spring back?"

"That's none of your business."

"You should know somebody else has already taken your place."

That was too close to the accusations Sam had once hurled around about Spring. Face burning, John took a step toward his brother. "You'd better watch what you say about my wife."

"It's not her I'm insulting," Logan flung back at him. "You're the idiot who's lost her."

"You little—"

Debra cut off John's curse. "Both of you, stop it. I will not have a brawl on my front porch."

"Would the backyard be better?" Logan demanded. "That way we can hide it from the neighbors."

Debra pulled at Logan's arm. He jerked away. She stumbled and might have fallen if John hadn't moved fast enough to catch her.

"Don't be a jerk!" he shouted at Logan, quickly thrusting Debra out of the way.

For the space of a heartbeat, the brothers stood nose to nose, neither backing down.

Then Logan laughed. An ugly sound. A sound so familiar John's flesh crawled.

"Damn funny, isn't it?" the young man said between shouts of laughter. "You protecting Mother."

Debra stepped forward, hands pressed to her cheeks. In her gaze, which caught John's briefly before bouncing away, was the same helplessness she had displayed every time Sam tore into him with his cruel words and his hard fists. That powerless role was one of her best, he thought. A real act. Because Debra Nelson was nothing if not capable and strong. She was weak only when she chose.

Logan was right. It was strange for John to protect Debra from anything.

John had been arguing with the wrong family member. He wasn't angry with Logan. It was Debra he hated.

He left without another glance back. Even a lonely, empty room in the Pine Cone Lodge was better than the viper's nest his only blood kin called home.

Only Spring could force John to remain in this town with his mother and half brother. He had to get her away from here soon, away from the poison that was his family.

"Pancakes are good for the soul." Mustering her first smile of the day, Spring poured maple syrup over the remains of a stack of buttered pancakes.

Across the booth, Dan Strickland's handsome features wrinkled into a grimace. "I don't get how you can eat that stuff before 9:00 A.M."

Mouth full, she darted a look at his black coffee and dry toast and swallowed. "What I don't get is why anyone would go out to breakfast and order that."

"I told you I didn't plan on going out. I was jogging, saw your car, and figured you were here at Ebbie's."

"Like I am every Saturday morning," Spring retorted, pretty sure he had jogged in this direction because he might find her here. They had been meeting here most Saturdays since the school year began. "Good thing I don't eat like this every day. Otherwise, I would weigh at least three hundred pounds."

"Yes, well . . ." His brow furrowed, Dan watched her consume the rest of her food. "You do have a healthy appetite."

Spring struggled not to laugh at his discomfiture. Dan was a very nice guy. Thirty-five, he had family in this county, where he had moved several years ago in order to enjoy the hiking and canoeing afforded by the mountains and to escape the problems plaguing so many big-city schools. He drove a conservative American-made car, exercised regularly, ate bran, and probably worried because his light brown hair was beginning to thin in the front. He was young for a high-school principal, having worked his way up with a quickness not normally seen in a place like White's Creek. Spring liked to think it was his youth, not his ambitions, that made him knuckle under so frequently to the higher-ups in the county.

He often didn't know what to make of Spring. She was too much for him. Laughed too much. Ate too much. Argued too much about changes that needed to be made in the schools. Dan was certainly attracted to her, and she wasn't averse to him, either. So far, however, their relationship had progressed to only a few tame kisses.

She scared him. With her appetites and her opinions and her temper. And her marriage. There was that one, small detail. As Rainy had pointed out, Dan was taking a risk by seeing a married woman, even a separated woman. White's Creek was a conservative place. Yet it was that hint of adventurousness in him that had aroused Spring's interest in the first place.

Lately, however, she had begun to think she had been fooled by that hint.

Spearing her last link of sausage with her fork, she considered if she should tell Dan about John being in town last night. Probably. Dan's attendance at an out-of-town football game last night was the only reason the gossips hadn't told him already. If John hung around for any length of time, there would be lots of talk. Dan could be affected. On the other hand, after arguing with her last night, John might have gone back to Chicago.

Then what was she going to do? The question Rainy had put to Spring last night on the phone was still chasing around in her head. Could she live with herself if she had allowed John to leave town without her talking to him about their marriage?

Yet knowing he might still be here was the reason her craving for pancakes floating in syrup and butter had been more intense than on most Saturday mornings. Comfort food was high on her list of priorities when she was stressed. Right now, her stress level was screaming for another shot of fat and sugar, even though her red sweater wasn't feeling as oversize as it had when she threw it on earlier that morning.

Ebbie stepped up to their booth, coffeepot in hand, and offered a refill. The diner was so crowded, the owner had done little more than wave since Spring arrived. Now she smiled. Slyly. That made Spring nervous.

"I hear you have a visitor," Ebbie said.

"My brother Clay?" Spring parried innocently. Ebbie loved nothing more than witnessing a juicy confrontation in her diner, but surely she wouldn't come right out and ask about Spring's husband with Dan sitting right here.

Ebbie's smile turned downright wicked. "Not Clay, honey. But I'm glad to hear he's come up for a visit. Your other brothers coming to town, too?" Completely ignoring Spring's negative answer, Ebbie patted her vibrant-hued hair. "I thought your folks might be having some kind of family reunion or something, seeing as how the family was gathering."

Trying to transmit a discreet warning with her eyes, Spring said no.

"Really? No family reunion? I just thought since you had out-of-town company . . ." The woman pretended to be pondering that information while Spring gave up discretion and glared at her. Dan was shooting both of them puzzled glances.

"Don't I hear somebody calling you?" Spring asked Ebbie.

"I don't think so, sugar."

The bell over the front door jangled. Ebbie straightened suddenly. Spring prayed she had been reprieved.

But instead, the diner owner's face was lit up like a float in the town's annual Christmas parade. Not a good sign. "Well, what do you know, Spring. Here's your guest right now."

Pancakes and sausage rumbled in Spring's stomach. Her gaze riveted on her plate as Ebbie called out to John. She could feel Dan staring at her, but she couldn't meet his eyes, couldn't frame a single, intelligible sentence, even after Ebbie had motioned John back to their booth.

Ebbie was barely covering her glee. "John, you won't mind sharing a table, will you? We're full up this morning."

Slowly, Spring lifted her gaze to her husband's face. His eyes were bloodshot and puffy, clear evidence he had slept no better than she. His ancient, threadbare jeans and flannel shirt were creased with wrinkles. His hair was still damp, as if he had just grabbed a shower. Since she knew he could barely stumble from the bed in the mornings without a cup of high-octane coffee, she had to admire the effort that had gone into getting all the way to Ebbie's without passing out.

But that didn't matter. What mattered was the awkward, heavy silence as her husband stared at the man with whom she was sharing breakfast. Facing the inevitable, Spring offered up the introductions. Dan's eyes widened when she said John's name.

In the moment's pause that followed, she added, perhaps unnecessarily, "John is my husband."

Ebbie chuckled while Spring willed the pot of coffee to pour down the woman's prominent bosom.

Dan, bless him, recovered his poise, stood, and shook John's hand. But there was more than a little irritation in his glance at Spring. She supposed she deserved that and much more.

Ever helpful, Ebbie said, "Spring, why don't you slide right over and let John sit down."

She started a protest, but John cut her off with a deceptively mild, "Yes, *dear*, why don't you slide over?" There was a gleam in his gaze that plainly said he hoped she would pick up a splinter in her butt.

She wanted to refuse, but Spring knew John was perfectly capable of causing a scene. People were already staring at them. She should pretend there was nothing unusual about this. So she darted an apologetic look at Dan and slid.

John sat beside her. Dan folded himself into his seat, as well, looking like he'd much rather face a roomful of irate parents. Ebbie got John coffee and took his order for exactly the same meal Spring had just finished.

When the older woman was gone, John said, "Best pancakes in town if I remember correctly."

"I was just discussing that with Spring," Dan replied. "I've watched her eat pancakes here a lot of Saturdays."

Spring stiffened. By saying they had shared many breakfasts, Dan was issuing a challenge. Surely that wasn't deliberate.

Whether it was or not, John didn't miss the implication. Spring could tell by the way the coffee cup wavered on the way to his mouth and his thick eyelashes dropped to shield his gaze.

She held her breath until he said, innocuously, "Spring, I'm surprised you aren't having blueberry pancakes."

"Not on the menu," Spring mumbled, thinking that if she barely answered him he would shut up.

He grinned. Dangerously. "Remember that time we were on vacation on Mackinac Island? You ordered blueberry pancakes for breakfast and dinner two days running."

"Did I?"

"You went wild over those berries."

"I don't remember."

"Forget berries this big?" John's thumb and forefinger formed a circle nearly the size of a nickel.

"Sounds as spectacular as something Callie would harvest out at the farm," Dan put in.

If Dan expected John to react to his casual use of Spring's mother's name, he was disappointed. John was intent only on Spring. "You have to remember. The pancake stacks were this high." He picked up her hand and lifted it several inches off the table.

She swallowed, trying hard not to remember, trying to think of some way to include Dan in this conversation. John's intimacy was deliberate and dismissive. He was trying to start a pissing match with Dan, a distinctly masculine "I know Spring better than you do" game. And judging from the pinched look around Dan's mouth, John's plan was working much too well.

She tried to stop him. "John, this is not—"

Ignoring her, he pressed on. "Remember? That inn where we stayed served fresh whipped butter and maple syrup in old-fashioned tins. We ate every meal at a corner table by the window."

A reluctant smile curved Spring's lips. She could almost taste that maple syrup, could see the table they had shared by the window overlooking the sun-drenched lake. A week on Michigan's

Mackinac Island had been their first real vacation after John made some money on his first book. Those fair, perfect days came long before her desire for a child and his increasing remoteness and ambition opened a chasm in their marriage. Spring recalled other, more intimate details of that magical interlude.

Triumph flashed in John's dark eyes. "I knew you would remember that week."

"The berries really were special." Forgetting the huge breakfast she had just consumed, forgetting Dan, Spring licked her lips.

John's voice deepened. "You called them fruit orgasms."

Across the table, Dan choked. Spring realized John still held her hand. She jerked free. Color flooded her cheeks.

Dan's face was flaming, as well.

John, damn him, looked cool and amused. Only the arrival of a waitress with his breakfast stopped Spring from pushing him out of the booth.

Fruit orgasms? Good God.

While an appropriate response eluded Spring, Dan pointedly changed the subject. "You in town for long, John?"

"I'm not sure." John drowned his food in syrup. "How long are you planning for me to stay, Spring?"

"Stop it," she warned in a low voice.

John's eyes rounded. "Stop what?"

A vein she had never seen before popped out on Dan's forehead.

John sliced off a section of pancake. His smile in Dan's direction was beatific. "The length of my stay is all up to Spring."

She kicked his shin.

He rewarded her with only a flinch. Then he laughed and dug into his food, ruining her pleasure at his slight discomfort.

Dan's fair skin took on a purple tint. Spring willed him to hang on. By rising so quickly to John's baiting, Dan was making this comically easy.

"I'm glad this is so funny to you," he muttered to John.

"Lighten up," John retorted.

"You've made Spring uncomfortable."

John's laughter turned sarcastic. "Spring doesn't get uncomfortable, buddy. She gets mad. After all those breakfasts you guys have shared, I'd have thought you'd know that much about her, at least."

"Shut up," she snapped at him.

"Now that's more like the Spring I know." Still laughing, John attacked his breakfast with renewed vigor. "Must be my presence that arouses her passionate nature. It's nice to know I still have the touch."

Dan got to his feet so fast he turned over his coffee cup.

Snatching his plate off the table, John protested, "Jeez, fella, watch the food."

Spring grabbed napkins from the holder and

mopped up the spreading coffee. "John, for God's sake—"

"He made the mess," John pointed out, sounding as peevish as a child.

Dan stalked away.

In the silence that reigned over all nearby tables, John asked Spring, loudly, "Does your boyfriend expect me to pay for his breakfast?"

Jaws clenched, she demanded he let her out of the booth. She was surprised when he complied without protest. She called out for Dan, but he didn't look back. Everyone in the diner was looking at her, including thin-faced, disapproving Willa Dean, who was seated in the booth by the front door. Spring met the old gossip's gaze with a defiant toss of her head as she hurried outside.

By that time, Dan was jogging up the block between the piles of pumpkins and cornstalk harvest decorations put out by the Downtown Merchants' Association to celebrate Thanksgiving.

Spring had to run to catch up with him. Even then, he didn't slow. "I'm sorry," she said, trying to keep pace beside him.

His face was tight. "You knew your husband was in town. You might have warned me."

"I was going to tell you, but I didn't know he'd show up at the diner."

Dan's jog slowed to a fast walk. "Is he here to get your divorce started?"

"I don't know."

"Then why did he come?"

She fought a spurt of annoyance. "I just told you, I don't know."

"Then you'd better find out."

The commanding note in Dan's voice set Spring's teeth on edge. She caught hold of his gray sweatshirt sleeve, swinging him to a halt. "I'd *better* find out?"

He shook off her grasp. "Don't I have a right to know what your husband wants from you?"

Several dates and a few mild kisses gave him few rights in Spring's estimation. "I told you I was married the first time we met, and as far as I'm concerned nothing that's happened between us entitles you to know anything more than that right now."

"I thought you were getting a divorce."

"I don't believe I've mentioned that word to you."

"Then you're not?"

"I never said that, either."

He made a dismissive gesture. "I should have listened to what everyone said about you."

She bristled. "What was that?"

"That you were playing with me, waiting for your husband to come running to get you."

Appalled, she said, "That's not true."

"Well, you didn't do much to avoid that scene back there. I think you enjoyed it."

"I did not!"

"We're going to be the talk of the town."

Spring was shocked to see just how much Dan feared that talk. She knew he was a small-town high-school principal with a reputation to consider, but she wasn't interested in anyone who could come this unglued about other people's opinions.

"Teachers will be telling this story in the lounge Monday morning." From the look on his face, Dan viewed this event as a tragedy.

Such inanity irritated Spring into striking back at him. "Nothing might have come of all of this if you hadn't gone into a jealous pout that egged John on."

Dan's eyes bugged out in a most unattractive way. "You're blaming me?"

"You didn't help."

His mouth thinned, further diminishing his good looks. "How about if I just stay away until you get this situation under control. Then you can call me."

"Don't sit by the phone," she advised. Spring turned and walked back toward the diner.

She heard Dan's feet pounding on the sidewalk as he jogged away.

She felt curious gazes from shoppers going into the furniture store and gave them a dazzling smile.

It faded when she realized John stood beside a pile of pumpkins outside the diner, grinning. She glared at him and kept walking.

He followed her to the Corvette. "Your boyfriend owes me about seven bucks for your breakfast and his."

"I'm sure a hotshot author can afford to pick up the check."

"Affording and wanting are two separate things. And your boyfriend—"

"He's not my boyfriend."

"Thank God. I was afraid moving back to this 'burb had forced you into lowering your standards."

Trying to disregard him, she turned again to the car.

"Your friend Dan struck me as a pompous ass."

Sweetly, she replied, "You should know quite a bit about asses, being of that species yourself."

"I wasn't the one having breakfast with someone other than my spouse."

"Get a grip. We were sharing a meal, not making love on the table."

"Have you?"

The sharp question took Spring by surprise.

"Have you made love with him?"

"On a table?" she parried flippantly.

The last glimmer of amusement faded from John's gaze. "Anywhere."

"I don't think you have a right to ask me that."

"We are still married."

"For now." She dug her keys from her front jeans pocket.

John blocked her from using them. "Are you saying you want a divorce?"

She turned the question on him. "Is it what you want?"

"I'm not the one who started this."

"I suppose that means you consider yourself completely blameless in this situation."

"I didn't leave. You did."

Spring took a breath to slow her runaway temper. She'd had about all she could take of arguing with pushy men on the sidewalk this morning. "Get out of my way, John."

He didn't comply. "Don't you think it's about time we talked about a few things?"

"You want to hash out the problems in our marriage here on the sidewalk?"

"I'd talk to you on national television if it meant we had a real conversation instead of just hurling accusations at each other."

That made her pause.

In a softer, more even tone, John added, "I want to work this out. That's why I've come here."

She studied his familiar, earnest features. "Are you saying you've changed your mind about having a family?"

He hesitated. "Is that really the issue?"

"It is for me." Finally getting past John, she unlocked the Corvette and swung open the door.

He took hold of the edge of the window. "What's the plan, Spring? Are you going to throw our marriage away just so you can go out and find somebody who wants to be a daddy?"

"Of course not."

"Then why won't you give us a chance?"

"A chance?" she repeated, startled. "We've more than given our marriage a chance."

"If that were so, you wouldn't have run away."

"Stop making me out as the bad guy because I left. Lots worse things had already happened between us before I decided I had to go. You know that. So stop preaching at me about running away like Mama does."

"I think Callie has the right idea. She said last night we both have to stop running."

"Mama should mind her own business."

"You're talking about Callie. She can make anyone's business her own."

Spring crossed her arms and tapped one foot impatiently. "Would you let go of the door?"

"Better be careful, Spring. I could ask her to put a hex on Dan."

"She wouldn't do that," Spring said, though not questioning her mother's ability to cast a spell. Callie had learned a variety of unusual skills at her grandmother's knee. "Mama would only hex someone for a member of the family."

"I'm still part of the family. And I might want my competition eliminated. He wouldn't be the first rival for your affections that Callie took care of for me. Remember Tony Travers?"

Tony was someone Spring had dated in high school. In fact, the summer John appeared in White's Creek and in her life, she had still been seeing Tony.

"Right after we first met and went out, Tony did

everything he could to get you back. Your mama told me years later that she fixed him."

Frowning, Spring tried to think back to that summer. When Tony realized she had fallen for John in a big way, he had reacted in typical young, male fashion with taunts and threats, but she couldn't believe her mother hexed him. "You're full of bull, John Nelson."

"So why was Tony sick in bed for a week that summer while I went out with you every night?"

"Mama wouldn't make anyone sick, not anyone who didn't really deserve it."

John's eyebrow cocked. "Oh, really?"

The certainty on his face gave Spring pause.

"Callie told me Tony just felt a little poorly. He didn't feel like crossing his threshold. His whole family felt that way."

Spring's eyes widened. She knew enough of her mother's mountain ways to figure this out. "Mama threw graveyard dirt on their porch, didn't she?"

"Grave dirt dug at midnight, I think she said." John looked downright gleeful.

"It kept him in his house."

"Callie said she took food over there, looked in on all the Traverses all week."

"Good of her," Spring muttered.

"The important thing is that I had a whole week without Tony vying for your attention."

Spring swore. "I'd like to throw something on Mama's porch."

"A dead cat, maybe?"

Alarmed, Spring pushed at his chest. "Don't even joke about hurting one of Mama's cats."

"Not one of hers. Some stray."

"Any cat would be the same," Spring protested, eyes darting from side to side, as if Callie might be able to hear their conversation. "You'd better not be laughing about such things." Her round-eyed horror was much too funny for John to keep his laughter inside.

Immediately, the cool November wind picked up, whipping Spring's black hair across her face. A bundle of cornstalks rustled. Spring sent another warning look at John before a pumpkin dislodged from the top of the stack beside the diner door. It fell to the concrete sidewalk with a hollow crack.

Shivering, Spring moved nearer to John.

He liked that. Liked her clean, soft scent. Liked how her eyes were more gray than blue on this crisp autumn morning. Liked that she still could make him react simply by stepping close.

The wind blew hard again, whirling dry leaves into the street.

Spring said, "I think you'd better do something to atone for your transgression against cats."

"Drive around the cemetery three times while holding my breath?"

Spring sent him another reproving look.

"We could ask Callie for forgiveness," John said.

Somewhere down the street, a car misfired.

Spring jumped.

An undeniable chill moved up John's spine.

"You might want to avoid Mama today," Spring advised. "Besides, she'd probably tell you to do something you'd think foolish."

"Like what?"

"Throw something you prize over the falls up at Devil's Point."

"Okay. Let's go." John took hold of Spring's hand. "You come with me."

She hung back, shaking her head.

"Come on, Spring. I'll get lost going up the mountain without you."

"On Potter's Mountain? There's only one road up and down."

He threaded his fingers through hers. He noticed, with a quickening pulse, that she didn't resist. "I dare you to spend the day with me."

Her widening eyes told him she recalled another time, years ago on this very street, when he had issued this same challenge to her. "What do you say?" he whispered. "It's just a day."

The beginning of a smile tipped one corner of her mouth. "I know what you can send over the falls."

He grinned. "You volunteering?"

At that she tugged her hand away. "I was going to suggest your favorite Springsteen tape."

"Is it still in the 'Vette?" he demanded.

"Right where you left it."

"Then we can listen to it on the way up the mountain."

Spring hesitated, as if she might refuse again. Then she dangled the keys in front of him. "Want to drive?"

mountain."

Chapter Eight

∼ On the flat rock overlooking the water
rushing down from Devil's Point, Spring made
John turn around and close his eyes. From this
vantage point, mountains stretched in either direction. Ribbons of autumn orange, gold, and red
still lingered although Thanksgiving would come
next week.

To the south lay the twisting path she and John
had taken up from the road. Farther down was the
steel-spired bridge spanning the whitewater creek
below the falls. The scenery was as beautiful as it
was wild. Spring felt at home here in a way she
had never felt on a city street. There was definitely magic in the air.

"What's next?" John prompted her.

"Say you're sorry for what you said. Then
throw the tape over your shoulder."

He opened one eye. "Are you sure about this?
This tape might be a collector's item. Last time I
looked in a music store, CDs had taken over."

"All the more reason to let it go. Your sacrifice
has to be something you prize."

"All right." He squeezed his eyes shut once more and lifted the tape.

"Say you're sorry," she cautioned.

"I'm sorry."

"You have to mean it, John."

His brow wrinkled in concentration. "I'm sorry and I mean it." With that, he sent the cassette high in the air.

Spring watched it sail toward the churning water at the base of the falls, nearly a hundred feet below. "It's gone." She turned back to John. "Feel any better?"

"Some."

"Good. Then we can go home."

"Wait a minute," he protested, catching hold of her arm. "I'm not sure it's safe for me to go back into town yet. That wind might kick up again and blow down Ebbie's awning or knock down the statue in front of the courthouse."

"You have nothing to fear if you made your sacrifice with a sincere heart."

John tucked a tendril of hair behind her ear. His dark eyes were solemn. "I wish I could banish all my fears so easily."

Without pausing to consider her words, Spring whispered, "What do you fear?"

"Losing you."

She turned. "Let's go back to town."

"There you go, trying to run again."

He was right. She hated admitting that, but from the minute she had seen him last night, her first impulse had been flight. She was afraid to talk to him about anything significant.

But this was the place for banishing fears. She had nothing to throw over the falls, but she could try to face what frightened her most. "I'm sorry," she told him. "I have been running." She held up a hand when he started to speak. "I'm not talking about when I left you. I don't think of that as running away."

"Then what was it?"

"Surviving, maybe. I had to get out of there. Breathe again."

"I didn't realize you were smothering in Chicago."

"I felt as if I was in a box."

"In the city."

"In our marriage." She could see her words hurt him, but they were the truth. "When we first left here, first got married, there were all these possibilities, a wide-open slate. Then came the walls."

"My refusal to have a child?"

"That and more. I stopped feeling part of your life."

He stared off at the horizon where the mountains rolled one into the another. "I never meant to cut you out of any part of my life."

"I don't think either of us intentionally did any of the things that brought us to this point."

His pause seemed to go on forever. "But what do we do now?"

"That's just it, John. That question is the one I

keep running from. Maybe that's the real reason I left you. I was afraid if we kept on together, we were going to reach the worst sort of conclusion."

Voice husky, John said, "For me, there's nothing much worse than being apart from you."

The emotion in his face made her chest ache. She hated having to face these decisions. With him in Chicago, she could drift along in limbo. But now he was here. A decision about their future was here. In her face.

John glanced at the falls and sighed. "I guess there's only one thing we can do."

"What?"

"Jump?" His laughter cut the tension that had been building between them.

It didn't get them any closer to reaching a conclusion about their marriage, either. Spring decided not to care. She was a coward. She couldn't face letting John go. Not yet.

So she let him take the conversation away from dangerous territory. "How come you never told me about throwing things from this rock?"

"You never talked about killing cats before."

"Is that the only kind of forgiveness available here?"

Spring smiled and took in a lungful of the clear air. She smelled damp earth and pine needles and the hint of woodsmoke from the ashes of a campfire they had found just east of the rock. "Smell that," she told John. "How can you smell this perfect, clear air and not feel forgiven for just about everything?"

John tucked hands in his pockets and sniffed at the air like a bluetick hound on the trail of a coon.

She punched his arm, laughing. "You have no respect for the majesty of nature."

"Comes from growing up in prep schools instead of running wild in the woods like you DeWitt rascals," he said with a smile.

"The stories around town about Mama leaving us on our own to run with wildcats in the hills are simply not true."

"You sure? There is a wild streak in you."

"That came naturally."

"And for that, I have been always thankful." In John's gaze was a warmth Spring knew very well.

It would be easy, she thought, so easy to give in to the familiar sexual ache strumming low in her belly. But what would that prove or solve? After the physical pleasure passed, they would face the same problems that had wrenched them apart. The problems she couldn't talk to John about last night or on this gorgeous late-autumn day.

Hastily, she pulled away from him.

He frowned, but didn't protest.

She turned to the trail leading away from the rock. "It's time to get moving. Unless you brought something for lunch that I don't know about."

"You're hungry?" John demanded. "After that breakfast?"

She held up her wristwatch for his inspection. "It's nearly one o'clock, and it'll take us at least a half hour to hike back to the car."

"And if we keep driving north, we could be at Reebo's by two-thirty. They haven't closed Reebo's, have they?"

He referred to a restaurant in the next county. It was little more than a dive, actually, where liquor had been sold illegally out of a back room since long before John or Spring was born.

Ned DeWitt had always told Spring the do-gooders in that dry county might have shut Reebo's down if it weren't for the pit barbecue they served six days a week as a front for their more lucrative sideline. It was also rumored the Reebo family flavored the sauce with moonshine, along with a combination of secret ingredients selected to ensure their recipe couldn't be copied. And they closed down on Sundays, to encourage everyone to go to church. Granddaddy Reebo was a deacon and a choir member, the most generous tither in his Baptist church.

Spring's mouth began to water for the old gentleman's barbecue. "I guess Reebo's is closer than going back to town," she said by way of justification.

John smiled in triumph.

And that's how they wound up at a roadside picnic table, eating sloppy barbecue pork sandwiches with mayonnaise-drenched slaw dripping out of each side. Best of all was the big dill pickle she bit into after each mouthful of sandwich. She tried stealing John's. He gave it up only after she traded him half a package of vinegar potato chips.

And he laughed when she consumed the last bite of sandwich and tried to discreetly undo the top button of her blue jeans.

The moment was almost like old times.

Dangerously like old times.

Especially when Spring let herself gaze too long across that table and into John's brown eyes.

She didn't want to admit how good it felt just being with him. Nor did she want to confess how many memories were stirred by the smoky tang of the barbecue. By the landmarks from years gone by that flashed past the car window once she insisted they start the drive back to White's Creek.

Spring fell silent, intent on the falling leaves that rained down on the sun-dappled road as the Corvette hugged the twists and turns of the mountains. Was John remembering, as she was? Surely he recalled it was Reebo's they had visited on the day they first made love.

She glanced over at him. His profile was somber. His hands were light on the familiar steering wheel. John had driven another car on that other afternoon. His mother's light blue Cadillac. It had been winter then. The week before Christmas. The weather had turned cold.

Despite the freeze warnings, Spring and John had been so eager to be alone, they had taken their Reebo sandwiches and driven this very road, then pulled off onto a logging trail. They had eaten in the car, with her worrying the whole time

about dropping food on the expensive leather and
suede seats . . .

John laughed at her. "Would you relax?"

"But she'll know it was us."

"So what?"

Spring was surprised by his tone. John was usually
more careful about antagonizing his mother and stepfather. "What's gotten into you?"

"I don't know how much more I can take of being in
their house." John never claimed the house where he
lived with them as his home.

She recognized the defiance in his voice. He was
always this way after a run-in with Sam Nelson. He
had assured her there had been no beatings since his
last bruises had faded, but Spring wasn't sure she could
trust John to tell her the truth about that.

She placed her sandwich on the dash and turned to
face John. "What's happened? What's he done to you?"

He set his mouth in the grim line she had come to
know too well.

She put her hand on his arm, pressing lightly. "You
can tell me."

John looked down at his half-eaten sandwich, folded
the edges of the wax-paper wrap, and thrust it in the
paper sack from Reebo's. He avoided looking at her. "I
don't know how to tell you this."

Alarm made her breath catch. "What?"

"My mother told me all this . . . stuff. About you."
The ugly lies Debra had heard about Spring spilled out
of him, each word like a rock to her heart.

When he was through, she was trembling. Sick, almost. But angry. "So you think this is true?"

"No." His denial was bullet-quick. He took hold of her arms, his gaze burning into hers with a fierceness that was almost frightening. "Of course I don't believe their lies."

"Their lies? What did Sam say about me? What does he think he knows? The only time I've ever spoken to him has been when he came in the diner, and I waited on him."

John wouldn't tell her what Sam had said. She figured it must be bad.

In the silence that fell between them, she expressed her deepest fear. "Are they going to make you stop seeing me?"

Another explosive denial tore from John. "They couldn't." His hands went to her face. "They won't." His fingers threaded through her hair. "I won't let them."

"What choice would you have?"

In his expression was misery. Raw and unchecked. Instead of answering, he reached for her. His kiss was flavored with desperation. And Spring, so long the one who had resisted recklessness, gave herself completely to this kiss.

She welcomed the dance of his tongue against hers. The sureness of his fingers undoing the buttons of her blouse and the snap of her jeans. The urgent whispers and tender strokes as his hands moved over her body. From her breasts to her belly, to the curls that covered her mound.

They had ventured this far before. Many times. In the gathering twilight of this December day, however, she threw no caution flags in his way. No pleas for him to wait. This time, she gave in to the strength of his need and the power of her answering passion.

In the wide backseat of his mother's Caddy, on the sleek leather upholstery, beneath a blanket Debra Nelson had placed in her trunk in case of emergency, John took Spring for the first time.

Despite all the rumors and lies, it was her very first time.

John tensed above her, the hard muscles of his back bunching beneath her hands as he withdrew from his first, awkward, not-so-successful thrust into her body. She looked into his eyes, half-fearing she would find surprise or disappointment, or some other clear evidence he had believed in the reputation she didn't deserve.

But all she found was joy. A wide, heart-stopping smile she could lose herself in. So she had. They lost themselves in each other. . . .

Now, as the miles sped by as quickly as the afternoon, Spring let the cool breeze blow in her hair. She gave a slight smile. Wouldn't some people be surprised to learn John Nelson was the only man she had ever made love with? The only man she had ever, truly wanted?

That almost made her laugh out loud. For what other man had she ever even looked at with more than casual interest? The boys she had dated before John had been just that—boys. Even Dan Strickland, attractive as he was, had paled when John came into the diner this morning. John had been her world from the moment they met. She used to think he felt the same way about her. But he had changed, and that's when she had first started living with the soul-emptying fear she felt right now.

She wasn't completely sure when this fear first took her by the throat, just as she couldn't define the exact moment when John started not needing her in the way he had for most of their relationship. If she could work out a time line, she might be able to untangle the mess they were in.

But all she knew, with absolute certainty, was the hollowness that had overtaken her heart in the past few years. Trying to live with the ache had been impossible. Leaving John hadn't filled the emptiness, either.

Would ending their marriage bring her a measure of peace?

That was hard to contemplate when her head was thick with memories of all they had shared. She wasn't sure if she was strong enough to walk away from the history they shared. She and John had become adults together. Struggled to find their own true selves together. Could she truly stand alone, without him?

Spring didn't realize she had made a sound until John's voice broke through her thoughts. Even then, she turned to him with a blank stare. "What?"

He took his attention from the dangerous curves at the base of Potter's Mountain to glance at her in concern. "Are you okay?"

Looking at him made Spring want to cry. She had no solutions, and she knew better than to turn to John for answers. No matter that he claimed he wanted to talk things out, he hadn't been talking honestly with her for a long, long time. Logically, she knew they had to confront the issues between them. But emotionally, she still couldn't face the very real possibility that they would never live together as husband and wife again.

"I want to go home," she said with quiet finality.

John was silent as they reached the tree-lined streets of White's Creek.

With removed appreciation, Spring noted the purple shadows edging over the familiar homes and buildings. In contrast, the brilliance of the setting sun sparkled off the plate-glass windows of the storefronts along First Street. Through her half-open window, she heard the raised voices of children and spied a big group gathered on an empty lot near the high school. They were playing touch football, trying to wring enjoyment out of every last ray of the remaining daylight.

Spring could remember the go-for-broke feeling of a fading Saturday afternoon. Each moment was a gift, a reprieve from the parent's voice that would call, from the homework and chores that had to be done, from the darkness that would soon smudge its inky fingers over a bright world.

She envied those kids with a keenness that shocked her. For they could live in the moment. Spring couldn't.

"We have to talk," she told John. "We've avoided it all day long."

"Then can't we put it off a little longer?"

Surprised, she turned to face him. "Talking's what you wanted to do last night."

"And we ended up in an argument. Today was so nice, I don't want it ruined."

She knew exactly how he felt, but that wouldn't get them anywhere. "Then I guess you better get back to the Pine Cone Lodge, and I better go home."

His laughter was dry. "Sad commentary on us, isn't it? The only way we can avoid fighting is to ignore the hard subjects or just stay apart."

She moistened her lips. "John, if you would really talk—"

"Let's not start the argument right here," he interrupted. Thrusting a hand through his dark hair, he nodded toward the intersection they were approaching. "Can't I turn right here to get you home?"

"What about your car?"

"I walked down to the diner from the motel this morning. I'll take you home and walk back, too. It's not far."

"It'll be dark soon."

He threw her a bitter look. "That doesn't bother me nearly as much as going back to that motel room."

John drew the car to a stop in the drive beside her little house. He looked so sad, so lost, that an invitation trembled on Spring's lips. She bit it back.

He walked away. She went inside. To a meowing cat and an emptiness so real she could feel it swallowing her. The night stretched ahead of her like an endlessly unfurling bolt of black cloth.

Wearily, she wandered through the house to the kitchen. On the counter was a small jar and a note in her mother's handwriting. "Use these raspberry leaves and skullcap in a hot bath before you go to bed. They'll help you sleep. Love, Mama."

Trust Mama to know what I need.

Spring smiled as she unscrewed the jar and sniffed the herbs. It didn't smell all that pleasant, but she was sure it would work in the way of all of Mama's remedies. Spring could take a soothing bath and go to sleep early.

If sleeping was how she really wanted to spend the evening.

At her feet, Basil let out a plaintive, almost angry meow. He hissed, turned with feline quickness, and tore out of the kitchen.

"What in the—" Spring began, following the cat's path down the hall.

A knock at the front door sent Basil into another hissing fit. Not knowing what to expect, Spring flipped on the porch light and turned the doorknob while telling the cat to calm down. Basil retreated to the living room, fur ruffled and teeth bared.

Spring found John standing on the other side of the screen door. Before she could protest, he said, "Don't be angry. I just couldn't go back to that motel. Not tonight. Not yet."

And Spring realized she had wanted him to come back from the moment he walked down the street.

She opened the door and didn't resist when John came in and took her in his arms.

"I hate this," he muttered. "I hate being here, but not being *with* you."

"I know." Her voice was thick, clouded by the conflicting desires swirling inside her.

"Let me stay. We don't have to talk. We can . . ." He swallowed and leaned his forehead against hers.

Spring drew back. "This isn't a good idea."

"It's better than both of us sitting alone, wanting each other."

"John—"

"I know you want me." His hand cupped the back of her neck. "No matter what else has gone wrong, you want me. Not that guy you were with today. Not any other guy."

She didn't bother with false denials. "That isn't the point."

"But it should be the point." His breath was hot on her face, his mouth just inches from hers. "We belong together, Spring. You know we do."

His kiss stopped her next protest. She didn't have time to think. It was all-consuming. Potent. As familiar as his kisses were, their separation flavored this with a new power.

His hands were in her hair. Moving down her body. She pressed herself against him, shamelessly grinding her hips into his. If she lowered his zipper, he would be velvet, hot and hard against her touch. One or two moves and he would be inside her. She was wet from just his kiss. Aching to feel what she had missed. It had been so long. Too long.

He edged her toward the wall, pushing her sweater above her waist. His voice was a low croon. She was lulled by his words, by promises of how he wanted to touch her, fill her. Spring almost let that happen. If she had allowed her body to take over, it would have happened.

But there was this voice in her head that wouldn't shut off. It kept asking her what this would prove or change. The answer, of course, was nothing.

"Don't, John. Stop it. Slow down." He came after her, but she held him off.

For a moment, he leaned against her, breathing hard. "Don't tell me to leave, Spring, please. I'm not going back to that room. Not now."

"I don't want you to go," she admitted. "Just

stop . . . this. I can't handle making love to you right now."

"But why?"

"Because then I won't be able to think."

"There's nothing wrong with just feeling." His lips swooped toward hers again.

She turned her head. "Please, stop."

At that, he let her go.

She waved him toward the living room. "Just go in there. Sit down."

"You come with me."

Eluding his outstretched hand, Spring retreated a few steps down the hall. "I'm going to the kitchen for a minute. To get . . . something . . . tea or a beer. I just need a few seconds to . . ." Not bothering to complete that sentence, she escaped to the kitchen.

Just inside the door that swung shut behind her, she covered her face with her hands. She should ask John to go. If he stayed a minute more, he would stay the night. She would wake up tomorrow feeling like a drunk after a binge. Making love with John wouldn't give her the answers she needed. If anything, more questions would be raised.

A shout sounded from the living room. Then a crash.

Spring raced down the hall and rounded the corner as her cat, claws extended, launched himself at John's denim-clad leg.

Basil dug in and held on. Shaking his leg and

dancing in a circle, John yelled at Spring, "Do something. Get this crazy cat off me."

Diving for her pet, she shouted back, "I knew you weren't sincere when you threw that tape off Devil's Point. Basil knows it, too."

"I'm sincere now. With all my heart, I'm sincerely sorry for insulting the cat population."

Basil let go with one last hiss. In the cat's green eyes, Spring detected genuine satisfaction.

Chapter Nine

〜 "Ouch!" John jerked away from the pungent-smelling cloth Spring pressed against the red welts on his shin. They were in her small bathroom, him seated on the commode, with his jeans off and his injured leg propped on the edge of the tub. The wound burned like fire when she touched it again with the cloth. "Spring, are you sure this is what your mother said to do?"

"You heard me call Mama. This is what she recommended." Spring, who looked uncomfortably close to laughter, bent over his shin once more. "Stop being a baby and hold still."

"But I thought she'd give you the formula for some kind of soothing herbal potion."

Spring again doused her cloth with liquid from a brown bottle. "Mama said to clean it first with plain old hydrogen peroxide."

John winced. "I think Callie is just trying to make me suffer."

Again Spring's lips trembled. "I told her they were shallow scratches."

170

"Shallow? That cat damn near tore the skin to the bone."

She laughed out loud. "Let me assure you that if Basil had wanted to inflict a real injury, he would have."

The feline in question was sprawled in the doorway to the bathroom regarding the goings-on with what John interpreted as cynical glee. But John wasn't about to criticize. "Nice kitty," he said, gritting his teeth against the continued sting of the antiseptic.

"Mama gave him to me, and he's actually a very good cat. He has excellent manners, unless provoked somehow."

"I'll remember that."

Spring rummaged through the medicine cabinet over the sink and withdrew a plain white tin. "Aloe vera gel," she explained, chuckling, when she screwed the lid off and John resisted the application. "Mama makes it for all of us."

"I remember," John mumbled, as the cool ointment began to counter the peroxide's sting. "She used to send it to us in Chicago. We were always burning ourselves on that stupid gas stove in that first awful apartment."

It had often taken both him and Spring to coax that recalcitrant stove to life. They had made it a game, with the one who actually managed to get the stove on able to claim the most intimate of prizes. The phrase "light my fire" had become a secret, shared joke.

Those memories, coupled with the close confines of the bathroom, turned John's thoughts down the very path he had abandoned when the cat came at him. Spring's special scent was all around him. Her touch was light and soft against his skin. He was all too aware of the rounded thrust of her breasts beneath her red sweater, the sweet curve of her bottom under worn jeans.

It had been over five months since they had been together.

Five months.

Forever.

No wonder he had practically attacked her in the hall. No wonder all he could think about right now was getting her out of those clothes and into bed.

Spring had to be aware of his growing arousal —his shortening breath, the tenting of the front of his boxers. But she kept her eyes on her task as she strapped some gauze over his injured shin. "Mama said she'll make you an oak-bark poultice if this gets infected."

"Sounds lovely."

"It's actually not so bad." After settling the last corner of the bandage in place, she put away her medicines and washed her hands, still not looking at him. "I'm going to make us some tea. You can get dressed."

He reached out and took her arm. "Do I have to?"

"You know you do," she insisted, shaking him off. If John didn't know her so well, didn't see the slight tremble of her bottom lip, he might have imagined she was unaffected by their closeness, by what had passed between them only a short while before. She was struggling as hard as he. So he let her go.

He sat in place and stared for a moment at Basil, whose unblinking regard seemed vaguely accusatory.

"I'm still her husband," John muttered to the cat. "And I still want her. I can't help it if I'm horny. You're a young guy. Surely you can understand why I would like to lay your mistress across her kitchen table and have my way with her."

Basil meowed. But not in an angry way.

From another room, Spring called, "Don't be afraid of the cat. I don't think he'd attack you again."

John wondered what she would say if he confessed it was the animal inside of himself that he was most afraid of right now.

Sighing, he stood and pulled on his jeans. Unless Spring weakened considerably, he was not going to get lucky tonight. She was being sensible, focusing on their real dilemmas. Lord knows, sex had never been a problem. Funny thing was, he hadn't come back to her house in search of sex. He just couldn't bear to be away from her tonight. It made no sense to him that they shouldn't be together.

The living room was chilly, a reflection of how the November temperature dropped once the sun set. Logs and kindling were laid in the fireplace, so John opened the flue and used one of the long matches in the pottery jar on the mantel to light a blaze. The dry tinder sparked immediately, snapping and popping as the flames spread.

A movement beside him made John look down. He was surprised to find Basil at his side, staring intently into the growing fire. John set the fire screen in place and grinned down at the cat. "So you've decided I am good for something." John sat on the sofa, and the cat followed, perching on the broad, rounded arm beside him.

Spring appeared in the doorway with two steaming mugs. "I see you two boys have made up." Grinning, she handed John some tea.

"I won't insult his species, and he won't try to maim me."

"Good deal." With a weary sigh, Spring curled into the far corner of the sofa. Well away from John. "That fire's going to feel good when it gets going."

"You've always loved a fire. That was your one requirement when we went shopping for our apartment. Remember?"

Not answering, she appeared pensive as she looked toward the fireplace with the same rapt attention as Basil.

It was a nice room for firegazing, John thought. The rich colors and homey touches would make anyone feel right at home. He had to wonder if Spring had entertained Dan Strickland here.

He hadn't intended to be combative, but there

was an edginess in the air. John knew it was sexual frustration, but that didn't keep him from saying, "I hope my coming back here tonight hasn't put a crimp in your social life."

Spring didn't even look at him.

"How long have you been dating the good principal, anyway?"

Finally, she turned her gaze to him. "Do you really want to get back into this?"

"You're still my wife. I think I have a right to ask about the men you see."

"You and I have been separated for five months, and in all that time you haven't bothered to call. I've had no hope that our marriage would continue. I didn't think there was any reason for me not to see any man I wanted."

"How would you feel if I told you I've been dating?"

Raw emotion glittered briefly in her eyes. "Have you?"

"I'm not sure you deserve an answer."

She set her mug down hard enough to splash tea onto the old trunk she was using as a coffee table. "I don't want to argue with you about something that doesn't matter."

"Doesn't matter?" John repeated. "I think honoring our marriage vows matters a lot."

"Right." Voice laced with sarcasm, Spring stood and went to the hearth.

John was right behind her. "Just what are you implying I did to dishonor our vows?"

"Infidelity isn't the only type of betrayal."

He felt as if she had punched him. "You think I betrayed you? How have you made me feel with your obsession about having a child? That's what feels like a betrayal to me. I still don't understand why it is so important to you."

"You act as if it's this weird craving," she retorted. "Wanting a family is basic. To most people, it's all-consuming. I'm tired of you making me out as some kind of freak because I want to have a baby."

"You never wanted a child before that . . . that crazy vision. I always thought Callie convinced you that was a sign from God."

"I didn't need convincing. All that vision did was make me realize I had been ignoring what I truly wanted. I wanted a child long before that day. I just ignored the signs. Mainly because I knew how you felt, what you would say. I edited my needs to suit you."

He thrust a hand through his hair in frustration. "The strength of our marriage used to be how much we wanted the same things."

"People change. Needs change. Maybe that's the real danger in getting married so young."

"So now you regret marrying me?"

"I didn't say that." Turning away, she seized the poker and stirred the fire with sharp, vicious motions. "I wish you wouldn't try to twist everything I say."

He backed down from his aggressive mode. It would lead them nowhere except to another argument. And that's not what he wanted. So he held out his hand. "I'm sorry, Spring."

She looked up, obviously surprised by his concession.

He repeated his apology. "I don't intentionally twist your words. I'm just trying so hard to figure out where we went wrong. I know it's deeper than your wanting a baby."

Her eyes widened. "You're finally admitting there were other problems?"

"I think the baby thing is probably just a symptom."

She shook her head. "I don't want you fooling yourself. My desire for a child is more than a symptom of the problems between us. It's very real. I'm not going to kid you about it or hide my feelings. I did that long enough."

He returned to a question he had asked her this morning, one she hadn't fully answered. "Is having a baby all you want from a marriage?"

"I could go to a sperm bank if I wanted a child alone. It's the whole package I want. A *family*. The real thing."

He thought she had idealized the notion. "Did you think Dan Strickland was a candidate for this perfect little picture?"

She made a disgusted sound. "Just forget about Dan, will you? He's history. I came to that conclusion this morning."

John didn't bother to hide his pleasure at that news.

"You shouldn't look so pleased with yourself."

Her chin lifted. "I did go out with Dan. I let him kiss me, and I kissed him back."

Despite the pang that confession caused, John straightened his shoulders and chuckled with confidence. "I'll stake a few kisses against thirteen years as a couple. The odds are in my favor."

"You think so?"

"Yeah, I do." John felt his confidence returning. Spring loved him. They had fire between them. Years of warmth and love. In the end, that would bring her back, keep her close.

She regarded him with suspicion. "What's that smile about?"

"Can't a guy be happy when he finds out his wife has given her boyfriend the boot?"

Spring's frown followed him all the way back to the sofa. He sat and unconcernedly held out a hand to Basil, who sniffed his fingers. John was determined to be as pleasant as possible. He knew he wasn't going to get anywhere with Spring by being belligerent. Switching conversational gears, he said, "Did I tell you I finished my book?"

Spring, who had crossed her arms and was regarding him with suspicion, nodded. "You mentioned it last night."

"I know you don't care about it, but—"

"Please stop accusing me of not caring."

He went on as if she hadn't spoken. "It'll be out next spring. The publisher has big hopes for it. They're going to send me on a book tour, put some advertising money behind me. They're hoping to take me to the next level."

"That's wonderful."

The flatness of her tone stirred resentment in him, making him forget his vow to keep the mood pleasant between them. "Why do you hate it so much?"

"Since you stopped telling me what you were working on, I barely know what this book's about. I can't hate it."

"Not the book. Why do you hate my writing?"

"I don't."

"You were never this way when I was a reporter."

"At least then you seemed to care about real people."

John sat forward, puzzled. "Real people?"

"As opposed to a fictional world. Now you want to spend more time with your characters than with anyone who is real-life flesh and blood."

"Getting caught up in the story is the way I write, Spring, the way I've always written everything—fact or fiction. You used to understand how much I get into my work."

"But when you were a reporter, you didn't ignore the world around you." She exhaled slowly, and added, "You didn't ignore me."

He made an impatient gesture.

"Don't brush me off," Spring told him. "I'm telling you the truth, no matter how much you don't want to hear it. Everything changed after your first book came out and they wanted you to write a novel."

"Yeah, we actually had enough money to pay the rent in full every month."

"I've never cared how much money we had. I cared about the way you were locked up inside yourself while you were writing that first novel."

"I don't think I was any different than when I was working on a big story."

She took a deep breath. "But you were. And I can't help but think it all had something to do with Sam's dying."

That brought John to his feet. "Don't start that nonsense again."

"But he died just before your first book came out. He never knew about the movie option or the novel or your really big success. That's when you changed."

"And you changed, too," John insisted, deciding to give voice to feelings he had never been able to express before. "When I signed the contract for my first two novels is when you made it clear you didn't like my success."

"Now you're being absurd. I celebrated with you. I was so proud."

"I think you were jealous. I think you still are."

Her mouth opened, but no sound escaped.

In the silence, John continued, "You don't like it that I'm making money, that I'm not struggling. You hate it that I have something in my life that I love as much as I love creating these stories."

Spring's denial was swift and heated. "That's the stupidest thing I've ever heard. There's never been any jealousy between us. I want you to love what you do. I have a job I love, too."

"And it's such a noble job," he retorted. "That's at the root of your jealousy. All I'm doing is writing about cops and robbers while you're dedicating yourself to children in need. But I'm the one pulling in the big bucks."

He wasn't surprised when she said, "Money is no barometer of success."

He laughed, bitterly. "You're not living in the real world about this, Spring. Money is important. It's important to me." It felt damn good just admitting that to her.

"You didn't use to care about money. Neither of us did."

"I used to be an idealistic fool, running from everything and anything that reminded me of my mother and stepfather." He held up his hand before she could interrupt. "I know you think I'm still running. But making money and enjoying some success is when I finally believed in myself, when I finally started freeing myself from all the garbage Debra and Sam fed me about my abilities and my potential."

Spring's eyes had grown wide, more silver than gray in the flickering firelight. Her voice was quiet. "I always believed in you."

"This isn't about you. This is about *me*." John thumped his chest with one fist for emphasis. "Just me. This is about what I think of *myself*. It has nothing to do with you or your image of what I should or shouldn't be. It has to do with me."

John could see he had knocked Spring for a loop. Until the day she burst into his life, John's life had been a study in misery. She had, indeed, believed in him from the start. For many, many years, their lives had been completely intertwined. There was nothing they didn't share. Without her love and encouragement, he didn't know where he would have ended up.

But some time ago he had realized it wasn't enough for him to be the man reflected in a mirror Spring held up. That was why he grabbed the chance to do his first novel.

And while Spring said she was excited for him, hesitation had tempered her enthusiasm. She feared he would fail, and that wasn't a normal reaction from the woman who had always given him unconditional support.

So maybe Spring was right about him withdrawing. While writing that first novel, he hadn't shared all of his own fears of failure with her. He also hadn't shared the joy either, his exhilaration over the newfound freedom of writing fiction as opposed to reporting the facts. He hadn't felt he could share with her.

For the first time in their marriage, a wall had come down between them. The box she had been talking about up at Devil's Point this morning. The wall had become a barrier. But he knew, with absolute certainty, that he hadn't built that obstruction by himself.

Now, he said, "No matter what you say, Spring, the problems between us are not all my fault."

She cocked her head, her expression thoughtful. "Is that what I've said?"

"That's what I've heard."

Spring began a reply, but a knock on the front door cut her short. She started and glanced at the clock. It was nearly 10:00 P.M. Late for unexpected visitors in White's Creek. "Who can that be?"

Not pausing to consider this was her home and she might resent him taking over, John strode to the hallway. Through the door, he demanded that the visitor identify himself.

Scuffling sounds and low, urgent conversation greeted his query. Then a feminine voice called out, "Miss DeWitt, it's me, Mollie. Open up, please."

John looked at Spring. "Who's Mollie?"

Instead of answering, she pushed him aside and flung open the door.

A frightened-looking teenage girl literally fell across the threshold. Holding on to her, swaying, was a young man who was bleeding profusely from a gash in his forehead. Only when the youth slipped to the floor did John realize who he was.

Logan.

Spring quickly knelt beside John's half brother. The girl with him whispered, "I think he's really hurt."

Logan lifted his head, and looked right at John. His voice was a sad parody of Sam Nelson's swaggering machismo. "Hey, bro. If you think I look bad, you should see the other guy."

John dropped to one knee at the boy's side, shocked by the genuine fear that gripped him.

"What are you doing?"

Ignoring John's low, angry question, Spring concentrated on collecting what she needed from her bathroom medicine cabinet. "You Nelson brothers are taxing my limited nursing skills tonight."

"Logan needs to get out of here."

"He's hurt, John."

"Then let's get him to a hospital."

"Is there any harm in cleaning him up a little?"

"He's got a head injury. He belongs in the ER."

"But you heard him when I suggested that. He refused."

John swore, and took the ointment and bandages out of her hands. "I don't understand why you feel the need to get involved with him."

Anger kindled inside her. "He needs someone to get involved before he self-destructs."

John thrust a hand through his hair. "What about this girl who's with him? Who is she?"

Spring briefly explained her relationship with Mollie, then bit her lip. "I have to admit I'm not thrilled that she's involved with Logan."

"Then warn her away from him."

"Maybe I will. After I clean up that cut on his forehead and try to talk him into going to the hospital." With that, Spring brushed past John and headed for the kitchen, where Mollie and Logan were waiting.

The young man was sitting at the table in the center of the room, holding towel-wrapped ice against his lips. In the bright overhead light, his handsome face was a real mess. His nose was already swelling. A huge purpling bruise decorated one jaw. Various cuts were oozing blood, which had splattered on his white cotton shirt. He held one hand against his ribs. And yet there was still something cocky in his posture. A deeply ingrained defiance.

Mollie sat beside him, pale and shaken.

Efficiently, Spring set to work cleaning Logan's face. She was relieved to find that the gash on his forehead was more bloody than deep. His nose was bleeding, as well, but didn't appear to be broken. He insisted his ribs were only tender and that no bones felt broken. Spring would feel better, however, if a doctor looked him over.

Aware of John lingering in the doorway to the kitchen, she finally asked Logan what had happened.

Logan was silent and stoic, not even wincing as she smoothed on ointment and bandaged his head.

"Mollie?" Spring asked, turning a reproving glance on the girl.

The young redhead took a deep breath. "There was a fight," she explained, before looking imploringly at Logan. He glared at her, and Mollie clammed up.

Spring didn't like seeing the girl looking to him for permission to speak. "You'd better tell me everything, Mollie, no matter what Logan says you should do."

Logan's blue eyes shifted toward John.

John stepped into the room. "By coming to my wife's house for help, you made this my business, too."

"So you two are back together." He looked at Spring. "You're really taking him back?"

"That is not the issue right now," she said.

"But you don't want him back," Logan insisted.

John broke in, "Stuff your wise-ass attitude and tell us what happened."

Spring glared at him. "Please—"

"No, I'll tell him what happened," Logan cut in. He sounded proud. "Some guy was ragging on me at a party tonight. So I kicked his butt."

"Looks like he got a piece of you, too," John retorted.

Logan jerked away from Spring's ministrations. "They ganged up on me."

"That's right," Mollie insisted. "There were a couple of guys. They all jumped on Logan."

John cocked an eyebrow at her. "Was this before or after Logan beat the hell out of the guy who was giving him a hard time?"

Mollie's uncertain glance at Logan told the whole story.

Logan started out of the kitchen chair, but Spring caught his arm in a firm grip. "You sit still." The ease with which he complied made her think his injuries were more serious than she thought.

"You're a real hothead," John said to Logan. "Last night it was me you wanted to tangle with."

Spring looked at John in surprise. "You didn't tell me you had seen your family."

He shrugged. "It wasn't important."

"He came sniffing around," Logan jeered. "He came to see what he might have had if he hadn't been such a jerk to my father."

"Let me tell you who the jerk was," John began.

Spring stopped him. "There's nothing to be gained by arguing with him. He's the kid, and he's hurt, and you're the adult. Try to keep it in perspective."

John's face colored.

Logan snickered. "Looks like she's got you pussy-whipped, big brother. I'm not surprised."

"You little—"

Whatever insult John was preparing to toss Logan's way was lost to the pounding that sounded from the front door. Before anyone could react, a voice called out, "It's Sheriff Kane, Spring. Open up. I know Logan's here. I need to talk to him."

Logan bolted toward the back door. But John was faster. He caught his younger brother by a bloodstained sleeve and quickly barred the door. While Mollie shrieked, the brothers struggled. Spring ran for the front hall and let in Sheriff Kane and two of his deputies.

Their appearance sent Mollie into hysterics. Spring grabbed the girl and held her back while the men closed in on Logan.

Angry and frightened, he struck out at everyone and kept trying to escape, even when Sheriff Kane yelled that he just wanted to talk. A scuffle ensued. The kitchen table was upended. A chair crashed against the wall. Logan spewed filthy curses, most of them directed at John.

Spring chilled at the venom in his voice. *Why did he hate John so?*

She could have forgiven John if he had smacked Logan for the things he said, but he didn't. Instead, he held on to him, clearly to keep Logan from doing more damage to himself and those around him. Finally, John wrestled Logan to the floor, holding him there while one deputy cuffed him.

"You asshole!" Mollie screamed at John over Logan's continued abuse. "How could you do this to your own brother?"

Sheriff Kane, big and imposing in his blue uniform, jerked around to glare at her. "I'd advise you to hush right now, young lady."

Mollie shrank against Spring, who kept her arms around the girl's slim, trembling body while a still struggling Logan was hustled out the door by the two deputies.

John, breathing hard, knelt on the floor where he had brought Logan down.

The sheriff put out a hand and hauled him to

his feet. "I'm sorry about this," the older man said, directing his glance from John to Spring.

"What's Logan done?" Spring asked, though she feared she knew the answer already.

"Beat a kid almost senseless."

"They beat him up, too," Mollie protested, slipping from Spring's restraining grasp.

"Did you see everything that happened tonight?" the sheriff demanded.

Mollie's reply lost some certainty. "I saw enough."

But Sheriff Kane just shook his head. "There are a dozen witnesses who swear they saw Logan attack Jeff Lott for no good reason. They were both drinking a little, but weren't obviously drunk. Supposedly, Logan just went after Jeff."

Spring spoke up. "Logan told us that this other boy was giving him a hard time."

Taking off his cap, the sheriff wearily raked a hand through his silvering hair. "Spring, you ought to see this boy Logan beat up. His head is damn near cracked open. Can you imagine what he might say that would deserve that kind of beating?"

Mollie's swift protest was cut off by another sharp look from the sheriff. He turned to John. "This isn't the first time Logan's been in trouble. But Jeff Lott's parents aren't much like the other folks your mother and brother have tangled with."

"So they're not for sale?" A bitter smile curved John's lips.

The sheriff slapped his cap back on. "Not yet, anyway." Explaining that Logan was being taken in for questioning and that an assault charge was a strong possibility, he turned toward the front of the house.

Spring didn't bother seeing him to the door. She was afraid to leave Mollie alone in the room with John.

Sure enough, as soon as Sheriff Kane was gone, the girl raged at John. "How could you keep him here? He could have gotten away."

"And then what?" John tossed back at her. "He couldn't go far on foot. The sheriff's department would have found him right away."

Mollie, normally so sensible, seemed blind to the consequences of what Logan had done. She wanted to blame John for everything. "Logan told me you hated him. We should have gone the minute we found out you were here."

Openly scornful, John asked, "That's right. Logan should have run home to his mommy."

"She's mad at him," Mollie replied, tears welling up in her eyes. "He told me she said he'd better not come home in trouble again."

"But why come here?" John asked. "This is none of Spring's concern."

"Yes, it is," Spring insisted. "Logan and I are friends. He should have come to me."

Mollie dashed a hand across a damp cheek. "Logan didn't want to come, especially when he saw you here. But I talked him into staying, and now look what you've caused." Her voice rose again. "You're as rotten as he said, as—"

"Stop it!" Spring took hold of the girl's shoulders, then spoke gently. "This is not John's fault. Get hold of yourself, Mollie. Be smart."

With a sob, Mollie went back into Spring's arms.

As she comforted the girl, Spring looked at John. "Aren't you going to call your mother?"

"I'm sure the sheriff knows her number."

"John—"

He held up a hand. "Don't lecture me, Spring. I'm not getting in the middle of this mess."

"Logan's in serious trouble. Don't you care?"

His expression was incredulous. "Did you catch any of what he said to me?"

Over Mollie's continued sobs, Spring said, "That was anger talking."

"No," John snapped. "That was Sam Nelson talking through him. I felt as if the bastard was right here in the room with us."

"All the more reason for you to get involved."

He gaped at her. "What?"

"The world doesn't need another Sam, does it?"

She could see her statement affected John. He glanced toward the door.

"Go on," Spring urged him. "If you won't call Debra, at least go down to the sheriff's office and try to help Logan."

He hesitated, but indecision was clear in his posture.

"The car keys are on a hook by the front door," Spring murmured.

Saying nothing, John turned and stalked out of the room. A moment later, the front door slammed.

Her tears at last under control, Mollie lifted her head from Spring's shoulder. "Logan won't want to see him."

"But John needs to see Logan." Spring couldn't stop the hope that was lifting through her. Maybe, at long last, this was the opening John needed to make some peace with his past.

Chapter Ten

John wasn't surprised to find Debra already at the sheriff's office with a lawyer. No matter what Mollie said about Debra being through with Logan, John had known she wouldn't walk away from this.

Not out of concern for her son's welfare, of course. As always, Debra was only interested in herself.

When John found her waiting in Sheriff Kane's outer office, Debra was stalking back and forth, fuming. "I can't believe Logan's done this to me again."

A man John recognized as Sam Nelson's best friend, attorney Gregory Stanton, patted her on the shoulder. "Now, Debra, calm down. We'll smooth this over."

Pausing in the doorway, John cleared his throat. The two people in the office faced him.

Debra hastily covered her surprise. "John. I didn't expect to see you here."

Surveying his mother's sequined black dinner suit and upswept hairdo, John drawled, "It doesn't look as if you expected to be hauled down to the sheriff's office, either." In fact, she looked as out of place amid the shabby fake-leather furniture and tattered magazines as a debutante would look at a barn dance.

Before she could reply, Gregory Stanton greeted him and asked how he had found out about Logan's latest escapade.

John explained what had taken place at Spring's house. "I guess the sheriff called you."

"Gregory and I were just back from the club when a deputy came to the door and said Logan was being brought in for questioning," Debra replied. "I had other guests, as well, coming for coffee and drinks. They heard everything the deputy said."

No wonder she was pissed. Not only had she been embarrassed in front of friends, but an evening of socializing had been interrupted, as well. John didn't know what Debra loved most—her money, her position in the community, or her parties.

While White's Creek might not be a social playground, the larger town of Gainesville, Georgia, was a short drive to the southwest and had much to offer. Debra and Sam had always taken advantage of that. Saturday evenings and Sunday lunches at the club were sacrosanct, reserved for hobnobbing with peers.

John wasn't surprised to see Debra was carrying on the tradition. From the looks of things,

Gregory Stanton was her willing escort. How convenient for Debra to date her attorney. Especially with a son as trouble-prone as Logan.

Stanton slipped back a starched white cuff and studied his wristwatch. A Rolex, of course. Gold. His work for the Nelson family was obviously paying well. "I wish the sheriff would get this show on the road."

"What show?" John was puzzled by the terminology and Stanton's almost jocular tone.

"The questioning," the attorney replied. "Logan's a juvenile, so he can't be questioned without his parent or guardian present. And before that happens, I need to talk to him, too."

"I know that, but with the way he resisted being taken in, surely he'll have to spend a night in the juvenile wing before any questioning."

The attorney chuckled. "Not if I have my way."

A deputy appeared in the door, with the news that Stanton could see Logan now for a talk.

Debra said, "You go ahead, Gregory. You know better than me what to say to the boy about this."

Nodding, Stanton picked up a briefcase and left.

John turned back to Debra. "Do the two of you understand that Logan really tore up some other kid?"

Debra nodded, betraying not one iota of concern.

"It also took me and three other men to get him to go along with the police. That in itself should earn him a night in jail, even if he is a juvenile."

"I know." Debra was still unfazed. "I can't believe the idiot thought he could get away. That was foolish of him."

John blinked. "Aren't you worried at all?"

"Gregory will fix this."

"Can *Gregory* fix that other kid's skull?"

Debra speared him with her dark-eyed gaze. "I sincerely hope the boy who started this fight will be okay."

John couldn't believe she was already putting her spin on the situation, implying the other boy had brought on his troubles himself. She had deduced all this without even talking to Logan about the incident.

"My main concern is getting Logan out of trouble," Debra continued.

"I think it would do him some good to cool his jets in here for at least the rest of the night."

She paused, as if considering that possibility. It was quickly dismissed. "Everyone would wonder what I was thinking of, letting him sit in jail for the night."

"*Everyone* isn't involved in this," John retorted. "You're the one who has to deal with him on a continuing basis. Maybe it's time to stop worrying about what the neighbors think and start considering what's going to help Logan."

Debra's beautiful features hardened. For the first time, she looked like a fifty-one-year-old. "I don't need your criticism," she told John. "I've done the best I could with Logan since Sam died. It hasn't been easy."

"Oh, I can see that. Logan's a punk, just like Sam. And you were never able to control Sam, either."

Diamonds flashed on Debra's tennis bracelet as she unnecessarily smoothed one wing of her perfect hair. "Don't start in on Sam, John."

He started. "I can't believe you have the nerve to say that to me."

She gave him a hard look. "I know it's popular nowadays to find fault with everything your parents did. I get tired of hearing that. Everyone makes mistakes."

John could barely force words beyond the obstruction in his throat. "You call what Sam did to me a mistake?"

"He had his flaws, but he gave you a lot. Think of the schools you attended."

"I figure I earned the prep school education," John retorted bitterly. "I paid in bruises."

"You're exaggerating," Debra said. It was the same line she had always used when John used to try and talk about Sam's violence. Even when faced with a bloody nose, the woman had been able to tell John not to make a mountain out of a molehill. Maybe denial and indifference was how she had lived with herself all those years. But it made John sick.

She was wound up now, focusing on what she called John's ingratitude to Sam. "When Sam was a boy, he wanted to attend the schools you went to, John. Lord knows his family had the money. But his father was cheap. He decided Sam should stay here. Sam always felt that held him back in business. So many of the men he had to deal with at other companies were old schoolmates. He felt locked out of the group."

"Poor Sam," John sneered.

"He wanted Logan in those schools, too. It was a real blow when that didn't work out for Logan."

"And why didn't it?"

"Logan was too emotional. Young for his age. He didn't like being away from home."

"Probably because at home someone was always ready to get him out of trouble."

Debra frowned at John. "Sam wasn't easy on Logan. Neither was I. We were both disappointed when he couldn't perform in prep school."

John felt some sympathy stir for his brother. "I guess you let him know how he had let you down."

"Well, we didn't reward him," Debra snapped. "And we did all we could to get him the help he needed."

"I bet."

Debra sniffed at his sarcasm. "I guess you think we didn't do enough for him. I can tell Spring thinks that. But that's not the case. Sam was patient. For a long time, he . . ." She stopped, biting her lip. Then she continued, "For a very long time, Sam and I were very patient."

"And after that you settled for just paying his way out of whatever scrapes he got in?"

Her expression froze. "You're pretty disdainful of money, aren't you?"

"As a matter of fact, I like having money a great deal. I just wouldn't use mine as you do yours."

"Don't be too sure." Debra laughed, a hollow sound. "Doing without money can change you."

"I know about being broke.

"Not the way I do."

John figured she was talking about when his real father had died, before she married Sam. That was a time she had never discussed. But surely she couldn't say she had ever been as poor as he and Spring had been while in college. "Spring and I left here with almost nothing, remember?"

"I made Sam let you have that car. You could have sold it."

Obviously, she thought that car made up for letting him go and never bothering to check and see how he was surviving. He didn't bother explaining that car had become a symbol of freedom to Spring. Debra, he was sure, couldn't identify much with symbols.

She had a strange look in her eyes, a fevered glitter to replace the usual coldness. "My parents wouldn't have done that for me," she whispered. "They wouldn't have given me anything."

John was shocked. All he had ever heard about his maternal grandparents was that they were aristocrats, descendants of the family which had founded White's Creek. To his knowledge, Debra had never said a word against them.

"What are you talking about?" he asked.

But Debra was through with true confessions.

She paced to the door and stood, arms crossed and tapping one high-heeled shoe on the floor. "Where is that sheriff? It's awfully late, and I may have to take Logan to the hospital. One of the deputies said they were having him checked out by the paramedic on duty tonight."

"Spring cleaned him up pretty well," John assured her. "She didn't think he was hurt too badly. You may not have to waste any more of your evening seeing that he has medical attention."

"I'll have to thank Spring for looking after him."

The image of Debra beholden to Spring for anything was almost comical. "Looking after people is something that comes naturally to Spring. She gets it from her mother."

Mention of his mother-in-law drew an arch look from Debra. "It's amazing to me how well all of those DeWitt children have turned out."

Rancor colored his tone. "Yeah, amazing how far love and attention go. Far as I know, those are what kept all the DeWitts out of the gutters—and *jails*." He paused to let the gibe sink in. "Just proves it doesn't take money for people to know how to parent."

Debra turned away again, but her jaw was clenched.

Score one for me, John thought, though he was curiously joyless at the victory. In fact, being here with Debra at all made him sick. He was wrong to have let Spring prod him into this.

He started for the door. "You don't need me. You've got your lawyer and plenty of money."

"No, John . . . wait."

Against his better judgment, he paused beside her in the doorway.

"Your being here . . ." Debra hesitated, then plunged ahead, not quite meeting his gaze. "Maybe you can help Logan."

John laughed. "He won't talk to me. He hates me about as much as Sam did."

Turning away again, Debra sighed. "I suppose you're right." She rubbed her temples. "Sometimes I think nothing's going to help him. It's been this way since Sam died. Maybe that was it. Maybe being there, seeing his father die—"

"Wait a minute," John cut in. "Logan was with Sam when he died?"

"Logan's the one who called for help. It was too late, of course. Sam was dead from a heart attack before they got there."

John frowned. Sam had died just over four years ago. Logan would have been only thirteen. No matter what kind of monster Sam had been, witnessing his death couldn't have been easy on a kid that age.

But that still didn't make Logan John's problem.

"If he manages to wriggle out of this trouble, get him some help," John advised Debra. "Put him in a clinic somewhere."

She looked horrified. John could imagine she was thinking of how to keep everyone from finding out.

"Send him to Europe," John added. "You can pretend he's in one of those fancy boarding schools. Or you could lock him in his room for a couple of weeks. I remember how that worked for me."

A faraway look came into Debra's eyes.

"Don't you remember?" John muttered. "I got expelled for cheating on a final. Sam locked me in a room and fed me bread and water. Surely you remember."

In some eerie way, Debra didn't seem to hear him.

John waved a hand in front of her face. "Are you listening?"

"Of course."

"Then why don't you say you remember?"

She moistened her lips, but didn't speak. Perspiration dotted her forehead.

Stomach churning, John stared at her. Denial was such a deeply ingrained reaction she couldn't make herself speak the truth.

Debra suddenly lurched forward. The sheriff and a deputy were leading Logan down the hall, Stanton following them.

Logan was calm now, though his gaze flicked angrily from John to his mother and back again.

Sheriff Kane greeted Debra with a curt nod. "Let's talk in my office." When John hung back, the lawman invited him in, as well. He quelled Logan's protest with a sizzling glance.

They went into Kane's office and Logan told them about the party up at Silver Lake. A bonfire.

A wiener roast. Some beer, of course. Logan claimed to have had only two drinks. The sheriff agreed he didn't appear inebriated.

The trouble started, Logan claimed, when Jeff Lott brought up an incident that had happened at school. Specifically, when Logan was caught making out with Jeff's girlfriend. This previous altercation had resulted in Logan breaking Jeff's nose. Tonight, Logan said, Jeff came after him with a stick of firewood. He defended himself, finally shoved Jeff out of the way, and in falling, Jeff hit his head on a rock.

When Logan was finished, Sheriff Kane was silent, his hands folded on his desk, just looking at the young man.

Stanton spoke up, smoothly. "Of course Logan deeply regrets that Jeff is badly hurt."

"Does he?" the sheriff asked, graying eyebrows lifting.

John wondered if anyone else noticed that Debra nudged her son with her foot.

"I'm very sorry," Logan said. And damned if he didn't look and sound sincere.

The sheriff's chair squeaked as he sat forward. "A lot of people told me a different story about tonight's party."

Logan just shook his head. "It all happened pretty fast, sir. I guess some people did get the wrong impression."

"And weren't a lot of the kids making accusations drunk?" Stanton asked.

Kane's eyes narrowed, though he didn't reply.

A slight smile appeared on the attorney's mouth. "Since you're still gathering facts, I'm assuming you can let Logan go home tonight."

When the sheriff nodded, John couldn't stop his exclamation of shock. Logan shot him a baleful, but triumphant look. John felt sicker to his stomach than ever.

Stanton didn't waste any more time. He hustled Logan and Debra out of the sheriff's office. John trailed them to the parking lot, was close enough to hear Debra order her lawyer, "You get up to that hospital and talk to the Lott boy's parents, first thing tomorrow."

With a plan in motion to take care of Logan's troubles, Debra seemed to have forgotten about John. No surprise there. But as Stanton's car turned out of the parking lot, it was as all John could do not to bend over and retch.

He had always known Debra was cold, but her disregard for the condition of the boy Logan had beaten was a particularly heartless display. Worse, however, was her disregard for her own flesh and blood. Until she made Logan suffer the consequences of his actions, he was bound to continue to self-destruct.

A day would come when her money and her position couldn't help.

Footsteps behind him made John turn. Sheriff Kane ambled across the lit parking lot toward him.

"I can't believe you let him go," John said. "If

he weren't Sam Nelson's son, he'd be in jail right now."

Kane came to a stop. "My, my, John, a person could get the impression you want your brother locked up."

"I happen to think that's where he belongs."

"Juveniles are almost always released to their parents' custody."

"Even when charged with a serious crime?"

"I got a call from the hospital. Seems that Jeff Lott's injury isn't as bad as it looked to me and the paramedics."

"That's a relief, but it doesn't take away what Logan did."

"Stanton's right. A lot of the kids who say Logan started the fight were flat out drunk."

"That doesn't make them liars."

"But it could make them unreliable witnesses if this thing goes to court."

"So you just let him go."

"For now." Sheriff Kane took off his cap and sighed, kicking at gravel on the ground. "But like I told you, Jeff Lott's parents aren't the types who just roll over. They moved here a few years ago. They don't work in one of the mills your mother inherited from your father—"

"My stepfather," John corrected brusquely.

The sheriff gave him a hard look. "All right, whatever you say. But the point is, the Lotts don't rent one of the Nelson buildings or depend on Debra Nelson in any way. I'll lay money that they'll push me to come down hard on Logan, especially since this is the second time he and their son have tangled."

"I hope you listen to them."

Kane looked confused. "It's clear you aren't close to your family, but you act as if your brother would be better off in a juvenile-detention facility. Hell, at his age, he would end up with some pretty hardened criminals. Logan is trouble, yeah, but he's not like that. Surely you don't want that for him."

"Why not? His mother isn't going to make him straighten up. All she's interested in is covering up."

"And what about you?" Kane shot back. "What's your sudden interest after all these years away?"

That made John falter. For all the noise he had made about not getting involved in this mess, here he was, arguing about his half brother's fate.

"Come on," the sheriff said, jerking his head back toward the building. "Why don't you and I go in and have a talk about Logan?"

John resisted. "He's none of my business. I shouldn't even be here. I came back to town to patch up my marriage, not my family. That's been over for a long time."

"Hear me out," Kane insisted. "I know Logan pretty well. He's been making regular appearances here at the office since his daddy died. I think he needs someone's help."

"There's nothing I can do to help him."

"I'm not so sure about that," Sheriff Kane said.

"I am."

"And how are you going to feel if you don't try?"

John shrugged, though the question gave him an uncomfortably guilty pang.

"What if he really explodes one day? Kills someone, maybe? Are you going to be happy that you walked away without trying to reach him?"

John's breath caught and held. "Hellfire," he muttered. "You've been talking to Spring, haven't you?"

The sheriff's smile was enigmatic.

"All right," John agreed, reluctantly. "Let's go talk."

Spring spent an hour talking with Mollie before calling Mollie's brother, Larry, to come take her home. But she wasn't sure if she got through to the girl about how troubled Logan was and how much trouble he could bring to Mollie's own life.

For Mollie was in the throes of first love. She wasn't looking much beyond Logan's handsome face. And like so many quiet, shy girls, the allure of a bad boy was difficult for Mollie to resist. She had spent most of her life as a caretaker and nurturer for her brothers and sisters. It was a role she thought she could play for Logan, as well. She thought she could help him.

How well Spring understood that desire.

Maybe her own experiences with John explained why she was so worried about Mollie becoming involved with Logan.

The good news was the relationship hadn't progressed much beyond infatuation. Mollie had gone with a friend to the party where the fight took place, only lending Logan a hand when he was hurt. Since Mollie was so very different from the more mature and flamboyant girls Spring had seen Logan with before, she hoped nothing but friendship would develop. Mollie wanted more, so she would be hurt. But better a broken heart now than later.

When Mollie and her brother were gone, Spring waited for John to come back. As the hour grew later and later, she tried calling him at his motel room. She hesitated, however, over calling the sheriff's office. To relax, finally, she took a long bath, using the soothing herbs her mother had left for her earlier.

As she soaked, it wasn't worry over Logan's situation that pulled Spring. It was what John had said earlier tonight, about her being jealous of his success. That wasn't true. Surely it wasn't true. Certainly, he had started changing about the time the opportunities began to open up for him. But she didn't resent him for the success. She resented the change in him. She feared the emphasis he put on the money and the prestige of success.

How in the world could he think she would begrudge him his achievements? What had she done to give him that impression?

Spring fell asleep with those questions gnawing at her.

When she awoke, she found John asleep, bare-chested but draped in an old quilt, on the chaise lounge in the bowed window of her bedroom. Even more startling was the sight of Basil curled at his side.

Infuriated, Spring threw a pillow at the pair of them. She missed, however, and the pillow bounced off the rattan stand which held her only plant, a spider fern.

Cat and man came suddenly awake. Basil scampered. John yelled, "What's the matter with you?"

"With me?" Spring demanded. "You're the one who has broken into my house."

"I had your keys, remember?"

"You could have knocked."

"I did. But the lights were out, and I got worried when you didn't come to the door. I found you in bed, dead to the world, snoring."

"That's a lie." Flinging back the covers, Spring gasped at the coolness of the morning air. She shivered and reached for the robe she had draped over the iron footboard of her bed. "I've never snored in my life."

"You looked drugged."

"Maybe I was," Spring muttered, thinking of the herbs she had bathed in before coming to bed. Just what had her mother put in that mixture, anyway?

John sat up and rubbed his face, blinking in the sunlight that streamed through the window. "Every bone in my body is aching."

"You could have slept on the sofa."

"I tried."

"I bet." Spring didn't like seeing him here in her bedroom. She was reminded, sharply, of all the mornings when they had awakened in each other's arms. "You should have gone back to your motel."

He shuddered. "It's a dreary place, Spring."

"Then move to the bed-and-breakfast over on Third Street. It's pricey for White's Creek, I hear, but I know you can afford it."

Not rising to the bait, he turned back the quilt and got up. In the mirror over the dresser, Spring brushed her hair and covertly studied his lean physique revealed by the boxers that rode low on his hips. It would help matters if he had grown unbearably skinny or fat during the months they had spent apart. Apparently, however, he had been spending the requisite hours at his gym and finding enough sustenance to keep going.

She was intent on her admiration of his washboard abs when she realized he was looking into the mirror, watching her watch him. Nose lifted in the air, she flung down her brush and headed for the bathroom. "Too bad if you have to go," she said, before shutting and locking the door with an emphatic click.

When she emerged, some ten minutes later, she was disappointed not to find him dancing from foot to foot in the hall. Instead, he was in the kitchen, clad in his jeans and unbuttoned shirt, brewing a pot of coffee.

Hands on hips, she stopped in the doorway. "I don't recall inviting you to stay for breakfast."

He grunted. "Too bad. I need coffee."

For the first time she looked, really looked at his haggard face. An alarm sounded deep inside her. She knew him so well, it was easy to see he was very upset. "John? Is something wrong? Is it Logan? Or the boy he beat up?"

"They're both fine."

"Then what's wrong?"

Hands braced on the edge of the counter where the coffeemaker was sputtering to life, he bowed his head.

There was such despondency and pain in the lines of his body that Spring quickly crossed the room. Without giving any thought to her actions, she put her arms around him. "Tell me," she whispered. "What happened?"

"I . . . just . . . hate . . . her." The words were ground out. She could feel the effort it cost him to speak.

"Debra?"

"Who else?"

"What did she do?"

"It's more what she didn't do." He kept his head down.

Spring hugged him tighter, knowing from past experience it would take him a few minutes to get himself together enough to talk about his mother.

"Come on," she said at last. "Come sit down."

"No." John straightened from the counter and

turned, taking her in his arms. "Just let me hold you, Spring. Let me feel someone who is good and kind and decent. After last night, I feel dirty, just the way I've always felt after brushing up against my mother."

It never occurred to Spring to protest. Despite the angry words that had passed between them and the months they had been apart, John needed her, so she was there. That's the way it had been between them in the beginning. This fierce need in him had been missing for the last couple of years. She greeted it with familiar, answering warmth.

"Tell me," she coaxed when his arms finally began to relax about her. "What did Debra do last night?"

Tears glinted in his brown eyes when John met her gaze. "It's not last night, Spring. It's my whole damned life. Her life. Logan's."

"I don't understand."

Blinking back that betraying hint of moisture, John set Spring away from him. "It's old news."

"I still want to hear it."

He looked out the window over the sink. "I just don't understand why she sacrificed me to Sam."

"She wanted money, security. For whatever reason, she was afraid taking up for you would mean losing him."

"Then I guess the greater question is why he hated me so."

"You may never understand that."

Muscles working in his jaw, John shook his

head again. "You should hear all she's done for Logan."

"Like what?"

"Sheriff Kane filled me in on my precious baby brother's tangles with the law. The records are all sealed, of course, because Logan's a juvenile, and none of these cases ever came to anything. But Debra's bought Logan out of more trouble than I ever dreamed of."

Like a litany, John recited nearly a dozen drunken brawls and fights Logan had been involved in since he was thirteen. There had been a rape accusation thrown in, as well, though the girl and her parents had withdrawn the complaint so quickly that Sheriff Kane suspected Debra had paid them a hefty price for their silence.

"Rape?" Spring shivered, thinking of sweet and trusting Mollie. If Logan did anything to her . . .

"It was an accusation," John said. "Nothing proven or even really investigated."

"But still." Spring could barely get her breath. If that charge were true, Logan was even more troubled than she had imagined.

"He's a thug, but Debra protects him."

"Then she's sacrificing him, as well, by not holding him accountable for his mistakes. She's done no better by him than she did by you."

"But at least she tries to protect him. That's more than she ever did for me."

"John, don't."

"All I did was try to be a good kid. But nothing I did was good enough. My mistakes earned me a beating or a tongue-lashing. Hell, even when I was bad, I was trying to please her or Sam. I cheated on that final exam that got me expelled because I knew there'd be hell to pay if I failed chemistry. When I brought home C's in science and math, Sam used to laugh at me. The A's in English made me a wuss in his eyes. He said I'd never amount to anything."

Feeling his anger starting to grab hold of him, Spring took John's hand and forced him to look at her. "Stop it, John. Stop thinking about what Sam wanted and thought of you. It doesn't matter now."

He was too deep in his fury to listen to her. "But what she did does matter. Why didn't she care when Sam beat me up? The first time I remember him laying into me, I was maybe four years old. I was trying to play catch with this man my mother was married to, the man she said I was supposed to call Dad. But after I threw the ball over his head a few too many times, he called me a couple of choice names. Like stupid. Clumsy. Retarded."

"John." Spring laid her head against his chest, unable to bear the horror in his face.

"Then he hit me. With his belt. I was so sore I couldn't sit down for days. But when I cried to my mother, she told me to hush. She always told me to hush."

Spring could feel his heart pounding. No matter how hard she hugged him, his anger kept churning. It had always been this way. There were some hurts not even her love for him could heal. And perhaps that was the biggest failure of their marriage. Perhaps that was why he had withdrawn from her these past few years, because she had never been able to ease his deepest agony.

The harshness in John's voice grew stronger. "Debra was clever. The times when she didn't pretend he hadn't really hurt me, she told me that if I let anyone know how Sam treated me, he would throw us both out in the street. She said we'd have to eat dirt." His laughter echoed like a lonely wail from the rock at Devil's Point. "You can't imagine, Spring. You just can't know how that frightened a little boy."

"I do know."

"That's why I can't do anything for Logan."

Spring went still and drew back. "What does Logan have to do with what Debra did to you?"

"Haven't you been listening?" John demanded. "I can't stay in this town. I can't be near her."

"She can't hurt you now, and maybe you could help Logan, save him from her."

"You and Sheriff Kane seem to think I have a duty to help him."

She stepped away from him. "There's a difference between doing what's right and just being dutiful. I think you should do the right thing. Logan needs someone to help him. It's obvious Debra won't."

"But it's not my fault that he's had her jumping through hoops for him while she wouldn't lift a hand to keep Sam away from me."

"Is it Logan's fault then?"

John blinked. "Fault?"

Sensing an advantage, Spring rushed ahead. "Exactly how do you figure that Logan made Sam beat you or made Debra stand back and let it happen without protest?"

"That's not what I've said. I'm blaming Debra. Haven't you listened to me."

"But if you blame her, why should you punish Logan?"

John squeezed his eyes shut. "Goddammit, Spring. You're not going to shame me into getting involved with Logan and my mother."

"But you are involved, whether you like it or not. They're your family."

"We were never a family."

"You could change things."

"Not when I hate her."

"If not with Debra, maybe Logan. Maybe there's still a chance with him. You may be the only person who can understand him. You share something, John. You don't want to see that, but it's so clear to me. Sam did no better by Logan than by you."

For once John didn't protest that Sam would never have hurt his real son. Maybe he was beginning to see what was so obvious to Spring.

"Logan needs someone who can understand."

"Not me. Last night was my final attempt at family togetherness."

"Then Sam won, didn't he?"

John growled, "What does that mean?"

Spring stepped right up to him again. "He never wanted you to be part of his family. He separated you from your mother. He didn't want you to be a part of Logan's life. The best revenge you could have on that man is to be better than he ever was. Think how he would feel if you and Logan wound up as real brothers."

"It won't happen."

"But if you walk away from Logan without trying, then you're no better than Sam."

Dull red color crawled up John's neck as he recoiled from her.

"You always said becoming like him was your worst nightmare," she continued, fighting to keep her voice from breaking. "You let that fear keep us from having children. You've let him control most of your life."

"I broke free of him," John insisted, as he had so many times. "I don't know what in the world I have to do to convince you of that."

"Prove it to me," she challenged. "Be the man Sam never was. Do something right. Do something for his son."

"Just stop it!" John threw up his hands in disgust. "Cut the saintly do-gooder act, Spring. No matter what you think, the world can't be saved. You can't adopt every child who's been abused. You can't turn every bad kid's life around. Some people are just lost causes. Logan is a lost cause."

His taunts struck home, painted a picture of Spring as a sanctimonious Pollyanna. It wasn't flattering. It certainly wasn't the way he had once viewed her. And that showed how desperately their relationship had changed. Desperately and irrevocably.

Trembling, she pressed a hand to her mouth.

John stepped close to her once more. His voice was low, thick with anger. "Maybe I'm a lost cause, too. Maybe that's why you left me."

"That's not true."

"You can't change me or the bitterness I live with, Spring. Face it. Accept it. Stop trying to change me. My God, you knew what you were getting when we married."

His tone gentled. His eyes grew moist again. "Why can't you love me like you used to, Spring? Why did that die? What did I do that was so wrong? Is it truly the writing you hate? Or is it just me? What is it that made you change so much?"

She wanted to tell him love wasn't the problem. Her love for him would continue forever, but the black hole the past had drilled into his heart was keeping them apart. For years, they had managed to hold back the darkness with the power of their love. But that wasn't enough now. The insecurities and frustrations of John's past had reached down through the years to strangle him and tear their marriage apart.

She believed, with all her heart, that the path back to happiness lay in John's finally slaying his childhood dragons.

"Come home with me," he pleaded. "Let's get out of this place like we did once before. We can make it good again, Spring. We can find our way back together."

Bowing her head once again, she whispered, "No, John, that won't help. We can't just run away. I don't want to run away again."

"But you can push me away, can't you?"

There was devastation in John's face. Naked pain. The emotion made Spring hurt. "I'm not pushing you anywhere."

"Then hold me. Please." He put out his arms. "I need you, Spring. I need you so much."

She knew what would happen if she stepped into his embrace.

Yet she couldn't stop herself.

She moved forward, lifting her lips to his.

Chapter Eleven

∼ The sweet forgetfulness John sought was found in Spring's arms.

In the breasts she offered to his tongue and hands.

In the mouth she slipped over his skin.

In the thighs which she opened to take him in.

They made love quickly the first time. Right in the kitchen, beneath the window where Callie's good-luck clover was pressed between pieces of glass.

Later, in Spring's sun-drenched bed, there was time to linger, to savor. With each touch, each taste, John distanced himself from the anger and the hurt he had been feeling. As she had done so many times, Spring's love gave him the escape he needed.

When they awoke, she was awkward with him. Distant. She said making love didn't mean she was ready to resume their marriage. She asked him to leave.

John was able to keep himself from pushing. He went back to the motel without arguing. Yet the walls between them had been breached. He had needed Spring, and she had been there for him. Just like always.

Winning her back would now be a simple matter of wearing her down.

He held on to that confident thought, even when that evening came and Spring said she didn't want to see him.

"I'm not making love with you again," she told him firmly over the phone.

He ignored her, of course, and headed straight for her house. All he found was an empty driveway and a locked door. Her family said they didn't know where she was. Callie assured him with typical serenity that Spring was fine. Rainy advised him to give her some space.

So he did. He turned on his laptop and got to work.

He didn't get angry until Monday evening came and all Spring could say to him was, "Leave me alone."

This was delivered just before she slammed the door in his face.

On Tuesday, he went to seek Callie's counsel. She put him to work helping with preparations for Thursday's Thanksgiving feast.

Sitting in her warm country kitchen, surrounded by the delicious aroma of baking bread, John understood why Spring had always felt compelled to visit home. The peacefulness here, the feeling of love and security, was a powerful tonic for a troubled soul.

At the table where he was shelling black walnuts, he sighed. "I should have come home with Spring more. She needed to see her family, and I kept her away."

Callie, busy pulling loaves of bread from the oven, merely grunted.

"Don't you agree?" John asked.

His mother-in-law pushed a tendril of black hair back from her heat-flushed face. "Spring needs to *live* where she can see the mountains."

"You think that's why she wants to end our marriage? Because I won't live here?"

"Lord above," Callie murmured, whipping around to face him. "Why is it you men want to break everything down so simple?"

"I don't know," John retorted. "God knows, nothing is simple about you women."

She laughed. "Nothing that involves the heart is simple for anyone, son, not for men or women."

"You and Ned seem to have perfected married life. How'd you do it?"

"We've had our battles. Especially in the beginning and when the babies were small. Life wasn't easy."

"To hear Spring tell it, Ned laid his eyes on you and that was it. He was hunting with a friend, met you, carried you down the mountains, you got married the next day and have lived happily ever after. No troubles at all."

"It was a little more knotty than that." Callie

sliced two thick wedges of bread, placed them on a plate, and carried them with a tub of homemade butter to the table. She sat down with a heavy sigh. "Land sakes, I'm tired. I'm getting old, John."

"Never," he claimed as he buttered a piece of warm bread. "You're enchanted. A witch, some say. You'll never grow old."

That brought a sparkle to her eyes. Eyes so like Spring's. "I'll tell you a secret, John. I'm no witch. I just believe in the powers that surround us. Powers in the air and the earth and the water and inside us. My granny taught me to believe in and to use a bit of those powers. Only God can harness them all. He just lets me do a bit of good now and then."

"But you have the sight. That gives you a definite advantage over most of us mortals."

Her face clouded. "Being able to see beyond what's in front of me hasn't always been a blessing."

He sat forward, suddenly anxious. "What do you see for me and Spring?"

"I won't tell you."

"It's that bad?"

She shook her head. "I won't tell because it's not clear to me. But there is a path. You've taken a step by staying here in town. I know you almost left."

He didn't question how she knew, for she was right. Last night, long after he had left Spring's house, John had impulsively packed his bag, closed his laptop, and started toward the office to check out of the Pine Cone Lodge. He was ready to admit his marriage was over.

Then he had stopped. He stood for a long time in the cold, November night, beneath a black sky dotted with stars brighter than he had ever seen. The wind was calm. The world was silent, with not even a passing car to disturb the hush. And for the first time since he was a little boy and gave up on prayer, he bowed his head and asked for guidance. He didn't get a message like Spring had once received. No answers came booming down from the heavens in a splash of light. But John knew he shouldn't leave White's Creek. Not just yet.

He returned to his room.

He hadn't thought about leaving again.

Sheriff Kane had called that morning, to tell John the Lott boy was doing fine. As predicted, his parents were pushing for Logan's arrest. Kane was proceeding methodically, questioning everyone at the party. At least two of the kids who had stepped forward that night had now changed their story to support Logan's version. John had to wonder if they had been paid off.

"Spring's going to be here soon," Callie announced into the silence that had fallen between her and John. "She told me she wanted to help me make some pumpkin pies for Thursday. I like to make them ahead of time, so they set up nice."

Sighing, he pushed the bowl of cracked nuts away. "She won't be happy to see me here."

"That girl always did resist taking medicine, even when she needed it."

John chuckled. "Is that what my wanting to put our marriage back together is? Bad-tasting medicine?"

"You could coat it with honey, if you wanted. Try being sweet to her."

He would have thought their lovemaking was the right sort of honey. He had been wrong. "Your daughter has developed quite a resistance to my particular brand of sweetness."

"If she's told you that, then she's lying. The feelings between the two of you still run about as strong as the falls up the mountain."

John chuckled, remembering Spring moving beneath him. "Now that is true."

From behind them, Spring's voice interrupted. "What are the two of you conspiring about?"

John turned and found her standing just inside the door, a beagle at her heels. Shadows smudged the skin under her eyes. She looked tired. He had to wonder if she was sleeping as poorly as he.

"We're not conspiring," her mother said with spirit as she got back to her feet. "John's cracking black walnuts for the cake I'm going to make, and I'm giving him sage advice in return."

"Sage is an herb that belongs in the stuffing for the turkey," Spring retorted. Ignoring John, she crossed to the kitchen counter where the loaves of bread were cooling. She sliced off a piece and fed it to the dog, then carved another for herself. "You got any honey?"

"Ask John," Callie said, bursting into laughter.

He grinned while Spring darted a suspicious look between the two of them. "I wish one of you would tell me what's up."

"Don't be so nosy." Her mother passed her the honey jar and surveyed her jeans and sweater attire. "You must have left school early to be changed already and out here."

"I had a bad day."

"Boyfriend give you a hard time?" John's quip earned a hard look from Spring.

"I haven't spoken to Dan since that scene you made Saturday morning."

Callie rubbed her shoulders. "Something at school is worrying you, though. I can tell."

"A little girl I've been working with."

"She'll be okay," Callie murmured reassuringly. "You don't have to fret over her."

"I sure hope you're right." Holding a piece of bread dripping with honey, Spring turned back to John. "Have you heard anything about Logan?"

He told her what he knew. "I guess the school's been buzzing about this."

"Of course." Her gaze narrowed. "I didn't expect to find you here. I figured you might be gone."

He met her gaze straight-on. "I gave it some thought."

"I thought that motel room was too dismal to be borne."

"I'm adjusting."

"Well . . . suit yourself." Her shrug was a shade too elaborate to convey genuine disinterest.

Callie's shoulders shook with laughter once more. For a moment, John imagined he could hear the sound of rushing water, the strength of a waterfall. Certainly, he could feel the tension running fast and deep between him and Spring. Nothing new about that. But the sound of water? Eyes widening, he glanced at Callie.

Spring frowned. "I didn't come out here to play guessing games. Let's get started cutting up pumpkin for the pies."

"All right." Callie nodded toward the windows. "Your daddy picked out the best pumpkins of the crop and put them in the root cellar last week. You and John can bring up two or three. Maybe four. The whole family's coming for dinner Thursday and staying all weekend."

Sparing him only a brief, irritated glance, Spring headed for the door, the beagle at her heels once more.

As John followed, Callie murmured, "Remember, now. Be sweet."

Once outside in the unseasonably warm air, Spring turned on him. "What are you doing out here with Mama?"

"She brewed me up a couple of love potions to try out on you."

"Don't be silly."

"Do I have to have a reason to come here? I've always cared a lot for your mother and father. I enjoy being with them."

Spring snorted and started around the corner of the house. "Yeah, you cared so much that you wouldn't even come visit them. They had to come see us in Chicago."

"You know the reasons why I stayed away."

"How come those same reasons haven't chased you out of town, like you threatened?"

Remembering Callie's advice, John kept his temper in check and his voice gentle. "You're the reason I'm still here. I can't leave until we get things settled between us once and for all."

"I thought I might have made everything crystal clear."

"What's clear to me is that you still care. You couldn't have made love with me if you didn't."

"There's never been a time I didn't care. That doesn't change a thing about our problems."

Forgetting his vow to be sweet, John took hold of her elbow, forcing her to look at him. "So do you want a divorce? You think I'm a selfish bastard like my stepfather and you want rid of me?"

She gasped. He didn't know if it was the hard grip he had on her arm or his words which caused her shock. But whatever the reason, her expression wasn't that of someone whose mind was made up about booting her husband.

John loosened his grasp on her arm. "I'm

sorry," he whispered. "I didn't mean to grab you like that."

"You didn't hurt me," she said quickly. "I just . . . oh, God . . . I knew we shouldn't have made love. I didn't know what to do before, and now I'm so confused I can't think. I don't know what we're going to do."

"That's what your mother and I were talking about," John confessed. "I was asking her what she saw for us."

"She won't tell."

"Nope. But it seems to me that if I was going to disappear from your life, she might not continue being so nice to me."

Some of the sadness eased from Spring's face. "You'd think so, wouldn't you?"

"There's something else." John lifted a hand to her hair, fascinated as always by the blue-black strands, legacy of some Cherokee ancestor from Callie's side of the family. "If you and I aren't destined to get back together, you'd think we'd stop generating sparks."

"Sparks?"

He focused his gaze back on hers. "All you have to do is walk into a room, and I'm lost. I want you. Just you."

At the intensity in his voice, she slipped away, a move she seemed to have perfected in the months they had lived apart.

John caught up to her at the bulkhead doors to the old-fashioned root cellar. He took her hand. "I wish you would stop running from me."

She broke free of him and threw the dead bolt on the door. "I don't want to get into this with you."

"But you can't keep denying your feelings." Tenderly, John pushed her hair back from her cheek.

"Cut it out." Spring tossed her head.

John stepped back, still mindful of Callie's admonition about sweetness. So instead of kissing Spring senseless as he wanted, he reached down and opened the cellar doors. The rich scents of roots, vegetables, and earth washed out as he and Spring peered down a steep flight of concrete steps.

John shivered. "Your daddy found a rattler down here once, didn't he?"

"Only because he forgot to sprinkle peppermint oil around the walls. He hasn't forgotten since that snake nearly got hold of him."

"You really think peppermint works?"

"Of course. There's never been a snake up in our house, and that's not something everyone out in the country can claim. Mama takes care of it."

"So why are you looking down there like something's waiting to get you?"

"I'm not," she claimed, stoutly, but with some hesitancy.

Chuckling, John took hold of her hand once again. "Come on, chicken. I'll protect you."

"Fat lot of good you'd do if we ran up on a snake," Spring retorted, though she let her fingers entwine with his as they descended into the cool, dark cellar. "You're just a city boy. You couldn't tell a copperhead from a water moccasin."

"I have to admit I've never gotten close enough to do much comparison of the various types."

At the bottom of the steps, Spring reached forward and pulled a string to switch on a dusty lightbulb. John didn't want to admit how grateful he was for the dim light. It wasn't much, but it revealed bins of white and sweet potatoes and shelves full of jars of corn and green beans and jellies Callie had harvested and preserved.

"Clay and Stuart and Paul were forever bringing snakes in from the woods," Spring continued. "I hated them."

"I bet your mother made your brothers let them go."

"She doesn't much believe in killing anything that's not threatening you. But I did see her cut a copperhead in two one evening when we were hoeing the garden. He was three feet long and coiled to strike at Rainy."

Spring pointed to the far corner, where the pumpkins were laid out in two neat rows. "There they are."

"Yep."

Neither of them made a move.

"This is silly," John said at last. "There's no snake waiting down here at this time of year." At the doubtful look on Spring's face, he added, "Is there?"

"Of course not." Straightening her shoulders, she led John toward the pumpkins.

Quickly, they hauled two plump specimens from the cellar to a table on the screened porch, where Callie had spread a couple of newspapers to catch the juice and scraps from the carving. They returned for two more. John led the way up the steps while Spring paused to cut off the light.

Then she screamed.

He spun around, fully expecting to find her wrestling with a rattlesnake. Instead, he was hit by a yelping beagle, who bounced off John's legs and kept going.

The pumpkin John held flew in the air and came down hard, narrowly missing a wide-eyed Spring, who ran up those steps with the same speed of the dog.

"What in the world?" John demanded, just before she hit him. He landed on his butt on the top step.

Spring fell in his lap, still peering down the steps in horror. "Something brushed my leg down there!"

John held her wriggling body, trying to calm her down. "It was the dog. He must have gone down in the cellar while we were around on the porch."

"Damn." Spring was actually shaking. "God, I hate snakes." Taking a deep breath, she punched John on the arm. "Why'd you have to mention that rattler Daddy found?"

"I was just making conversation."

"You got me all worked up."

He grinned at her choice of words. "That's never been too hard."

He kissed her before she could raise a protest. After an initial startled groan, she didn't resist at all. Her arms looped around his shoulders. Her body pressed against his. Willingly. Tantalizingly. He curved one hand over her breast. How right it was to feel her, hold her, lose himself in her scent.

"Let's go back down in the cellar," he whispered, when they drew apart. "Make love among the pumpkins."

"What about snakes?"

"They can watch if they want."

Framing his face with her hands, she kissed him again. A hungry, slow, deliciously naughty kiss. By the time she pulled back, John was about as hard as the concrete steps they were lying on. The way Spring was sprawled across him, he didn't think she could avoid noticing how very aroused he was. But just in case she wasn't paying attention, he took her hand and held it against his swelling crotch.

She spread her fingers, cradling his erection. Her smile was wide. "Impressive, Mr. Nelson."

"Right now, I could impress you in any number of interesting ways," he replied, nibbling at her lips.

"And then what?"

"Then we could do it again."

"John," she said, pushing him away. "We already know that's a stupid idea." A shadow crept into her beautiful eyes.

John stilled. "What do you mean?"

"Afterward, do we argue some more about what we're going to do? Do we split up? Or do we pretend great sex is enough to keep us together?"

Muttering a curse, John rested his head briefly against the soft knit of her sweater.

Spring eased out of his lap, though she remained beside him, her arm looped through his. "I'm sorry," she whispered. "I didn't want to stop, either."

"But you felt compelled to be sensible." He was too aroused at the moment to bothering hiding his frustration.

"I don't want our thinking muddied by sex."

"Right now, a little mud would clear my thinking considerably."

Her laughter was soft as she laid her head on his shoulder.

Her breast pressing against his arm did little to assuage the ache in his groin, but John pulled her closer. "I can't imagine being with anyone but you."

"I know. I feel the same way. But I don't want us to play games with each other. If I made love with you right now, I know I would start feeling everything was all right."

"We could pretend. It might catch hold and work."

"And what about the first time you close yourself off from me?"

"I'll try like hell not to do that."

"I think you've already tried," she said, sadly. "I believe you've tried as hard as you can to make things the way they were before, and you just can't. You always end up shutting me out, John. Even though you claim you don't, that's how it seems to me. Then I start feeling insecure and unneeded—"

"But I always need you," he insisted.

She closed her eyes. "That's not the way I feel, and I just can't live that way. I can't be with you and feel as if there's a crater separating us. Not when we used to be so together in everything we did."

"You could try. Try once more."

She looked at him again. "And what about children?"

He was quiet, not yet willing to let go of the sweetness of holding her, even though reality had now intruded.

Finally, he murmured, "You're right. You were right to stop us before we got all carried away."

Surprise lit her eyes. "I didn't expect you to see it that way."

He grimaced ruefully. "Neither did I."

She got slowly to her feet. "We'd better get started on these pumpkins. Mama probably thinks we are down in the cellar making out."

"I don't think she'd be all that unhappy if we were."

"She doesn't have to live with the consequences." Spring went down the steps again, picked up the pumpkin she had dropped, and nudged the toe of her sneakers at the one John had thrown. "These are cracked, but we were going to cut them up anyway, so there's no harm."

"I'll bring mine around in a minute," John said. "You go ahead. I want to sit here and think a minute."

Her gaze was full of concern. "Are you okay?"

"Just confused."

"Then that makes two of us." She blew out a frustrated breath. "This would all be so easy if I really knew what I wanted."

"But I know what I want," he retorted, looking up at her. "I want us to go back to the way things were."

"That's impossible. We're not the same people we were."

"But I still love you." The words flowed so naturally out of John that he didn't realize he had spoken aloud until Spring's expression grew even more pensive.

She leaned over and kissed him. "Wouldn't it be wonderful if love was all we needed?"

"I think it is."

She made no reply before leaving him to sit alone in the fading sunlight of the cool November day.

Only then did John admit to himself how frightened he was. He could lose her. Really and truly lose her. Maybe he had faced that possibility before, but at this moment, it felt more terrifyingly real than he ever remembered.

She loved him. He was sure of that. But she didn't want to live with him. At least not with the changes she found in him.

He could admit he had changed. He wasn't the same uncertain young man she had run away with twelve years ago. Maybe he didn't need her in all the ways he once had. Maybe her loving him had given him the courage and the confidence to reach for the things he wanted, to be the person he was now.

But Sunday, she had compared him to Sam.

The memory of those words made his heart pound. Was that who he reminded her of? John would rather be dead than like his stepfather. Spring's love would never last for a man like Sam.

And without Spring, maybe he would be better off dead.

He figured there was only one thing he could do. One chance to prove something to her and to himself.

He had to reach out to Logan. For all the reasons Spring had suggested on Sunday morning. Because reaching out, caring for someone he despised, was something Sam would never do.

"You're mighty quiet."

Lifting a dirty mixing bowl from the counter to the suds-filled sink, Spring glanced at her mother. The house was silent around them. John was long gone, and her father was out tending to his livestock. "I'm tired, Mama. Working all day and making eight pumpkin pies from scratch is wearying."

In truth, Spring knew her exhaustion came as much from the emotional scene with John as it did from physical activity. She shouldn't have let him kiss her. Certainly, she should have never kissed him back. She had been unsettled enough since making love with him Sunday. Today had just added to it.

"John was quiet, too, while you were working out on the porch. I didn't hear you talk much about anything but what you were doing."

"I guess we'd already said what we needed to."

"And what was that?"

Spring set the clean bowl in the other side of the sink for Callie to rinse. "Let's not talk about me and John. You probably already know what we discussed down in the cellar anyway."

"I don't know everything," her mother retorted.

"That's humble of you." Spring studied Callie in concern. "You're not getting sick, are you?"

The older woman laughed. "Not hardly. All my babies will be home for Thanksgiving. It would take a mighty strong sickness to lay me low with everyone coming."

"This place will be crawling with kids. All boys."

"Rainy's two. Paul's three. And Stuart's baby boy."

"I keep thinking there's got to be a girl baby in this clan sooner or later."

Callie grinned. "There will be. Just one. Every second generation produces just one girl. I was the one in mine. There'll be another for me to teach, like my granny taught me."

Spring knew the family legend well. "Maybe Clay will give you your granddaughter when he marries. When I was little, I always thought it would be me."

"Now, don't you give up yet. You've got a lot of childbearing years left."

"I have to find a man, first."

"I think John's the right man. You just keep working on him."

"Mama, even if I decided I could live with him again, he's never going to want children." Strange how saying something she knew so well could bring on such a fresh heartache.

"He might surprise you one day."

"Mama—"

"Hush, now. Don't be bringing bad luck your way by giving up."

"I might as well." With a sigh, Spring lifted her face to the breeze that came through the open window over the sink. Though cool, the wind felt more like mid-May than November.

Callie cocked her head, motioning for Spring to be still. In the forest that surrounded the house, the wind sang through the trees. Another gust sent chimes bouncing on the porch. From the mountains came an echo, almost a roar.

"Weather's changing," Spring said quietly.

Her mother nodded. "When the forest murmurs and the mountain roars, then close your windows and lock your doors."

The mountain saying was familiar to Spring. "Cold weather?" she asked.

"Rain, too. Your father's joints were aching this afternoon."

"That might have something to do with his hauling timber into the sawmill all by himself."

"John helped him load."

"So John was here all day."

"Pretty near."

"And I guess you invited him for Thanksgiving."

"Would you rather he were alone?"

"No," Spring admitted. Much as being with John would fill her with the sorts of yearnings she had a hard time controlling, she didn't want him lonely and alone on a day made for families.

"It'll be fine." Callie patted her shoulder. "We'll give John a baby or two to bounce on his knee. He might find out he likes the feeling."

"Don't get your hopes up."

"Life without hope ain't no life at all, girl." Callie's smile turned her face from pretty to startlingly beautiful, in the way that Spring loved so well.

Impulsively, she hugged her mother. "I'm so glad to be here. Home for Thanksgiving."

"It's right wonderful to have my baby home,"

Callie agreed. "Now come on, let's get these dishes put up. I've got to brew up some alfalfa tea for your daddy's rheumatism."

Chapter Twelve

John remembered that the car Logan had left outside Spring's house on Saturday night was a brand-new silver Miata. An expensive car like that shouldn't be difficult to find in a White's Creek high-school parking lot full of pickups and used sedans.

Sure enough, on Wednesday afternoon, John easily found Logan's car facing out across two slots at the edge of the lot. He perched on the hood about a half hour before the final bell. Overhead, the sky threatened rain, a perfect accompaniment to his mood.

But he was resolute in his decision to see Logan. He figured a surprise meeting like this was the only way he could get to his half brother, outside of getting Debra in on it.

At 3:25, Logan appeared, right on schedule, with the petite redhead—Mollie—who had brought him to Spring's. They were laughing, looking as carefree as most kids on the final day of school before a long holiday weekend. If Logan's face weren't bruised and cut and his forehead bandaged, John could almost believe these two had no cares. They pulled up short when they saw him on the car.

"Get off my car, asshole," Logan said, bristling with belligerence.

Obligingly, John slid off the hood. "I just want to talk, not fight."

"I've got nothing to say to you."

"Sheriff Kane thinks we should talk."

His key in the door lock, Logan paused. "That's bullshit, and you know it."

"He called me about the investigation." This was the only topic John could think of that Logan might be interested in discussing with him.

Mollie shot John an anxious glance. "Logan, maybe you should talk to him."

"He's nobody," Logan assured her. "He doesn't know anything about this. Mother's lawyer boyfriend has it all fixed up."

John framed his next comment with skepticism. "So you've got confidence in Gregory Stanton?"

"Why shouldn't I?"

"No special reason." John shrugged. "I guess he's handled plenty of this kind of stuff for you."

"Some."

"But he's not usually a criminal lawyer."

"I don't know," Logan mumbled, frowning. "I guess he takes care of business stuff, mostly."

"But he takes on criminal cases just for you?"

"For Mother. She pays him. Pretty well, I think." Logan's arrogance was enough to put anyone off.

John forced himself, however, to continue. "I guess Debra knows what she's doing." He started to leave, hoping he had whetted Logan's curiosity enough that the boy might want to talk to him.

Mollie, apparently, was curious enough for both of them. She called after John, "Do you know a lot about criminal law?"

"I was a crime reporter," John replied, facing them again. "I write police thrillers."

Logan sneered in derision. "Writers are pansies."

John could just imagine Sam making the same pronouncement. He bit back a retort. Nothing would be served by antagonizing the boy further.

"I'd love to be a writer," Mollie admitted. Evidently, her fascination for John's profession outweighed any anger she might harbor toward him for turning Logan over to the sheriff and his deputies on Saturday night.

"Maybe we can talk about it," John told her, smiling, hoping to charm her, at least. "I'd be happy to buy both of you a burger or something."

Shaking his head, Logan turned back to his car. "No, thanks. I've got better things to do with my time."

"Yeah, better take advantage of your freedom." John started backing toward his own car again. "Who knows what the future may bring."

Logan glanced at him once more. "What's that supposed to mean?"

"Just what I said."

The young man laughed. "You think I'm going

to do time over defending myself against Jeff Lott? You're nuts."

"It happens."

Mollie's pixie green eyes widened. "Is that what Sheriff Kane told you?"

At John's noncommittal reply, the girl turned to Logan. It took a few minutes, but somehow she convinced him they should go have a bite to eat with John.

At McDonald's, where the young couple had promised to meet him, John got a cup of coffee and took a seat. He wouldn't be surprised if Logan and Mollie decided not to show up. Truthfully, part of him hoped they wouldn't. Now that he had started this, he wasn't sure what he was going to say to his troubled half brother.

Finally, when John was about to give up on them, they came in the door. John sent Mollie to place a food order while Logan slouched in the seat across the booth. He played with the salt and pepper shakers instead of looking at his older brother.

"I only came because Mollie thought it was a good idea," he said once she was out of earshot. "She's got this thing about families. I tried to tell her we weren't a family, but she wouldn't let up."

"She seems like a smart girl."

"She's not dumb, that's for sure. Not like a lot of girls."

"So I guess Mollie's kind of special?"

With a resentful look, Logan retorted, "She's none of your business."

"Spring likes her a lot."

"Mollie thinks she's cool."

"How about you?"

Impatiently, Logan said, "Is this why you got me out here? To talk about your wife?"

"I thought the two of you were pretty good friends."

Logan shrugged, but at least he looked at John. "She was always nice to me when I was a kid. She's the same now."

"You remember when you used to tag around after us?"

"Some."

"You didn't seem to hate me much then."

"That was before you left."

John nodded. "Before Sam and Debra convinced you I was public enemy number one, right?"

The boy glanced away. "They didn't have to say much."

"Why?"

Rolling his eyes, Logan muttered, "You figure it out. You're the big, smart writer."

John decided to get down to business. "I wanted to talk about you. This trouble you're in."

A cocky smile curved Logan's still-swollen lips. "I told you, that's all going to be fixed up."

"What if it's not?"

"It will be."

"Sheriff Kane says you've spent a lot of time in trouble these last few years."

Anger replaced the confidence. "He needs to

keep his mouth shut. Sheriff is an elected office, you know, and Mother controls a lot of votes in this county."

John eased back in his seat. He could say one thing for his little brother. He thought he had all his bases covered. And maybe he did. "You've got it made, don't you?"

Logan met his gaze again. "Jealous?"

"Not hardly."

"I wouldn't blame you if you were," Logan continued. "Dad cut you out of the will. I get everything once Mother's gone."

"That could be a while. Debra's a young woman."

A frown creased Logan's forehead below the white bandage. "Why do you call Mother that?"

"That's just how I think of her. Debra." He made the name sound as cold and haughty as she was in his thoughts and his memories.

Maybe it was John's imagination, but he thought he caught a glimmer of admiration in Logan's eyes before Mollie came back to the table with their burgers.

For the next bit, she dominated the conversation with questions about how John became a writer. Where he went to school. His major. What he did as a reporter. How he came up with his stories. How he felt the first time he saw one of his books for sale.

Logan listened in silence, resisting every attempt by Mollie and John to draw him out. He was unimpressed with John's description of one of the many drug busts he had witnessed when he was a reporter. He clearly didn't care that John's first book might soon be a movie for television. If anything, he seemed resentful of the interest Mollie was showing in John.

Finally, pushing aside his half-eaten burger, Logan leaned forward, his expression ugly. "You know something, bro? I think you're as big a fake as my father said you were."

Mollie looked confused. "Logan, Miss DeWitt told me he was a writer. She showed me his books Saturday night. He's not lying."

"So big deal," Logan jeered. "He probably steals all his ideas. My dad said he was a cheat and thief."

John shifted in his seat, trying to stay cool. No matter that Logan looked and sounded like a man, he was just a kid, parroting his parent's lies. "I'm not surprised Sam Nelson told you that. Your father never liked anything about me."

"He said you were trouble from the minute he married Mother."

"I could have said the same about him."

"He adopted you. He gave you all kinds of chances, and you just kept screwing up."

"You're right," John agreed. Try as he might, he couldn't stop his voice from dropping into sarcasm. "But I bet he'd be proud of you. You're just like him."

"You got a problem with that?" the younger man demanded, leaning forward in challenge.

"Logan, chill," Mollie broke in, frowning at Logan.

He ignored her, concentrating instead on John. "Dad sure wasn't proud of you."

"Is that supposed to hurt?" John chuckled as he shook his head. "That's a compliment, considering your source. So thank you."

"You're a jerk-ass bastard."

John laughed again. "Is that all you can do? Mimic your father's simpleminded profanities?"

Logan went pale with anger, the purple bruise on his jaw stood out in stark relief. "You faggot."

"God, you sound just like him."

"Shut up!" Logan roared.

All around them, other patrons fell silent.

"Stop it." Mollie took hold of Logan's arm, as if to hold him back.

He shook her off. Too roughly for John to take.

He reached across the table and grabbed hold of Logan's shirt, jerking him forward, halfway across the table. "You don't treat her that way, you hear me."

"It's okay," Mollie whispered urgently, glancing around at their onlookers. "It's okay, I tell you. Let him go, please."

For her sake, John released Logan. The kid—he looked a little younger than he had before—fell back against his seat, gasping. He seemed shocked, like the last thing he had expected was for John to get rough with him.

In the silence, John asked, "What's the matter? Didn't you like getting manhandled? You ought to think about that the next time you start pushing someone else around. Especially a girl. And especially when she's someone like Mollie, who seems, for God only knows what reason, to be your friend."

Logan took Mollie by the arm. "Let's get out of here. This guy's a loser, just like I told you." Quickly, he hustled her out of the booth and toward the front of the restaurant.

John sat unmoving, trying to get his breath, trying to remember why he had attempted this meeting with Sam Nelson's mixed-up, smart-mouthed son.

He looked up, just as Logan pulled Mollie through the door, in time to catch the panic on her young, pretty face.

John realized he couldn't sit by and let Logan take her anywhere. Not when he was this angry, especially when that anger was John's fault. He got up and out of the restaurant as fast as he could.

Mollie and Logan were almost to his car when John came through the doors. He could hear the young couple arguing all the way across the lot. She started to walk away, but Logan caught her arm, obviously pleading with her.

"Wait," John called, hampered in getting to them by cars heading for the drive-thru lane. "I'll take you home, Mollie."

His half brother glared at him. Then he kissed the girl.

Even at a distance, John could see the violence in that kiss. He wondered just what Logan was trying to prove and to whom. When he released Mollie, she was rag-doll limp.

But she got into his car.

Still calling her name, John reached the passenger door just as Logan sent the sports car into reverse, tires squealing. He peeled out of the parking lot at top speed. By the time John got in his own vehicle and reached the road, Logan's car was nothing but a distant silver blur, heading away from town.

The long-threatening rain began to fall, fat raindrops collecting on John's windshield.

"Damn!" He pounded his steering wheel in frustration. He would never catch them. He had no idea where to start looking for them.

Why had he let Logan walk away with her? His half brother was an unpredictable, violent young man. A ticking bomb. And John had lit his fuse. Mollie could very well end up taking the brunt of the explosion.

John turned toward downtown. He had to tell Spring what had happened. Maybe she had some idea where Logan and Mollie might have gone.

Chalk and milk and crayons.

That unique combination of aromas assaulted John's senses when he walked in the bottom floor of the building where Spring's office was located. The schoolhouse smells flooded him with memories. Unlike some people, who went back to school and were reminded of only study and homework, John felt differently.

His best childhood days had been spent in the classroom. Discipline had been strict at all the private schools he had attended, but nothing compared to what he had faced at home. At least at school he had a few friends. There was often a teacher who took an interest in him. Sports to play for fun, not Sam's approval. Time alone without fear. At each school, John usually got in two good years before Sam decided he was too comfortable or too happy and moved him.

Maybe that's why he had escaped Sam Nelson with relative sanity intact, because he had been out of that house much of the time.

Unlike Logan.

Pausing just inside the school doors, John gave himself a mental shake. The direction his thoughts were going was crazy. Logan hadn't been hated. Logan had been the favored child, the flesh-and-blood son.

But he had grown up to be a bully.

Sam taught him, obviously.

By example. Or by force?

John got hold of his runaway thoughts. He was nuts, thinking like Spring. He would bet every dime he had ever made that Sam had never laid a hand on Logan. Sam wouldn't bruise the prince. That treatment was reserved for John.

And yet . . .

Shunting foolish notions aside, John rounded a

corner from the front vestibule. He pulled up short, however, spying Spring just down the hall. She was talking with a woman and a little girl. Because their expressions were serious, he paused at the corner. No one in the little group even looked his way.

The girl, who couldn't be more than six or seven, was all dressed up. Deep blue dress with a broad white collar over a white sweater. White tights with shiny black shoes. But her head was down. Shoulders slumped. She clutched books to her chest.

As John watched, Spring dropped down to the girl's level. She told her something, and the girl looked up, smiling. Her face lit up as she gave Spring a big hug. Spring returned the embrace with equal fervor.

The scene reminded John, sharply, of the child Spring had wanted them to adopt. Chrissy had been about the age of this girl. Just as forlorn. But he had seen Spring bring Chrissy to life with a smile and a hug, just as she had done with this little girl.

One of the counselors Spring had worked with in Chicago had told John she had a gift for mending angels' broken wings. Certainly, she had rescued many children, who had been beaten, raped, and abandoned by the adults who were supposed to care for them.

With the way Spring had always felt about all children, it probably shouldn't have shocked John when she wanted her own. He remembered the way she had put it to him, again and again, "I need to do this. I need a child."

He realized, with the clarity of hindsight, how desperate she had sounded.

While John pondered that, Spring rose from the little girl she had been hugging. The woman took the child by the hand and walked toward John. As they passed him, he smiled. The girl gave him a solemn look, then glanced over her shoulder at Spring.

Arms folded, face set, Spring looked every bit as upset as the child.

When John reached her, his hand closed instinctively on her shoulder, in comfort. "What's wrong?"

She pursed her lips.

"Come on, you can tell me."

"It's nothing, John. At least not anything I can control."

"But you're almost in tears. What did that little girl's mother say to you?"

Spring took a deep breath. "That was Nan's caseworker, not her mother."

"Caseworker?"

"Nan's been a ward of the state for about six months. Ever since her mother left her and her baby brother by themselves for a whole weekend while she went partying with her boyfriend."

John waited, knowing there was more to the story.

"They're letting Nan go home for Thanksgiving," Spring explained, as the front door clanged shut down the hall.

"I take it you're afraid the mother's not ready to have her daughter back."

"Nan's scared to death to go home. She had a panic attack in class this afternoon. A six-year-old having a panic attack . . ." Sighing, Spring shoved her hair back from her face. "No one but me thinks that's reason enough to keep her away from her mother."

John slipped an arm around her shoulders. "You can't save everyone."

"So you keep reminding me," she retorted, shrugging away.

Upset as she was, John hated to tell her about Logan and Mollie, but he had no choice.

Alarmed, Spring led him quickly through the deserted administrative office to her small cubbyhole. She looked up a number and punched it into the phone. Her relief was palpable when she said into the receiver, "Mollie, thank goodness you're home."

John's chest eased, as well. At least Logan hadn't skidded on a wet road and wrapped his spitfire of a car around a telephone pole. John sat and rubbed a hand over his face while he listened to Spring's end of the conversation. She told Mollie he had been worried about her because of Logan's mood when they left the restaurant. It was clear from Spring's expression that Mollie said little to reassure her.

Frowning as she said good-bye, Spring set the phone in its cradle and took a seat behind her desk. She looked up at John. "I don't know what to do about Mollie. I talked to her Saturday night and again yesterday about Logan. I've kept telling myself that they're just friends, that she's not his type of girl, that they won't get really involved. But now I'm not so sure. You said he kissed her, right in front of you. That doesn't sound like Mollie."

"She didn't have much choice. Logan was showing off. I wanted to take her home. He was already pissed because she was interested in my writing."

"He felt threatened by you."

"Believe me, Spring. That's not what I set out to do."

"I know." Her tone gentled. "I know just how hard it was for you even to approach him."

"Maybe you should go to Mollie's parents. Warn them."

"Her grandmother's all she has," Spring reminded him. "There's a brother, a year younger. I don't know that Larry has too much influence over her. Mollie has played mom to her siblings for a long time. She's an authority figure."

"Logan said family is important to Mollie. Surely she'd listen to them."

"I don't know." Wearily, Spring rubbed at her temples. "Getting Larry or her grandmother involved could just make things worse. Mollie has always been a model kid. With all she's been through in losing her parents, she's had good grades. She's never been in trouble. But there comes a time in most every teenager's life when they rebel. And a boy like Logan . . . he fits the bill perfectly."

John gave that some thought. "Is it possible," he suggested, slowly, "just possible that Mollie might be good for Logan?"

"Now you sound like her," Spring retorted. "Mollie thinks she can save him from himself."

John paused. "Sounds like someone else I know."

Spring shifted uncomfortably in her chair, avoiding John's gaze.

"You rescued me once upon a time."

"It wasn't the same. You weren't the sort of boy Logan is."

"I could have been."

"It's not in you to be violent or destructive."

"Okay," John conceded, still studying her thoughtfully. "Maybe I was quiet and lonely instead of brash and trouble-prone like Logan. But you have to admit, I was just as angry. I turned it inside, instead of out. It was you who kept me from exploding."

"Perhaps . . ."

But John was insistent. "You rescued me. Just the way you rescue these kids you work with. It's your mission in life."

"You were more than a mission."

John paused and straightened his shoulders, his expression clearing. "Maybe I wasn't."

She protested. "What are you saying?"

"I think I'm beginning to understand when our troubles began," he murmured. "It all started when you didn't have to rescue me anymore."

"That's ludicrous."

"Think about it." He got to his feet. "Writing my first novel was the only thing I had ever attempted that you weren't behind one hundred percent. And then, when I was successful . . ." He hesitated, a line appearing between his eyebrows.

"That's when I got jealous, remember?" Spring was still smarting from John's accusation that she envied his success.

He was distracted, as if trying to sort through his thoughts. "You were jealous and afraid, I think. Because my success had taken away what our marriage was based on."

"Yesterday, you claimed love was all we needed for our marriage."

"All I needed maybe," he replied. "You needed more, I think."

"So you're blaming me for all of this."

"I'm just saying you were always rescuing me. Shoring me up. And when I didn't need that . . ."

His words touched her deep-seated fear that he really didn't need her. For anything. No matter how many times he had claimed it wasn't true, his actions had said otherwise. Now, hearing him say it, was more than she could take. It opened the door to the terror she had been running from since the day she left Chicago—the terrifying possibility that it really was over between them. Every time they got close to recognizing that, she backed away, started an argument, pushed him aside.

Sunday, she told him she didn't want to run away any longer. But yesterday, after she let him kiss her and they were talking in an honest, forthright way, she had walked away again. She was running away right now. And she couldn't stop herself.

She stood, holding up a hand. "Please, John, don't say anything more."

"But Spring—"

"Please."

He bit his lip, shoved one hand in his jeans pocket, and stared at her.

She tried to explain without revealing how much his words had upset her. "I don't want to get into this right now. All this stuff with Nan and then Mollie and Logan . . . it's been a long day and I'm tired . . . I just can't think about what you're saying to me. I can't."

Hesitating only a moment, John nodded. He surveyed her with genuine concern. "Are you going to be all right?"

"Of course." She knew she would have sounded more convincing if her voice hadn't trembled so.

"Let me take you home."

"No, John, that's stupid—"

"It's even stupider for you to sit here in this empty building."

"I'm not going to sit here. I'm going to call Mollie back and see if I can talk to her tonight."

His smile was somewhat sad. "Going to save her from Logan, are you?"

"John—"

"Sorry." He backed away from her desk. "I'm going. I'll see you tomorrow."

"Tomorrow?"

"Thanksgiving," he explained. "At the farm." He left.

Spring dropped to her chair.

What was she going to do? She couldn't live with John, but didn't seem able to let him go, either.

The next day, with him across the table and her family surrounding them, Spring prayed not in thanks, but for help. She definitely needed divine intervention to show her the way out of this mess.

She needed God or one of Mama's spells to do something.

Fast.

Looking up, Spring saw from the sparkle in Callie's eyes that she had read her youngest daughter's mind.

Spring steeled herself mentally, knowing just about anything could happen.

Chapter Thirteen

～ "There are some really good things about everyone being home," Spring confided to Rainy as they sat at the kitchen table Thanksgiving afternoon. "Mainly, it keeps Mama focused on someone other than me."

Rainy downed the last bite of her second piece of pumpkin pie and laughed. "Yes, ma'am, I was real happy to see Clay come in with a new girlfriend. It distracted Mama."

"With that and all the kids around, she's been very well occupied." Spring wasn't sure what she had expected since her mother's enigmatic smile over the blessing, but nothing had materialized. So far.

Right now, Callie was out in the shed where she dried herbs and mixed her homemade remedies, showing off for her two daughters-in-law and Clay's date.

"It's been a nice day," Rainy added.

Spring nodded to the far end of the big room. The men were sprawled on two sofas, chairs, and the floor in front of a televised football game. "They sure seem content. Like pigs in slop."

John was right in the middle of her three brothers, Rainy's husband, and Ned, just as if he and Spring weren't separated. No one had said a word to Spring about the state of their marriage. Not even her sister, who was usually all too eager to express her opinion. No doubt, Mama had imposed a strict rule of silence for the day. Which was fine with Spring. She was so confused, she didn't know what to say to herself about her husband and their relationship, much less what to tell her family. Mostly, she was afraid to think too much about all the things that could bring her pain.

"Would you listen to those kids?" Rainy smiled as the sound of boyish laughter drifted in from outdoors. "I'm glad it stopped raining so we could send them out."

"All but this little guy." Bending down, Spring picked up the dark-haired baby boy who had crawled from his father, her brother Stuart, and into the kitchen. "Hello, little Will, is your daddy too busy watching football to play with you?"

"He looks a lot like my boys," Rainy said, patting Will's bottom as Spring tickled his belly and made him laugh.

"You had beautiful babies," Spring agreed.

Her sister smiled and leaned forward. She was about to say something when the screen door opened, admitting Callie and the other females of the family.

From the other end of the room came a chorus of groans.

"Halftime," announced Paul, the oldest DeWitt sibling. Short and rounded, much like Rainy, he rubbed his hands together as he walked toward the table. "After a sorry half like that from the Falcons, I need some more of Mama's black walnut cake for consolation."

Everyone, it seemed, was ready for another round of food. As plates and platters were unwrapped and the family gathered by the table, Rainy stood and gestured for her husband to come to her side. "Before you eat again," she said, beaming, "there's something Jess and I want to tell you. I was going to wait, because it's early yet . . . but . . . well . . . I'm not sure how this happened, but I'm pregnant."

Approval was loud and strong and included some rather pointed suggestions about how such an event might have occurred. Brothers twirled Rainy around and pumped Jess's hand. Ned and Callie beamed. The women cried and hugged.

Spring was grateful for the noise and confusion. She hoped it covered her shock. Her pain. Her out-and-out jealousy.

Over Will's head, she met John's solemn dark eyes.

And she wanted to die.

Nausea swept over her. Tears gathered and threatened. Finally, because she couldn't look at John anymore, she handed the baby to his father and grabbed Rainy.

"Mama said," Spring whispered, thickly, against her sister's ear. "She warned you."

Laughing, Rainy replied, "I'm not so sure she didn't make it happen."

"I'm so happy for you." Spring couldn't stop the sob that rose in her voice.

Rainy drew back. "Spring, honey, are you all right?"

"Of course." Spring hugged her again, just in case any of her jealousy had come through in the first one. "This is wonderful news."

Rainy said nothing more, and Spring broke away, edging toward the door. Studiously, she refrained from looking at her mother or at John. She didn't think she could stand it if either of them said a word to her.

But, of course, she couldn't avoid either of them forever. Just as twilight was falling, John found her out at the edge of the yard. She was feeding carrots through the fence to her father's old mare, glad to be away from the noise of the family.

John came up beside her. He stood quietly for a moment, then cleared his throat. "I'm sorry, Spring."

She merely grunted in reply, concentrating on the horse.

"Listen, I can see how upset you are—"

"I'm not," she denied, though she knew everything she had done since Rainy's announcement had said otherwise.

"I wish it could be different."

That made her look at him. "It could."

His gaze fell. They stood together in silence for a moment. Then he reached out and took Spring's hand. His fingers entwined with hers.

She wanted to pull away. Slap him. Scream. Do something to make him want what she wanted so desperately. But she did none of those things. Instead, she went into his arms. She hugged him as a sob rose in her throat. She held that back, along with the tears.

But she didn't look at John when he walked away. She went in the opposite direction, toward the gentle rise beyond the house, where Ned was spreading hay for his cattle. Spring stood beside her father and watched John's car drive away. For some reason, knowing he was gone made it safe to cry. It was easier still because her father was there when the first tears fell.

His arms felt strong and solid around her. His old coat was rough against her cheek, smelling of tobacco and hay and work. His farmer's hands were gentle on her hair. Ned seemed to know without words that she just needed to be held, the way he had held her when she was a little girl and his presence was all it took to set her world right.

Lord, how she wished he could slay her dragons now.

He stood with her for a long time. Until she could draw away.

"Better now?" he asked.

Nodding, Spring wiped her wet face and her runny nose with the back of her sleeve.

Ned offered her the crisp, white handkerchief he was never without.

She laughed through her tears. "You always have what I need, Daddy."

"I wish I did, Daughter. I wish I could fix this for you."

"Nobody can but John and me. We keep talking at it and around it, and we don't get anywhere. Because I'm afraid of where we're going."

"You're right to be afraid. Stayin' married is a hard ride."

"Today, when I heard Rainy's news . . ." Spring paused, shaking her head to stave off a fresh batch of tears. "I looked at John and I knew it would never be him and me making that announcement to the family."

"He's passing up the joy of life."

"He doesn't understand. He lived inside of himself for so long, without anybody he could trust. That caught up with us, finally."

"John just let you slip away. He can't blame that on nothing but himself. Not on his past. Not his parents. Not anybody."

"I wish I could believe that, Daddy."

"You had nearly twelve good years together. Why, all of a sudden, did everything go wrong? He made his choices, I think."

"And I made mine, I guess, by leaving him," Spring whispered. "He says I changed."

"Change is part of living. Why, I'm not the same handsome, young rascal your mother married."

"Still handsome," Spring claimed, tucking her arm through his. "Still a rascal when you want to be."

Ned chuckled. "The point is, me and your mother didn't give up on each other, even when things didn't turn out like we planned. You got to make adjustments in a marriage. It's like a house settling on its foundation. Some give here. Some take there."

"What about the cracks?"

"You mend. The funny thing about foundations is, sometimes the ones that crack last the longest. If you fill 'em in good and firm, that is." Her father gave her hand a final squeeze and turned back to his cattle. "If you're through crying, I've got to see that these ladies and gentlemen get their bellies full."

"I'm through," Spring said, grinning. "Let me help."

And maybe it was the cleansing power of her tears, or maybe it was her father's way of breaking the biggest problems down into simple parts, but she felt stronger than she had since John had come to town.

Strong enough to face some hard truths about herself and John and the cracks in their marriage.

Earlier today, she had asked for a sign. Maybe Rainy's pregnancy was that bolt from the blue, designed to make Spring wake up and see what was right in front of her eyes.

* * *

After a day with Spring's big, loving family, the last place John wanted to be was his mother's house. So why was he here, ringing the doorbell?

Because Debra had called and said she needed to see him.

Hours ago, John had gone back to his dreary motel room from the DeWitt farm. All he had been able to think of was the way Spring had looked when Rainy made her big announcement. Spring's pain, her yearning, had hit him like a blow from behind.

Maybe her features had once gone all soft and sweet when she had fantasized aloud about having a baby or adopting a child. Maybe he just hadn't been paying attention.

He was now. A child was something Spring wanted the way she had once wanted him. With everything inside of her.

Ever since Spring left him, John had been clinging to the possibility that she wanted a child to fill some lack he had caused in their life together. He thought that if he tried hard enough, showed her he loved her as he always had, the emptiness she felt would go away. Even when she told him it wasn't some passing fancy, he thought it was still something they could get around.

But he had to face it. Her desire for children wasn't going anywhere.

That sudden, painful knowledge echoed from the walls of his lonely motel room. He couldn't escape it, not even in the new book that called to him from his glowing laptop screen.

So when the phone rang, he grabbed it like a relay runner would snatch a baton. A desire to escape made him say yes when Debra asked him to come over.

And now here he was, at her door, thinking he was a fool.

Logan swung it open. The big chandelier above him was on dim, casting eerie shadows on the stairs and on Logan's face. If possible, he looked worse than he had the night he showed up at Spring's. There were no new bruises. Just a hollow, haunted look in his eyes. Strangely enough, he had no taunts with which to greet John.

That alone made John suspicious.

"Mother's in the family room," Logan said, stepping back for John to pass.

"I'm guessing you know what this is about?"

The boy shrugged. "Sheriff Kane was here earlier."

"Are you being charged with assault?"

A muscle worked beneath the fading bruise on Logan's jaw. "Not yet. But Jeff's parents are giving Kane a hard time." The boy tried but failed to adopt his habitual cockiness. "Mother's the one who's panicking."

"Doesn't she think Gregory Stanton can fix this up for you?"

"Why don't you ask her?" Turning on his heel, Logan led the way to the family room.

Along the way, John surveyed the house he hadn't seen for so many years. Not much was changed. The antiques, highly polished and well preserved, were still in place. The Tiffany lamp on the mahogany hall table was the same. The leaded glass in the bookshelves just inside the family room door. The crystal vase of roses on the rolltop desk in the corner.

The drapes across the wall of French doors were new. Green-and-white-striped. They matched the upholstery on the long, low couch where Debra lay with a cloth over her eyes and a highball glass in her hand.

"He's here," Logan announced. John stepped in the room behind him.

Debra sat up, dragging the cloth off her eyes. She blinked, staring at her older son. "Johnny?" she said, just like she had the first night he had been in town and came here.

"I wish you wouldn't call me that," he said.

She shook her head, as if to clear it, blinking again. "Of course. Your father was Johnny. Sam forbade me to call you that."

That was news to John. "He did? Why?"

She ignored his question with the adeptness she always used in dealing with anything she found too unpleasant or too close to the truth. Instead, she took a sip of her drink. Not her first drink of the evening, John deduced from the unsteadiness of her hand. Rising from the sofa, she straightened the skirt of her soft, blue robe.

"Did Logan tell you what the sheriff said to us?"

John glanced at his half brother. "Sounds like

the parents of that boy he beat up aren't responding to bribes."

Debra's beautifully symmetrical features hardened. "Is that what Logan said?"

"Of course not," John replied before the boy could. "I doubt he would be so indiscreet as to tell me you were trying to buy off yet another of his victims."

"I don't want them bought off," Debra said, her tone sharp. "I have offered to pay the hospital bill as a way of apologizing for Logan's part in that brawl."

"Aren't you afraid that looks like an admission of guilt?"

"It's just being decent, I think."

"Decent?" John rubbed his chin thoughtfully. "You know something about that, Debra?"

She straightened her shoulders. "I know about doing what's expected."

"But not necessarily what's right."

She closed her eyes, briefly. When she opened them, they were cold and calm. "I know your opinion of me, John. I'm not trying to prove anything to you. But what I've offered the Lotts is not, in any way, shape, or form, a bribe."

"Besides," Logan cut in, his usual brashness showing, "there are plenty of witnesses who say the fight happened just the way I said. Jeff came after me."

"I guess it's your reputation that's got so many having such doubts," John retorted.

The boy stepped forward, face flushing, hands

balling into fists at his sides. "I don't care what everybody else says about any other trouble I've been in. This time, the fight happened just the way I said."

For some reason John believed him.

"It's the truth. Jeff was drunk. He's been trying to get at me since I screwed around with his girlfriend. He came at me with that stick. I just fought back. Then I pushed him."

Coolly, Debra interrupted, "In case you're interested, John, the Lott boy's blood alcohol level was well above the legal limit. Ten witnesses have sworn statements to support Logan."

"I thought everyone at the party was drunk," John said.

"Some people," Debra replied. "Some people, like Logan, showed no sign of being drunk."

"How did that happen?" John asked, turning back to the boy. "From what I've heard, you're usually a big drinker."

He shrugged. "I was talking to Mollie for a long time that night. She's not into beer."

"Mollie?" Debra's eyes narrowed. "Who's that?"

"A friend," Logan told her, quickly. "Just a friend."

"Greta Stevens's granddaughter? A little thing? Scared of her shadow?"

"Yeah, that's her. She's nobody, Mother."

The deliberate way Logan downplayed Mollie to Debra told John there definitely was more between the kids than friendship. He could understand. He had hidden Spring from his mother and Sam for a long time, as well. He had learned early that when something was good, they would try to kill it. It surprised him, thinking Logan might understand that experience.

But that wasn't the point of this conversation. John asked, "Why am I here?"

Ice tinkled in Debra's glass as she drained the last of her drink. She set it on a silver coaster on the coffee table and took her time answering John. "Sheriff Kane said he had talked to you about Logan's past . . . troubles."

"So?"

"So I thought you could talk to him some more, perhaps convince him not to proceed with these charges."

Frowning, John glanced at Logan. "You've made it pretty clear you don't want anything to do with me. Why should I help you?"

Logan looked at the floor, his jaw clenched.

Debra spoke up again. "I think Sheriff Kane respects you."

"But I wasn't there that night. What can I say that would have any bearing at all on this?"

"You can tell Kane you believe Logan's telling the truth."

"But I don't," John lied, not wanting to go along with anything Debra suggested.

Logan's protest was cut short by a severe glance from Debra. She said, "I know you probably don't care, but this would mean a lot to me, John. I'd make it worth your while."

For a moment, John was too stunned to realize

what she was saying. It sank in, though, quickly. She was trying to buy him. The way she bought everyone.

She went on, digging a deeper trench. "This could be ugly, John."

"And public," he added, bitterly. "That's the worst part, isn't it? If Logan is charged, or if the Lotts bring a civil suit against you, everyone's going to talk even more than they're talking now. And you can't stand that. You don't want whispers following you around the pool at the club."

Two red dots of color had appeared in her pale cheeks. "I don't see why it's so wrong not to want people talking about me and my family. I had enough of that when I was young."

Intrigued at this latest slip about her family, John asked, "What did people say about your folks?"

"That doesn't matter," she replied, tossing her head. "But when this is over, Logan is going to behave. He's promised. There'll be no more talk for me to face about him."

John raised one eyebrow as he looked at his half brother. "Is that so?"

The boy said nothing.

Laughing, John turned back to Debra. "How are you going to make sure he toes the line?"

"Do what you suggested, I suppose. Send him away again."

Logan's startled exclamation made it clear this was news to him.

"Be quiet," his mother ordered.

"You can't send me away! You can't do me like you did him." Logan jerked his head in John's direction. "This is *my* father's house. I don't have to leave."

"It is *my* house," Debra snapped. "And you will straighten up once and for all or you will go."

John definitely understood what Logan was feeling. He watched as Logan's features reflected a range of familiar reactions. Rage. Fear. Resignation. Shame.

It was this last emotion that made up John's mind.

Debra, who didn't know that, was still making deals. "Will you help us out, John? If you can convince Sheriff Kane, then I'm prepared to—"

John cut her off with an impatient gesture. "Just stop it."

"But I can—"

"You can't buy me," he said, voice rising. "I'm not for sale."

Putting her hand to her throat, Debra said, "Then you won't go to the sheriff?"

John turned his back on Debra and faced Logan. "I'm going to do this," he told the boy. "But not for her. And not for money. For you."

Logan's eyes widened, but he didn't say anything.

"And I have some conditions," John added.

"Like what?"

"Like you see a psychologist."

"No way."

"You need some help."

"But shrinks never help," Logan claimed. "I've seen a dozen in the last few years. You can lie and tell them anything and they believe it."

"Then why not tell them the truth?"

Something in that challenge made Logan fall back a step, shaking his head even harder.

Before he could think, John offered another suggestion. "Then talk to me."

Logan smirked. "You?"

There was no backing down now that he had made the offer. Stoutly, John said, "We might have something to say to each other, Logan."

"I doubt it."

"But why not try talking to me instead of just hating me?" A sudden, unexpected tightness gripped John's throat. "A long time ago you didn't hate me, Logan."

The boy looked away, biting his lip.

John pressed him. "Maybe you'd stop hating me if we talked, if you stopped thinking like *him* and thought for yourself." He was certain Logan would know he meant Sam.

He did. Heatedly, he began, "*My* father said you . . ." Then the words trailed away as he realized he was just illustrating John's point.

Behind them, Debra cleared her throat. "John?"

He wheeled to face her again. "There's another condition to this, Debra. You stop trying to buy Logan out of trouble."

Her lips thinned.

"Don't bother pretending outrage," John told her. "You can deny your bribes all you want, but I know the truth. The only thing you know how to do is make deals. I know because I was once one of your commodities. You traded me for this house and your diamonds and your precious standing in this town. You'll deal in anything you can to make sure your life goes along just as you want it."

Her face gave nothing away.

John continued, "So here's another deal for you. If Logan agrees to talk to me and you stay out of this from now on, I'll go to Sheriff Kane and do what I can to make this all go away."

In the quiet that fell as John and Debra stared one another down, Logan said, "Mother, he can't do anything. He doesn't have any influence on the sheriff. You're panicking. Let Gregory do his stuff."

She ignored him and said, "All right, John. You've got a deal."

"This is bullshit," Logan protested.

John smiled. "You come by my motel room tomorrow afternoon. If you don't, I'm going to Kane and try and see what he can do about pressing those assault charges and recommending you get tried as an adult."

"Mother, surely you can't . . ." Fury deepened the color in Logan's face, but Debra regarded him in stony silence. He glared at her, then at John. Then he turned. His running footsteps echoed in the hall and up the stairs. A door slammed in the distance.

"Well." Debra put her hands together, rubbing

them as she might at the conclusion of a successful business negotiation. "Can I get you a drink, John?"

"No, thank you."

"Well, I'm having another." She picked up her glass and headed for the bar at the end of the room. "It's a holiday, after all."

From the hallway, the grandfather clock counted out twelve strokes.

Debra chuckled as she splashed some water in her bourbon. "Uh-oh. I guess that means the holiday's over."

"I think I'll go," John murmured, turning toward the door.

"You're welcome to stay."

The invitation caught him by surprise. He looked at Debra again.

"Your old room is available."

"I have a room somewhere else."

"The Pine Cone Lodge." Her tone was dry. "I hear it's charming since they remodeled."

"It suits me for now."

"Why aren't you staying with your wife?"

John glared at her. She didn't deserve to know the smallest detail about his life.

Debra waved a hand airily. "Sorry. I guess that's none of my business." She sighed and drained her drink with the speed of someone whose elbow was well used to the motion. Her profile pensive, she studied the ice in her glass. "Do you really think you can do something for Logan?"

"I don't know. I'm not even sure why I'm trying. Sam did a good job poisoning his mind against me."

"Yes, well . . ." She faced him again, very composed. "One thing you need to remember about Logan. He's a very good liar."

"I've noticed."

"So don't believe everything he tells you."

John had to wonder just what it was she was so afraid Logan would reveal.

Setting her glass aside, she avoided his eyes. "It's been a long day, John. If you'll excuse me, I'm going to bed. Can you let yourself out? You can lock the door as you go." Without waiting for him to reply, she swept from the room.

John was left alone with his thoughts.

And the ghosts of this house.

He could feel them, peeking around corners. Hear them, calling his name.

He had to get out of here.

Shivering in a sudden draft, he walked to the hall, dousing the family-room light behind him. The other rooms he passed were dark. He left the Tiffany lamp burning on the hall table, the stair-well chandelier on dim. His hand was on the doorknob when he found he couldn't take another step.

He turned and looked up the stairs, not sure what had drawn his attention.

"Logan?" he murmured, moving to the foot of the stairs.

There was no reply. Not one sound.

Curiosity got the better of John. He crept up the stairs. At the top, he paused. One end of the broad hall was bathed in the glow from recessed sconces. The other end, where his old room was located, was dark.

He hesitated only a heartbeat before walking into that darkness. By memory he counted the paces to the door at the end of the hall. Nineteen . . . twenty . . . twenty-one. He had always known exactly how long it would take to get to his room. He had always moved quickly and silently, trying to slip in without being noticed. That had been his goal for so many years. Just to get to his room without Sam remembering he was here.

Perspiration broke out on John's forehead. His chest tightened as he looked over his shoulder.

His stepfather was dead. What was he looking for?

But with his blood pounding, John wrenched open the door to his room and slipped inside. And shame followed hard on the heels of the fear, just as when he was a boy, sneaking, creeping into the house. "Sweet Jesus," he murmured into the dim room. "What's wrong with me?"

He fumbled for the light switch and stared, amazed. He had entered a time warp or something. How else could he explain this room? It was the same, the very same as the day he had left.

The neat blue corduroy bedspread. The spelling bee trophy on the pine dresser. The framed cowboy prints on the wall. Orderly rows of Hardy

Boy mysteries on the built-in shelves. A baseball signed by the '84 Braves in a case by the bedside lamp.

Only an empty shelf, once occupied by the stereo he had taken with him when he and Spring ran away, gave evidence that John had ever left.

The sense of déjà vu was strong. Bizarre.

Overwhelmed, John moved around the room, running his hands over the dresser. The frayed covers of the well-read books. The smooth top of the desk. He sat in the chair and, one by one, he opened the drawers. Here the illusion shattered. For the top two were bare, emptied of the coins and pens and keepsakes of his boyhood. The bottom drawer, however, was heavy when he slid it open. Inside was a photo album.

He pulled it out and lifted the cover and stared into his father's face.

Not Sam. Johnny, his real father. Dead twenty-eight years.

John had forgotten this album existed. He didn't think he had seen it since he was a boy. Vaguely, he remembered asking for it once and having Debra tell him to hush. Like always. Just hush.

Shut up. Put up. Be quiet. Disappear, Johnny-boy.

A squeak behind John made him jump.

He wheeled around just as the half-open door swung wide; he hated himself for the fear that raced up his spine.

Someone peeked around the edge of the door. Logan.

John breathed a sigh of relief. "You scared me."

For a minute in Logan's young man's face there was a trace of the little boy who had once sneaked into this room late at night to beg for a story from the brother he barely knew, the brother his father wished was dead.

"Sorry," he whispered, looking almost sincere. "I heard something. And for a minute, I thought . . . I was sure . . ." He swallowed, shook off his momentary lapse into civility, and demanded, "What are you doing in here?"

But John wasn't fooled. He knew, suddenly, why his brother had been sneaking around corners. Logan probably woke up some nights in a pool of sweat. Waiting. Fearing. Always wondering, why?

For like John, Logan had battled the ghosts in this house.

Chapter Fourteen

John took a step toward Logan. "What were you looking for?"

Again the boy's gaze slid away. "Nothing."

"Sam, maybe?"

"What?"

Shaking his head, John said, "Never mind. I was just thinking about ghosts."

Logan darted a look around the room and shivered. He hesitated, then confessed, "I used to think this room was haunted."

"It wasn't when I lived here."

"It was after you left," Logan said. "That's when I used to hear sounds. Late at night. I'd get up and come in here, thinking I might find . . ." He bit his lip. "I thought it might be you, back home."

Surprised, but pleased that Logan was in a more congenial mood, John decided to try to keep him talking. "It was probably mice."

"In Mother's house?" Logan laughed. "Come on, now. She would chase them out herself. Everything always has to be just so."

John set the photo album down and ran a finger down the clean, shiny surface of the desk. No trace of dust. "You're right. Even the rooms she doesn't use are perfect."

"Yeah." Again Logan sent a glance around the bedroom. His face tightened, and he looked at John. "Why are you still here?"

"Debra invited me to stay."

"And you're going to?"

John shook his head. "I just got curious about my old room."

"As you can see, nothing's changed."

"Why is that?" John asked.

"How should I know?"

"I would have thought Debra would turn it into a closet for her shoes."

"Sometimes I wished she would." The words were quick, edged in Logan's usual anger.

John decided to push for answers. "Do you really hate me as much as you claim?"

Logan looked startled.

"I know your father taught you to hate me," John continued. "But now that he's gone, is it still so important?"

"And what if I didn't," Logan retorted. "Are we suddenly going to become this big, lovey-dovey family? I can't see you and Mother becoming close anytime soon."

"We won't," John said, emphatically. "But does that mean you and I have to keep this war up?"

Logan's mouth twisted bitterly. "Don't go pretending you care about me. You've been gone all this time without a word."

"I knew I wouldn't be welcome here. Sam would never have let me write or call you." Surely the boy knew that much was true.

"So you drove off and forgot about me for twelve years."

When Logan put it in those terms, John felt some shame. He tried to explain. "I was young, you know. Spring and I were trying to get started. We worked all these jobs, went to school. There wasn't much time—"

"But now there is, huh?" Logan's laugh was an ugly sound. "Now that you're trying to get back into Spring's good graces, you're interested in getting to know me."

That probably was the way it appeared to the boy. John didn't want to lie. "You're right, Spring did bring me back here. And I am trying to put our marriage back together. But she has nothing to do with that deal I struck with Debra tonight."

"Yeah, right."

"I do want to help you get out of this mess," John said, as sincerely as he could. "But I want to do it the right way."

Logan rolled his eyes.

"I think I can understand you," John continued.

"Why? We're not much alike. You're this writer. I don't even like to read. I'd rather play football, if they'd let me. I don't think there's anything you can understand about me."

John didn't want to say anything against Sam. That had set Logan off yesterday. If it happened again, it would ruin this atmosphere that was running between them. He would rather end it here. So he picked up the photo album and smiled at Logan.

"Remember, I'll be expecting you at my motel room tomorrow afternoon."

The boy grunted.

John turned and left. For the first time he thought he saw the possibilities Spring saw in Logan. And as he drove away, he noticed the light was still on in his old room. A shadow moved across the blinds.

But not a ghost this time.

Just his brother.

The day after Thanksgiving had always been Spring's favorite day of the year. Not for getting a jump start on shopping. For a long time, she and John had been too broke to buy much of anything until the last-minute rush. But she always went out, mingled in the crowds, caught the holiday season's first rush of excitement and joy.

While in college, she worked at least two jobs this time of year, one of them in retail, so it was no effort to find herself in the middle of the hustle and bustle. Later, when she had the day off and John was free, she forced him to come out with her. She went alone or with a friend, but she never stayed home. Usually, she became so filled with spirit that she was up half the night, hauling out decorations and decking their modest halls.

This year, she planned to stay in bed.

Her sister and assorted family members called at daybreak, trying to tempt her with a seat in a minivan headed to Atlanta, shopping mecca of the South. Spring refused, rudely, hung up the phone, and tried to go back to sleep.

Basil, of course, had other ideas. Like being fed and petted and played with. Spring took care of her responsibilities to her pet, made herself some of the new herbal tea her mother had provided yesterday, and crawled back into bed.

She had a lot to think about. Mostly what she had come to realize yesterday. About babies. The ones she would never have. Babies with curling dark hair and John's brown eyes.

Her arms ached for John's babies.

But her life would be empty with no baby at all.

There was a difference. Children with John were not going to happen. But did that mean she had to give up any chance of nurturing a child, making a family?

If she got a divorce, she could find someone who shared her desire for children. He wouldn't be John. No one could be John. But there were other men. Good, decent men. With whom she could join the parade that was passing her by with every tick of her biological clock.

Basil, full of breakfast and lying on the chaise lounge in the morning sun, looked up, as if Spring had spoken her intent out loud. His meow was loud, vicious, and disapproving.

"You be quiet," Spring told him. Sighing, she drained the last of her tea and settled under the covers again.

Unfortunately, reproduction figured prominently in an erotic, vivid dream. She was pregnant in the dream, her belly big with child, her breasts lush and full. John was making love to her. In every imaginable position. In every possible way.

The dream disturbed her, left her aching for him, long after she awoke.

Because it would never come true.

By early afternoon Spring was still dragging around, ill-tempered and out of sorts, when knocks sounded at her front door. On the porch she found Mollie.

And Logan.

"Are we bothering you?" the girl asked, as Spring looked first at one and then the other.

Recovering her poise, Spring invited them inside.

Mollie perched on the sofa by Spring, while Logan stood, nervously shifting from foot to foot in front of the empty fireplace. He refused Spring's offer of a seat in the wing chair nearby.

"We won't stay but a minute," Mollie said. "I came by because I wanted to apologize. I think I was rude to you when you called me Wednesday night."

The girl had been curt when Spring phoned her

for a second time that evening. Mollie had refused to meet Spring to talk and wouldn't discuss what had happened with Logan and John earlier that afternoon.

Of course, Mollie had known Spring was going to warn her away from Logan again. Spring figured the girl's bringing him here today was a not-so-subtle message about Logan's growing importance to her. She was saying, "Back off." Spring wasn't sure she could.

"I could have called, I know," Mollie added. "But Logan and I were out riding around, talking, and we passed your house."

Spring patted her hand. "I'm glad you came by. Both of you." She studied the fading bruises on Logan's face. "You look as if you're healing fairly well."

"I guess." He stared glumly at the floor.

"Logan's going to see his brother," Mollie said, softly.

"Really?" Spring was surprised. She waited for details, but none were forthcoming in the awkward silence that followed.

Logan glanced at his watch. "I need to go, Mollie. I told him I'd be there at two."

The girl started to rise, but Spring stopped her, suggesting, "Why don't you go ahead, Logan? I'll make sure Mollie gets to work or home. Wherever she wants to go."

Mollie agreed, and Logan left, almost as abruptly as he had appeared.

Closing the front door, Spring asked her,

"What do you know about this meeting with John?"

The redhead shrugged, but Spring didn't buy for one minute that she didn't know why Logan was going to see his brother. Spring knew better than to press, however. The most important point was that she had Mollie alone without a class or a job or the girl's family calling her away. Spring invited her out to the kitchen for a leftover piece of the walnut cake her mother had sent home last night.

Once seated at the table, Spring wasted no time in asking, "You and Logan are seeing a lot of each other."

"Kind of."

"Last week, I didn't think you were really dating."

"It's changed. Sort of."

Spring sighed at the evasions. Of course, she had no right to be quizzing Mollie this way. No right except that she liked her so much, cared about her safety and welfare.

"Mollie, I can't tell you what to do—"

"Nobody's done that in a while, Miss DeWitt."

The gentle rebuke made Spring realize she had to stop talking to this girl as if she were a child. Mollie Stevens was more grown-up than many people twice her age. Which was one of the reasons Spring didn't understand why she wanted Logan. And she said so. "You and Logan," Spring told Mollie. "You just don't seem to go together. Or make sense."

"I didn't know love always made sense."

"You're in love with him?" Spring was dismayed. Mollie was wading in deeper than she thought.

"He's not like everyone thinks. He's smart, even though he tries to hide it. And he can be really sweet. Romantic."

This didn't match the picture Spring had formed in her mind of Logan, of the accusation of rape John had reported to her. "Mollie, he has a history of violence. Serious violence."

"I know some of the stories, Miss DeWitt. Some of them aren't even true."

"I'm sure that's what Logan has told you."

"He's also told me some of the bad stuff, the things he wishes he could change. He knows he has an attitude sometimes. He's trying to change. For the last few weeks, especially."

"Since the two of you got together."

Mollie clearly heard the challenge in Spring's tone. Her chin lifted. "I believe he can change. I can help him."

"Oh, honey." Spring wished there was some way to transplant all her hard-won wisdom with John into this girl's young mind. She put her hand on Mollie's arm, squeezing lightly. "Please don't put too much pressure on yourself to change Logan. He's really mixed-up, and he's in trouble over this fight."

"I believe what he says about that fight with Jeff Lott."

"But you didn't see exactly what happened."

"Logan wouldn't lie to me."

But lying was something he did quite well, according to his school records. Spring was very much afraid Logan was snowing this sweet, trusting girl the way he had snowed others through the years.

"Jeff's out of the hospital," Mollie added, nibbling at the last crumbs of her cake. "He says he doesn't remember much about what happened, but his parents are still really mad. They want the sheriff to do something."

"They could make a lot of trouble."

"I hope not." The girl sat forward, elbows on the table, chin cupped on her folded hands. "I think someone just needs to give Logan a chance. You have."

"That's different, Mollie. What you're doing is entrusting your heart to a boy who has proven he can be pretty immature."

"I'm not worried about being hurt. Logan really cares about me. And I can help him. Maybe his brother can, too."

Spring was intrigued by that observation. "John said Logan got really angry with him the other day. And abusive to you."

"I didn't appreciate the way he acted. I let him know it."

"And what did he say?"

"He was sorry for acting so weird to me, but . . ." Mollie frowned. "Logan's awful mad at his brother about something. I can't figure that out yet."

"There's a . . . history," Spring explained, proceeding cautiously. "They've never been much of a family."

"I know his mother is snob."

"Among other things."

"And his father sounds like a real jerk."

"Logan said that?"

"Not right out, but . . . I can tell. It's the way he talks about him. Sort of all mixed-up. Like I used to feel about my dad—my real dad."

Spring remembered that Mollie and Larry's biological father had deserted them when they were young. But by all accounts, their mother's second husband had been a good guy, a real family man.

As Mollie explained, "Sometimes I think I should be one of those girls who is all mixed-up about men. You know, looking for a father figure or something."

"But you're not?"

"My dad . . . he was my stepdad but I never called him that . . . he was really great. He treated me and Larry like we were his. With him around, I guess I figured out not every man has to be like my real dad."

"You were lucky," Spring said sadly, thinking of John's years with Sam Nelson's brutality. "I'm sorry you lost him."

"Me, too." Sighing, Mollie flipped a lock of red

hair over her shoulder. "I hope I can help my little sister remember all the good stuff about him."

"I'm sure you can."

Mollie sat back in her chair, her brow knitted. "There's one thing I'd like to ask you, Miss DeWitt—"

"After all this girl talk, I think you can call drop the Miss DeWitt routine and call me Spring."

Mollie agreed with a smile. "What I'm wondering is about you." She hesitated, then plunged ahead. "You and Logan's brother. Are you getting back together?"

Spring was silent, not sure where to start trying to explain or even if she should explain.

Taking their plates and forks, Mollie got up and put them in the sink. "I know I'm being nosy. My grandmother says that's my worst failing. But she's also the one who told me all about you and your husband, how you ran away together and got married when you were eighteen."

Mollie's dreamy tone told Spring there were stars in the young redhead's eyes. The sort of stars that occurred only once in your life, the first time you fell in love. That feeling, coupled with a story that sounded as romantic as Spring and John's, could turn the head of even a girl as sensible as this one.

"We did run away," Spring explained, choosing her words carefully. "And we were very much in love."

"But now you're not?"

The blunt question gave Spring pause.

"I'm sorry," Mollie said. "It's none of my business."

Slowly, Spring shook her head. She wanted Mollie to understand something of what had torn her and John apart. There was a lesson here. "Sometimes when you start out so young together, you change too much to stay married."

"Even if you're still in love?"

Spring nodded. "That's what makes it difficult. This would be easy if I didn't still love John. But I do. So it's hard to make the right decision."

Mollie's eyebrows drew together in a frown. "I've always thought that when you loved someone, everything would be easy."

"That's the way it is in fairy tales. Not real life."

"But maybe you'll work it out. I mean, if you really love someone . . ."

Once, Spring had been just as dreamy-eyed as Mollie. She had believed anything was possible with love. She had known she would love John forever, and because of that, they would always be together.

But that just wasn't true.

The rest of that day and evening, Spring waited for John to call. There was no reason to think he would seek her out, but if he had been the one to make the call, what she had to do would have seemed much easier.

She waited until nine that night. He didn't call. So she went to him.

His car was in the slot she expected at the

Lodge. A light glowed behind drawn curtains, but it took a long time for him to come to the door.

When he did, she could see he had been writing. His hair was standing on end, his shirt unbuttoned to reveal his smooth, muscular chest, his feet encased in slouchy white socks.

"I'm interrupting," she said, hesitating.

"Of course not." He drew the door back and gestured for her to come inside.

The room, more pleasant than he had described it, smelled of pizza and coffee. An open and half-empty cardboard box sat next to the sofa on a table, where the screen of his laptop also glowed. The television was on, but muted.

"You're working," Spring said unnecessarily.

"And watching the *Twilight Zone*."

"Without the sound?"

"It's a rerun."

"Aren't they all?"

"I keep hoping to see one I've missed."

The comment was so typically, completely *John* that Spring had to laugh.

He did, too.

Some of her nerves evaporated.

"How about some herbal tea?" he offered, walking toward the kitchenette.

"You have tea? A dedicated coffee drinker like yourself?"

"Frankly, I've had enough caffeine today for ten men. Your mother gave me some tea yesterday. Set me up with a jar of honey for sweetening, even a tea ball for steeping the leaves."

"It's probably the same as she gave me." Joining him by the small stove and sink, Spring took the small bag of leaves he held out. "Mama said it would stave off early-winter colds." She sniffed the fruity, faintly spicy scent of the tea she'd had this morning.

John put a pot of water on to boil and readied two chipped mugs.

"You're really setting up housekeeping here," Spring observed.

"I can't hoof it down to Ebbie's for every meal."

She glanced at his computer. "How's the work?"

He hesitated, sending her a sidelong glance.

"I really would like to know," she said, gently.

"It's . . . coming along."

"That all?"

"I just started this book. The characters don't feel like people yet."

"But it's the same main character as the other three novels, right? The drug dealer turned vigilante?"

"You think of him as a vigilante?" One hip braced against the counter, John crossed his arms and regarded her with a frown.

"He operates outside the law, trying to right wrongs."

"I think of him as operating with the law, just going where the police can't, taking the steps toward justice that technicalities and oversights keep them from taking."

"How can you be operating *with* the law when

you're going where it can't?" she argued. "M.J. is definitely a vigilante."

A slow smile spread across John's face.

"What?"

"You said his name. M.J. This is the first time I've heard you talk about him."

"That's not true," she retorted. "We've discussed him many times, discussed the books."

"Abstractly."

"John, that's not true."

"I was never even sure if you liked anything about the books, if you thought I could write worth a damn."

She couldn't believe what he was saying. "My God, I used to read your stories out loud from the paper, amazed at the way you put it all together so simply and straightforward, but with this . . . this . . . tension, I guess you'd call it. I always told you I loved what you did."

"That was the reporting."

"It's the same thing."

"Not to me. The fiction has always been different, more personal, more from *me*. When you read my books, you said you liked the plot, the setting, the theme. But I never got an emotional reaction from you. How did the writing make you feel?"

Afraid.

That word leapt into Spring's head with startling immediacy. Her first impulse was to cut it off, ignore it, never let him know how she felt. But she had decided last night, after her tears had dried, to stop running, once and for all. Today, she knew she had to follow through on that.

John was waiting, an expectant look on his face. So she told him.

"The story scared you?" he asked, confused.

"*You* scared me."

"Why?"

"Because you were so good, and you wanted success so badly."

John was silent, his gaze steady on hers.

Suddenly nervous again, Spring turned and paced the length of the room and back. She wanted to say this just right, to put into words the jumbled feelings and emotions that had become so clear to her over the past twenty-four hours.

Finally, she confessed, "You were right when you said I was jealous. I was. But not for the reasons you think, not because I thought you should have been saving the world instead of writing stories."

"Then why?"

"It's like I've said from the start, John. The writing took you away. But it was so good. There was so much power in the writing. I couldn't believe how good it was."

He pushed away from the wall as steam began to rise from the pot on the stove. "That's flattering."

"I wasn't surprised that you were good. But if you'll remember, you didn't talk about that novel, not the way we had always talked about everything we did, including your work. You kept it close to yourself and closed me out."

"You didn't seem interested. Even when that first novel sold and did well, you were removed from it, somehow. From the very first, when the editor called and talked to me about trying fiction, you weren't enthusiastic. You said the world was full of would-be novelists."

"That was because your first book, the nonfiction one, hadn't done what you hoped."

"What do mean? There was a movie offer."

"But it didn't get you Sam's approval."

The water on the stove boiled over, sizzling on the red coils of the burner. When John made no move to stop it, Spring foolishly grabbed the pot handle, jerked it off the eye, and burned her fingers in the process.

"Damn it, why did you do that?" John seized her hand in his, forcing her stinging fingers under the cold water from the tap.

"No," Spring protested. "You put butter on burns. Or warm, salted water. Cold water makes a blister."

He released her, cursing. "That's fine. Go ahead, take care of it yourself. You DeWitt women are so strong, so capable, so wise. You can take care of everything."

Spring knew he was talking about much more than a minor burn. And he was right. "Of course we can," she murmured. "We're fixers. *Rescuers*, remember?"

Ignoring her, John rifled through the contents of the tiny kitchen's cupboard and came up with a package of salt and a mixing bowl. "Here, fix your damn fingers."

Quickly, Spring poured some hot water from the pan into the bowl with the salt. She dampened a dishtowel with the mixture and wrapped it around her hand. Almost immediately, the salt began to draw the pain from the burn.

"Can I at least fix you some tea?" John demanded irritably. "Do you think I can do that?"

She got out of his way and sat down on the sofa. A few minutes later, John presented her with a mug of tea, aromatic and just sweet to the taste.

"Does that meet with your high standards?"

Spring sat back with a tired sigh. "Are we going to fight again, John?"

He took a long gulp of tea. "It seems to be what we do best these days."

"But what's left to say? I've already admitted you were right about everything. I was jealous and frightened because of your success with the writing, with something that seemed to exclude me so completely. I felt empty and really scared."

"And you started thinking having a baby would change things. But I didn't cooperate. So you left."

"That's a little simplistic, but . . ."

"But you still want a family. A baby."

Looking down at her mug of tea, Spring nodded.

"And I still don't."

Those were the facts. Just as they had been last week. And in June when she walked out of their life together. And five minutes ago. It was all spelled out like an accident report. She did this. He did that. They couldn't work it out. So they broke up. It was the formula for any average, garden-variety divorce.

So why did her heart still pump like a paddle boat when she tried to tell John a divorce was what she wanted?

The pumping image captured her imagination. Set it off in an erotic direction. Spring realized she was staring at John's mouth while he talked, though she wasn't hearing a word he said. She was thinking about the other, more exciting ways in which his lips could be occupied.

"Spring?"

Hearing her name, she tried to focus. "Yeah?"

"I said I spent the afternoon with Logan."

"I know." Shaking her head to clear it, Spring explained that Mollie and Logan had stopped at her place.

John continued, "He's a prime example of how parents can screw up a kid."

Spring wasn't having another conversation with John about how he would be a different parent from his own. There was nothing she could do to convince him. Much better to ask about Logan. "Did he talk to you at all?"

"Not much. I took him up to Devil's Point."

"Throw anything into the falls?"

"No, but I told him the story."

"I'm sure a smooth guy like him thought it was stupid."

"To tell you the truth, I'm not sure what he thought." John finished his tea and set the mug aside. "We're so different, Spring. It's hard to imagine we have the same blood running in our veins."

Spring closed her eyes, suddenly dizzy. Her own blood was rushing from her head. *Too fast*, she thought. And headed for all the wrong parts of her body.

When she looked up, John was studying her. And she knew that look. A sleepy, sexy, in-the-mood expression. The parts of her body so alive from the rush of blood responded much too strongly to that look.

He put out his hand and trailed his knuckles along her jaw. "Are you okay?"

"Yes."

"Really okay?" His voice dropped to a husky level. "Is there something I can get you. Do for you?"

He could, of course. He could make love to her. Right now. Right here. Just as he had in her dream this morning. Without thinking, she murmured, "What would you like to do?"

His eyes widened. "Everything."

Spring tried to keep her head on straight. She had come here set on asking for a divorce. So what was the matter with her now? Why couldn't she stand up and walk away, as she had the other day when he kissed her? They didn't need this.

So why did she reach out and take his hand? Why did she say, slowly, as seductively as possible, "Explain everything."

He lifted his hand and cupped her face, his thumb stroking across her lower lip. "First, I'd kiss you."

She leaned forward, until her mouth was close to his. "How would you kiss me?"

He demonstrated. Deeply. Soulfully.

Spring drew back. "What would come next?"

He cupped her breast.

"And then?"

He let his hand drift down between her breasts, her midriff, all the way to her crotch.

Feeling as if she was leaving her body completely behind, Spring thrust her pelvis against his fingers.

For months she had lived without John's touch. Without the feel of his long, smooth muscles moving against her body. Without the glide of his penis into her. In and out. But it seemed as if that was all she had been able to think of since they'd made love last Sunday.

And now, with his touching her, with this strange loss of control she was experiencing, Spring knew she was lost.

She tried one last time. She really did try to stop herself.

Divorce?
The word floated out of her head about as easily as John got her out of her jeans.

Chapter Fifteen

She made him pant.

And groan.

And very nearly beg.

All this without even getting naked.

By the time John got Spring halfway out of her clothes, he was almost gone, as out of his mind wanting her as he had been when they last made love.

Thankfully, Spring was just as crazy for him. She didn't wait for him to get undressed. Together, they got his essential clothes out of the way, and she crawled onto his lap, onto him.

He thought she climaxed instantly. Or sometime soon thereafter. He honestly couldn't say. Because it felt as if he exploded on his first slick, upward thrust.

And while those stars fell around them, he already wanted her again.

Maybe there was something to the celibate life John had led for five months. Perhaps it did something for his strength and stamina. Or time might have simply condensed, like the frames of a movie edited for television. For whatever reason, only moments after that first, earth-shattering orgasm, John picked Spring up and carried her to the bed.

Quickly, he got rid of his clothes. But slowly, with gentle reverence, he undressed Spring. She smiled at him all the while, with the sleepy, dazed eyes of a well-satisfied cat.

Lowering himself to her side, he whispered, "You're half-witch, I think."

"Only half?"

"Maybe all."

She turned to face him, her hand drifting down to his thickened, ready shaft. She stroked him once. Twice. "Does this feel like a spell you're under?"

"A magic wand?"

She laughed, pressing her face against his bare chest.

A wave of yearning went through him at that sound. Too many nights had gone by without Spring in his bed. Too many days without her laughter and her touch. What had they done to each other to have wasted precious time apart?

"Stop." She lifted her fingers to his face. "I don't know why or how, but I can feel your thoughts, John. Don't have regrets." She leaned forward, her mouth warm and eager against his own. "No regrets tonight."

He didn't question what she could feel or hear. He just lost himself in her.

He caressed the sweet, full curves of her breasts. Kissed the nipples that peaked and preened beneath his lips. He tasted her belly. Her thighs. Between them.

She moved and groaned and touched him everywhere.

When the tension was strung too tight to bear, he drew her leg over his and pressed himself deep into her. Face-to-face, watching each other, they found a rhythm, familiar and yet somehow new. It took them both where they needed to go.

Did John think this was wise? Probably not.

Could he have stopped himself from taking her? Absolutely not.

Holding Spring in the tingling, perfect moments after her body shattered around his own, he wondered how he had lived without her.

Tomorrow, after this night, how would he live again?

"Don't," Spring whispered again. "Don't think."

She fell asleep tucked as close against him as he could hold her.

Daylight sneaked through the crack in the curtains much too early the next morning. In those first, groggy moments of wakefulness, John lifted a heavenward plea that the night hadn't been a dream.

The woman at his side was his answered prayer.

Moving as carefully as he could, he rolled to his

side and looked down at Spring, sleeping still. There had never been a moment when John didn't think her beautiful, but in years of living and loving together, it was sometimes easy to forget, to stop really looking at her. So now he looked his fill.

Her ivory skin was stained with the slight flush of heavy sleep. Hair black as a midnight sky fanned across her pillow. Eyes, their color hung somewhere between the gray of a winter sky and the blue of Cuna Lake, fluttered open.

With a start, John realized Spring was awake and looking at him.

In shock.

"My God." She sat up, clutching the thin sheet over her breasts but leaving her back bare to his very interested regard. "John?"

Lazily, he braced himself up on his elbow. "You were expecting someone else?"

She glanced at him over her naked shoulder. "Did everything happen the way I think it happened?"

"Yeah. That and more." With a pleased chuckle, he drew a finger down her spine to the sweetheart curves of her bare bottom.

She wiggled away and twisted round to face him. "Good Lord, what have we done?"

"You want a play-by-play description?"

"John—"

"We could start with the first time we made love on the sofa. That was fast. How about the first time in the bed?"

"Would you stop?"

"I could remind you of exactly what you did with your sweet, sweet lips a few hours before dawn."

"John!" She smacked away the hand he had slipped under the covers. "Be serious for a minute. What happened here last night? One minute we were on the sofa, talking. Almost arguing, as usual. You made us tea . . ." Her eyes rounded as her words trailed away.

Her distress made him sit up, as well. "What is it?"

"Mama," Spring whispered. "The tea."

"What about it?"

"Mama drugged us."

"What? But that's stu—" John's protest died quickly, remembering the way arousal had first come over him. Like a landslide.

Spring threw off her sheet and stalked, adorably naked and furious, into the kitchenette. Seizing the plastic bag with the tea in it from the countertop, she tore it open and took a good, long whiff. "What the hell is this stuff? Some kind of mountain-grown aphrodisiac, I bet."

"I don't know," John murmured, rolling back on his side to enjoy the view she was so blithely presenting. "But if you want, you can rub it all over me. We can overdose together."

"I'd like to get hold of that meddling, nosy, bossy—"

"Watch out." Pretending fright, John covered

his head with his arms. "Better not say too much. Callie's probably listening. The roof could cave in. Go too far and we'll be heaving the 'Vette off over the falls at Devil's Point to make up for your nasty insults."

"But she had no right to do something like this."

He stretched, feeling the pleasant ache of muscles well used. "Come on, Spring, was it really all that awful?"

"But this is exactly what I didn't want to do."

"If your spirit hadn't been at least a little willing, would that magic tea have worked so fast?"

She flung the bag of tea to the side. "Just shut up, John. You're probably in cahoots with Mama. This is what you've been wanting from the minute you came to town."

"Longer than that."

Folding her arms across her breasts, as if she had just realized she was naked, Spring sent him a petulant look.

John folded back the covers in invitation. "Don't stand over there and freeze. Come back to bed."

"You know what will happen if I do."

"But hasn't the tea worn off?"

She took a deep breath. "Has it for you?"

Pushing the covers well down his hips, John said, "Come see for yourself."

She did. Twice more before they fell into another exhausted slumber.

* * *

About noon, John took a shower and made a run to Ebbie's for some sandwiches. While he was gone, Spring thought about leaving. She had a cat at home which was probably having a curtain-shredding fit. She had family at her parent's house whom she wanted to see one more time before the holiday weekend was over. And she had made a promise to herself that she was going to face the end of her marriage.

The rumpled sheets mocked her on this last point.

Some end.

Quickly, she took a shower, got dressed, and straightened the bed. John had said the motel had maid service every other day. She didn't know if that included today or not, but Spring could just imagine someone coming in, seeing her and this bed. The talk would be all over town.

And so what? You're married to the guy.

She was losing it. Truly losing it. And she had to get out of here. As soon as John got back.

But it was a mistake to wait. Because once he came back, with bags bursting full of thick steak sandwiches, Spring didn't want to leave.

She wanted to stay right here.

Snuggle with him on the sofa.

Fight with him over the french fries.

Hold on to him like they had never been apart.

Her decision to ask him for a divorce had disappeared about as quickly as the herbal tea she had washed down the drain of the sink.

The formula for divorce was still very valid. It was her will to do it that was gone.

Damn Mama, anyway.

"There's something I want to show you," John said when they had consumed the last morsel of food.

"Haven't you already shown me that?" Spring teased. "About six times since last night?"

He grinned, leaned over, and kissed her. "It's something else." He got up and crossed to the dresser, returning with a photo album he handed to her. "I found this at Debra's house. In my old room."

Spring was startled. "When were you there?"

He explained his Thanksgiving night visit, including the deal he had struck about pleading Logan's case to the sheriff. "Have you done anything about it?"

"If Logan shows up tomorrow afternoon, when we agreed to meet and talk again, I'll go to Kane on Monday and see what I can do. Maybe I'm crazy to think I can help him or that he'll talk to me about anything significant in his life, but I figured it was worth a try."

"Of course it is," Spring replied, beaming at him proudly. She had known he couldn't walk away from his half brother, no matter how hard he had protested. "He needs a sounding board other than Mollie. She's blind to his faults, I think."

John nodded. "And I'm not blind, at least.

When I look at him, sometimes all I can see are his faults. And then, there's a moment . . ." He shrugged.

"Do you believe Logan's version of that fight?"

John sat down beside her again. "Two days ago, I would have said no. Now . . . I'm not so sure."

"What's changed your mind?"

He leaned forward, hands clasped, looked ready to say something, then shook his head. "It's just a hunch. A feeling I have."

Spring held up the photo album again. "Anything to do with this?"

"This is about me."

Puzzled, she let him pull it out of her hands and open it up. A young man, startlingly like John, smiled up from the page. She gasped.

"My father," John said. "Johnny Clayton."

"You look just like him."

"Except for my mother's eyes."

Spring glanced from the photo to him and back. "I guess. It's hard to say. Without the military buzz cut, this could be you, a few years back."

"Look at this." Slowly, John turned the page.

A collage of snapshots showed a younger, softer-looking Debra mugging for the camera with John's father. The turn of another page revealed her pregnant, the man beside her with a smile wide and proud and loving. More startling, however, was the way Debra looked. All dreamy-eyed and maternal, her hands curved over her belly. And that was nothing compared to the way she looked holding a red-faced, tiny infant in her arms.

Incredulous, Spring went through the album, charting the first years of John's life. There were Debra and John's father, dressed up for a night out. With their son, in front of a Christmas tree. Holding him in a swing. Father and son, laughing into each other's eyes.

There was such love. Such warmth. It radiated from these pages. These images seemed to have nothing to do with the woman Spring now knew as Debra Nelson. She had morphed, somehow, into someone with the same features but an entirely different soul.

The album was only half-full. It ended abruptly. Much like Johnny Clayton's life had ended in a rice paddy halfway around the world.

Fighting her tears, Spring looked up at John. "Why have I never seen this before?"

John's smile was a bitter twist. "I barely remember it. Near as I can remember, Debra put it away about the time Sam started using me as his personal punching bag."

Spring slipped her hand into his. "I'm just glad you found it."

"I don't know if I'm glad or not."

"John, it's beautiful. You've always said you don't remember your father. This is a record. The only one you have."

"A record of what might have been? Maybe I'm better off not knowing there was once an alternative to Sam Nelson."

"Don't look at it that way. Just look at these pictures and know you were loved. Johnny Clayton loved you. Debra did, too."

"So what happened?" John took the album and slammed it shut with barely controlled rage. "Why'd she sell me out? Why'd she marry Sam?"

"You know why."

"But she had this." He thumped the album again. "What was Sam's money compared to this?"

"John—"

"Why don't I know anything about this man who sired me, Spring?"

"She wanted Sam to be your father. You've said that a hundred, a thousand times. She pushed you at him, over and over."

"But he didn't want me. Hard as I tried to please him, he didn't give a damn for me, right from the start. He didn't want another man's son."

"He was sick. Weak. Like anyone who has to prove his power over a child with his fists."

"It was more than that," John insisted. "When I looked at these pictures, I knew it was more. Sam hated me for something, hated me for being born."

Puzzled, Spring dropped her gaze to the album again. "Where do you get that from these pictures?"

"Because I can compare the pictures in this album to the ones in my head. To my memories of Sam. The things he said. The way he taunted me.

The names he called me. He wanted me humiliated. Crushed. And he damn near did it. Debra damn near let him."

"You were too strong for them. You got away."

"Yeah." A smile chased the shadows from John's face. "I got away. Because one day I walked into Ebbie's diner, and I looked into your face. You saved me."

"I wish that were true." If it were, they wouldn't be having this conversation. Sam Nelson wouldn't still be haunting John's life.

"But it is true. You know it is. You know it like you know there's magic between us. You feel it between us."

She drew away, resisting the temptation to let him persuade her that everything was fine.

John rubbed a weary hand over his face. "I think we've proven we can't stay away from each other, Spring. Let's take these feelings and ride them out of this town, just like we did once before."

"And what about the way you look over your shoulder?"

"What do you mean?"

"The way Sam and your mother hang on to you. I wish I could step back in time, figure out why he hated you, what motivated her—"

With a vicious curse, John slung the photo album to the floor as he stood. "Damn it, Spring, just stop it. Let it rest, for once and for all. Sam is dead, and Debra means nothing to me."

"You've been living for them all these years. Letting the mistakes they made rule your life."

"I lived for you. Spring." John stabbed the air for emphasis. "Only for you. I thought you felt the same way about me. Until you started changing the rules and walked out."

John's hands clenched into fists as he stood before her, swaying with the rage inside him. It frightened her. In the way his anger over a past that couldn't be undone had always terrified her.

He reached for her. "I want you, Spring. Just you. Let's go. Let's get out of here."

She went into his arms, as she always did. Throat thick with tears, she choked out, "I can't, John. I can't go back with you."

"Then be with me here."

Surprise rippled through her. "You'll stay here? In White's Creek?"

"Until I can't stand it. But only if you'll be with me."

"But John—"

He pressed his face against her hair. His heart beat hard against hers. "Last night, you told me not to think. Now I'm asking the same of you. Don't make any decisions now. And don't ask me for what I can't give you. Just let us be. Just for a while."

"And what will that do?"

"It'll stop the ache inside me. That's all I need for now."

Only a fool would give in. But Spring had never

claimed to be anything else when it came to John Nelson.

So she put her arms around him and held on.

But even as she met his kisses and reveled in the strength of his passion, Spring made herself a promise. She was going to find out why Sam had hated John.

She could try this one, last way, to rescue John from his past.

Chapter Sixteen

～ "So you and Spring, you back together or what?"

Logan's question was a good one, John thought. He wished he had the answer.

It was Saturday afternoon, just after Christmas. They were out at the DeWitt farm, on the heavily forested slope beyond the house, where Callie had sent them in search of water and a couple of smooth stones from a nearby creek. John hadn't bothered asking why. Since the aphrodisiac tea incident, which Callie had admitted to with something akin to glee, his respect for his mother-in-law's strange skills had grown quite a bit.

"Well?" Logan prompted John. "Are you back with your wife or not?"

That was a tricky question. He and Spring were sleeping together most nights. Had been since Thanksgiving. They took most evening meals together. They celebrated Christmas with her family. They had given each other gifts, made plans for New Year's Eve. Yesterday, they had gone to the movies with Mollie and Logan. But

they were still somewhere short of a reconcilia-
tion.

"I haven't moved in with her," he admitted to
Logan. Spring had thrown a fit at that. Rather
than disturb their uneasy truce, John had signed
on for weekly room rates at the Pine Cone Lodge.
He used it as an office and refrained from telling
Spring that it was a waste.

"Sounds complicated." Shaking his head,
Logan turned back to the worn path. "Women are
complicated."

"You got problems with Mollie?" John asked.
"You guys seemed okay yesterday."

"She's on me about my grades."

"What are you failing?"

"Chemistry."

That brought John up short. Logan advanced a
few steps down the path, then turned when John
didn't follow.

John started laughing.

"What's funny about me failing chemistry?"
Logan demanded defensively.

"It's not that," John hastened to reassure him.
"I just figured you for a science whiz."

"I hate it."

"I did, too. I failed chemistry. That's what got
me into trouble and home for my senior year in
high school."

Logan's eyes narrowed. "You got expelled for
cheating."

"Because if I failed that chemistry final, I knew
Sam would beat the crap out of me."

His brother swung around abruptly, turning away, as he always did when John talked about how Sam had treated him. But turning away was an improvement over the first couple of weeks of these brotherly outings, when Logan had hotly defended even the slightest criticism of his father. The more time they spent together and the more open John was about the abuse he had suffered, the more certain he became that Logan had been victimized as well.

Logan admitted nothing negative about Sam. But just as there had been desperation in his defense of Sam, there was now urgency in his avoidance of the subject. There was something there, John thought. Something had happened.

Following Logan through the cool, December air, John wondered when his brother and step-father's relationship had gone sour. John remembered Sam adoring his son. According to Debra, Logan's behavior and academic problems had disappointed Sam. And John knew firsthand Sam was a harsh taskmaster. But why hadn't Sam cut his true son some slack?

John might never know. The same as Logan might never admit to any abuse. Hell, John might not really be helping his brother by being so open. He had helped himself, however. Being honest about Sam felt good. Rediscovering the brother he had lost was even more gratifying.

There were still a long way from being bosom buddies. The boy had levels John could only guess at.

Last weekend, Mollie had reported to Spring that she and Logan hiked up to Devil's Point. True to the legend John had told him about, Logan had thrown a wrapped package over the falls. The girl didn't know what it contained, but she said Logan's manner creeped her out. When John brought it up, Logan had gotten angry about Mollie telling. John decided it was a subject best left alone.

The sound of rushing water cut through his thoughts. The creek was just ahead. It had rained a lot this past week, so it was no surprise the water was running off the mountains with such force.

Logan stooped at the creek's edge to fill the hollow gourd containers Callie had given him. No plastic for her. She said the water needed to be carried in something natural, to maintain its purity.

Looking up at John, Logan said, "What do you think she wants this for, anyway?"

He shrugged and bent over to dislodge a smooth, gray stone from the creek bank.

"I've heard people say she's a witch."

"Could be," John agreed.

Logan grinned. "I know a few people I'd like her to put a hex on."

"Ask her. Maybe she'll do it."

The boy just laughed. He seemed to like Callie. But then, she had that special way about her. The ability to look in your eyes and touch your hand

and make you feel safe. It was something John had a feeling Logan needed.

Logan cleared his throat and said, "Sheriff Kane came by last night."

"Oh, yeah?" John concentrated on unearthing a second stone.

"I'm not being charged."

John nodded. "He called me."

"You could have told me," Logan said, resentfully.

"I knew he'd let you know."

"He took his time about it."

"He told me Jeff's family finally backed off." John darted his brother a look. "I also hear you made peace with Jeff."

Shrugging, Logan said, "It's no big deal. We used to be friends. A few years ago, when we were kids."

"Jeff told the sheriff he had no hard feelings." John leaned over to rinse the mud from the rock, not looking at his brother. "I think you being man enough to go right up to Jeff went a long way toward making this all go away."

"It was Mollie's idea."

"But you did it. That took some guts."

"I just want everyone to shut up about that fight," Logan muttered, getting to his feet. "I'm tired of Mother yapping at me all the time, so worried about what people think of her for raising a criminal. She didn't care that the Lotts might sue us. She just didn't want people talking."

"That's how she is," John agreed, softly. "It used to really get to me."

"Still does, doesn't it?" Logan shot back, the faint trace of a jeer in his voice. There were times when he still seemed to delight in needling John.

John didn't rise to his bait. Instead, he admitted the truth. "Yeah, she bothers me. I guess she always will."

There was silence from Logan. The only sounds were the rushing of the water and the sighing of the winter wind through the pines.

John took in a lungful of the fresh air and admitted to loving the beauty of this place. He and Spring had come here often when they were dating. They had made love here once, back among the trees, on a bed of moss and pine needles. John had been scared to death her mother or father would come strolling by and catch them. Spring had laughed and done a slow striptease for him, like a naughty wood nymph. Soon enough, he had forgotten to worry about being surprised by her parents or anyone else.

He smiled at the memory. Maybe tomorrow they needed to come back up here. If sex could solve the problems in their marriage, they'd be just fine.

He freed a third rock and washed it clean, only then glancing up at his brother.

Logan was watching him, a pensive look on his face.

"Something wrong?" John asked.

"I was just wondering . . . about my father and you . . ."

John went still, waiting.

Logan took a deep breath. His voice was rough. "I wondered. Did you ever think of fighting back?"

John took his time answering. "Of course I thought about it."

"But did you do it?"

It was hard admitting, man to man, what John had to admit. But he had promised himself he would never lie to this kid. So he shook his head. "I didn't, Logan. I always took it. No matter what he dished out, I took it."

Swallowing hard, John added, "But in my dreams, sometimes still, I hit him back. Hard."

In Logan's nod, in his somber expression, there was understanding. But he said nothing.

Quickly hefting the two gourds he had filled for Callie, Logan turned back to the path. "Better get these to the witch's pot," he quipped, though there was no laughter in his voice.

It was a few moments before John felt steady enough to pick up the rocks and follow him.

Back at the farm, Callie met them at the edge of the woods. She lifted her quicksilver gaze to meet John's. Her warmth reached deep inside him as she framed his face with her hands.

"Someday," she promised. "Someday soon, it will stop hurting so much."

He hoped she was right.

Turning to Logan, she grasped the handle of

one of the gourds. "Come on, you sweet young thing. I'll show you how to make cough syrup from fresh water and cherry bark."

"How about a love potion?" Logan said.

Callie darted a sly look over her shoulder at John. "You might want to ask your brother about that one."

John laughed, the pain in his chest easing with thoughts of Spring and a very special tea.

Willa Dean had a secret fantasy.

It wasn't something she could tell anyone. Not her husband of fifty years. Not her sister who lived in Nashville. Not anyone who knew her as a scrupulous housekeeper and a cook on par with anyone in the Ladies Aid Society of the Baptist church.

Secretly, Willa would just as soon eat out every meal of the day.

She knew such thoughts weren't fitting for a Christian woman who prided herself on frugality and simple living. But she allowed herself to admit it privately. She just plain loved sitting down to a meal someone else had made, at a table someone else would clear, off dishes someone else would wash.

That was the reason she didn't hesitate one minute when Spring DeWitt Nelson called her up and invited her to Saturday lunch at Ebbie Ruth's place.

Now, Willa knew Spring flat couldn't stand her. Willa hadn't made much secret about her feelings for Spring or her weird mother, either. Willa knew going to Ebbie's with Spring on a Saturday would guarantee most folks in town would see them and set their tongues a-wagging. But she also figured Spring could tell her something a might bit interesting.

Like how come John Nelson's car was seen most nights at the little white house Spring was renting, although he hadn't given up his room at the motel.

Willa would like to hear that story, that's a fact. Eating out was just icing on the cake.

To her dismay, upon reaching the diner, she found that Ebbie herself, Willa's chief rival for the choicest bits of information in town, was going to lunch with her and Spring.

Worse still, all Spring wanted to talk about was old news. Very old news. About John's mother and daddy. *Both* his daddies.

Just after the waitress poured their iced tea, Spring produced an old high-school yearbook. It fell open to a page near the front. And there was Debra White, with her two beaux, Johnny Clayton and Sam Nelson.

"My, my." Clucking, Ebbie picked up the book and peered at the black-and-white photo of the beauty queen flanked by the two handsome young men in their football uniforms. "I had forgotten she was so pretty back then."

"She's still pretty," Willa put in. "Doesn't look a day over forty, though everyone knows she's fifty." Darting a look around the restaurant, she leaned forward and whispered, "I hear she's had some work done on her chin."

"Her nose, too," Ebbie added, not to be topped.

"You don't say." Spring let her eyes go wide, wondering why it had taken her two weeks to think of appealing to the two people in White's Creek who knew everything about everybody.

After several sessions studying the photo album John had found, Spring had become even more curious about his father and mother's relationship. She knew she couldn't ask Debra and expect a straight answer. Only days ago had she thought of looking for clues in these old yearbooks at the school library.

She had been startled to see Debra, Sam, and John's father together in photo after photo, all through their high-school years. She had asked her mother and father if they knew anything about the relationship among the three attractive and popular young people. Of course, they knew nothing, having made it a habit of ignoring just about everything that didn't concern them or their family directly.

That couldn't be said for Ebbie Ruth Denison and Willa Dean. So Spring had invited them both to lunch.

"Johnny Clayton was a handsome devil," Ebbie said, still peering at the picture.

Willa practically took the yearbook away from her. She studied the photo in question over her glasses. "I say Sam was the handsome one. Remember the way he dressed? Even as a boy, he was always turned out just so."

"He had money to dress," Ebbie observed dryly. "What did Johnny have?"

"His family was poor?" Spring asked, settling back in anticipation of a good story.

"They lived up in Rooster Holler." Willa's long, thin nose wrinkled. "A tar-paper shack."

"But Johnny's daddy was an honest worker." Ebbie took a sip of her tea. "He did some carpentry work for me on this place once. Didn't try to beat me on it 'cause I'm a woman, like some men do."

Willa agreed with Ebbie's assessment of the elder Clayton's character. "He would have been better off if he hadn't married Johnny's mother."

"She was sickly," Ebbie explained to Spring. "She died with her second baby. A boy it was."

"So John has an uncle somewhere?" Spring asked.

"He's been gone a long time." Ebbie's brow creased. "Willa, did he go off before or after Johnny died?"

"Before," the other woman said with frank disapproval. "He didn't even come back for Johnny's funeral. With his brother a war hero and all, you'd have thought he would come for that."

Sadness touched Ebbie's faded blue eyes. "I remember that funeral. It rained to beat the band."

"And Debra sat up there at the Methodist

cemetery, under an umbrella, until Sam went up and took her home."

"Sam took her home from the funeral?" Spring was intrigued by that information.

The two old gossips traded looks and giggled just as the waitress set their lunches in front of them.

Once their meals were in place, Spring demanded to know why they had laughed.

Again Willa sent a suspicious look around the restaurant, as if she was scared she was going to be overheard. "If you must know, Debra had a hard time deciding between Sam and Johnny. I guess it was natural that Sam moved right in after Johnny got killed in Vietnam."

Ebbie disagreed, vehemently. "Willa Dean, she didn't have a hard time. She was in love with Johnny Clayton from day one. Anybody with eyes could see that."

"But she loved Sam's money, too."

Conceding that point, Ebbie added, "I guess you couldn't blame Debra for thinking money might be the safest course. After all, her family used to be rich."

"By the time she was born, they were in a decline," Willa said, slicing into the crust of her chicken pot pie. As aromatic steam rose from the plate, she grinned. "Being poor didn't keep Debra from having airs."

"Being rich hasn't kept her from much, either," Ebbie claimed with a hearty chuckle.

"Wait a minute," Spring said, holding up a

hand. "Start from the beginning. From when both Sam and Johnny were courting Debra."

The story was simple enough. Debra White was the prettiest girl in town. Her family, who had founded the town, was broke, and she was the last of the line.

Johnny was the star of the football team and her main date.

Sam Nelson was a somewhat less talented athlete whose father happened to own two textile mills, a paper mill, half the buildings in downtown, as well as the big house where Debra resided today. The Nelsons were new money, Midwesterners who had come to Georgia after the Civil War and made a fortune. Ebbie thought Sam's daddy, a tough little bull of a man, wanted Sam to marry Debra because of her lineage. He thought she would add Southern gentility to the family.

But Debra married Johnny. He went to Georgia Tech on a football scholarship until she got pregnant. He dropped out and couldn't find a decent job. Finally, he enlisted in the service. And died.

"And Debra married Sam," Spring whispered.

"Six months after the funeral," Ebbie said.

Willa sniffed. "But they were living together before that. Everybody knew it."

"Debra was torn up bad after Johnny died." Bright red curls bounced as Ebbie shook her head. "She couldn't look after herself, much less her baby."

"Sam took over," Willa said. "Adopted your

husband, Spring. Treated John as if he was his own." She cut her eyes around a bit, her lips pursed. "Of course, then you and John up and married. I guess Sam thought you were too young, and that's why he cut John out."

The lift in Ebbie's eyebrow and the look in her eyes told Spring she might not share the other woman's generous opinion of Sam Nelson. "The man had a mean side to him."

"Folks did say he could be hard to work for." Willa buttered the last corn muffin thoughtfully. "He didn't take much nonsense. Of course, I hear Debra stands for even less."

"That's true," Ebbie agreed. "When Sam died, a lot of people thought she would hand over the running of the businesses to somebody else. She didn't, though. My oldest is a supervisor at the paper mill. Debra may not be down there all the time, but everyone knows she's the real boss."

Willa nodded her approval. "She's right to keep her finger in the pie. I imagine that's what Sam told her he wanted done. She is looking out for his son's birthright."

"I always wondered what Sam really thought about getting Debra secondhand," Ebbie said. "There are plenty of men who set some store by being the first."

"Goodness gracious." Willa's sallow cheeks turned pink. "Ebbie, how you do talk. Sam and Debra Nelson were married a good long time. They seemed happy to me."

Which only showed how little this old gossip

bothered to look below the surface, Spring thought. Spring believed the sturdy diner owner had made a very good point about Sam. She also thought Ebbie knew a lot about him that she wasn't telling.

"What's all this about, anyway?" Willa asked, settling back from her empty plate. "You researching John's family tree, Spring?"

"Something like that."

Ebbie pulled her considerable bulk from her chair with a sigh. "Sorry to break this up, ladies. But I've got work to do. I'll send over some dessert."

Once she was gone, Willa leaned forward, conspiratorially. "Spring, dear, I can tell you some stories Ebbie doesn't know. About Debra's family. Both her parents were drunks, you know."

Spring listened, because she figured everything she learned about Debra had some bearing on the way the woman had treated her son. But it was the relationships between Debra, Johnny, and Sam that she knew lay at the heart of what she needed to know. She had that pretty well figured out.

Later, after Willa had been fed some sweet potato pie and sent on her way, Spring went looking for Ebbie again. She found the older woman smoking a cigarette and running a calculator at a rickety old desk in her tiny, crowded office.

"I figured you'd want to talk some more,"

Ebbie muttered. She gestured for Spring to sit down in a chair in front of the desk.

"I want to know everything you can tell me about Sam Nelson."

Ebbie blew out a stream of smoke. "This isn't genealogy research, is it?"

Spring laid her cards on the table. "There are some things John has never been able to put behind him about his stepfather. I'm trying to help him."

"Sam was a bastard." Ebbie's generous mouth twisted around the words. "And I don't care what that old crone Willa says, I know he and Debra were miserable."

"How?"

"He had other women." Ebbie tapped her cigarette against a clay ashtray in the shape of a child's hand. "He had my daughter, for one. Not the daughter who lives here. The other one that I haven't seen for a while. Sam gave her the money to get out of town." The pain in the woman's face was palpable.

Spring eased back in the chair, releasing a pent-up breath. "I'm sorry, Ebbie."

"It's okay," she said stoutly. "She was wild. Sam was one of many men. But as far as I can tell, he was the only one who got his jollies by cracking her ribs."

"You're right about him," Spring told her. "He was a bastard. The worst kind."

"I knew he wasn't good to John, no matter what kind of front he and Debra liked to put up for everybody." Ebbie's voice deepened to a disgusted growl. "The kind of man Sam was, no way could he be good to another man's child."

"Or any child," Spring murmured. "Even his own."

Ebbie didn't seem too surprised at the implications of that remark. "When a man's mean, he's mean to most everybody. I've got it figured about the only person Sam didn't work over was Debra. I think that because she's hard and selfish as they come. She turned that way the day she buried Johnny, and she would have killed Sam if he bruised her lily-white self."

"I think you're right." Thoroughly disgusted by all she had discovered, Spring started to rise from her chair.

"Tell John one thing," Ebbie said quietly, before Spring reached the door. "Tell him his real daddy was a good person. Kind and generous. The kind of man who would have been a good father."

"I think John's always known that," Spring replied. "Somewhere, back in his mind, he remembers Johnny Clayton."

"I see his daddy in John."

"I'll tell him you said so." Spring managed a sad smile for Ebbie before she left.

Outside the diner, in the cold sunshine of the year's final Saturday, Spring wondered whether anything she had learned was going to make a difference to John. Knowing his stepfather and real father had been rivals for Debra's love explained the basics of why Sam had seemed to hate him so. Beneath Ebbie and Willa's not-quite-impartial observations were the facts.

But there was only one person who could explain the true reasons why Sam's hate had been used against an innocent child. That was the woman who had stood by and allowed it to happen.

It was time Debra was called to task for her sins.

Chapter Seventeen

～ Spring knew getting John to willingly go to his mother would be about as easy as leashing a mountain lion. So she brought Debra to him.

Sunday evening John went to the door and found her standing on the porch at Spring's house.

In the hall behind him, Spring released a pent-up breath. She hadn't known until this moment if Debra was going to show up. Spring had issued an invitation for drinks, insinuating she was having a number of people over. Debra had made no promises, but Spring had counted on simple curiosity to propel the woman here. She had been right.

Now, Spring stepped around John to greet her. John gave her a sideways glance and said nothing to Debra.

She looked uncertain, an unusual twist. "Did I misunderstand you, Spring? You did ask me to come over tonight, didn't you?"

"Yes, I did." Spring ignored John's glare. "Please come in."

Though her eyes narrowed in suspicion, Debra came into the house and greeted John. His reply was little more than a grunt.

Spring led Debra into the living room. A cheery blaze burned in the fireplace. The Christmas tree was still decorated in a corner by the front window. Colored lights twinkled. Pine scented the air.

It was a homey scene, marred only by Basil, who rose to his haunches in front of the fire and hissed in Debra's direction. Spring sent him a look, and he slunk, teeth bared and eyes glittering, to a spot beneath the tree.

Debra gave the cat a wide berth, taking a seat on the sofa. Somehow, Spring got through the next awkward moments. She sent John to the kitchen for a glass of wine for his mother. He escaped gladly, leaving Spring to make chitchat with Debra until he returned.

Even then, Spring kept up a stream of innocuous talk for several moments, managing to cover for John's continued silence. She thought Debra was lulled into thinking this was a purely social evening, and she was simply the first guest to arrive.

That's when Spring went over to the desk and picked up the photo album John had taken from his childhood room. Flipping it open to the first page, the photograph of Johnny Clayton, she held it out to Debra.

The woman went rock still. She looked at the picture, then up at Spring.

"I want you to tell John about him," Spring said. "About his father."

John stood, protesting. "This is ridiculous, Spring. Is this why you got her here?"

"I think it's time you heard some things about your father," Spring told him. "I want Debra to tell you."

Debra set her wineglass on the end table. Her eyes were hard. "John is right. This is ridiculous."

"What's wrong?" Spring asked. "Are you afraid to talk about Johnny Clayton?"

"There's nothing I can say."

"Then let me start." In the most succinct words Spring could choose, she relayed the information she had about Johnny, Debra, and Sam. John, who tried to interrupt her at first, soon fell silent. Debra just sat there, her face set.

In the quiet after Spring's recitation of the facts, John stared at his mother. "Were you involved with Sam when my father was in Vietnam?"

The question brought Debra to her feet. "Of course not," she denied hotly.

John didn't looked convinced. "That's the way it sounds."

"I loved your father!" That declaration, filled with anguish, ripped from Debra. She looked almost as surprised by it as Spring felt. Hand going to her throat, she took a step backward, stumbling against the sofa.

Spring reached out and grabbed her, letting the photo album fall to the floor. Debra gave her a dazed look and jerked her arm away.

"I don't want to talk about this," she said, her voice strangled. "There's nothing to talk about."

"But there is," Spring protested. "If you loved John's father, why did you marry Sam so soon after he died?"

"I don't have to explain myself to you." Recovering her habitual poise, Debra headed toward the hall.

But John blocked her path. "Explain it to *me*, Debra." She tried to sidestep him. He took hold of her arm. "If you were so in love with my father, how could you trade me, his son, for Sam's money?"

"You don't understand," she said tightly. "You can't understand what I went through."

"Then explain it." John now gripped both of her arms. His face was crimson with anger. "Tell me. Make me understand."

A muscle flinched in Debra's cheek, but there was defiance in the set of her jaw, in the sound of her voice. "I was alone. Completely alone. Your father was dead. And my family . . ." Her laugh was bitter. "They were no help. My father was dead, my mother was drinking herself into the grave. Neither of them had ever done anything much for me. The only person I cared about was gone."

"But what about me?" The hurt in his eyes tore at Spring's heart. "What about your son?"

"You were a baby," Debra snapped. "Helpless. I didn't know how I was ever going to raise you."

"People raise children alone all the time," John

muttered. "They get jobs and they take care of their own."

"I was devastated. *Alone.* I didn't know what to do."

"That's crap, and you know it." John released his mother, almost shoving her away. "You wanted the good life. That's why you married Sam. That's why you stayed with him, even after he . . ." Voice breaking with emotion, John turned away, toward the fire, as if he couldn't stand looking at her any longer.

Debra could have left then, beat a fast retreat to the front door. Spring gave her credit for standing her ground. Eyes flashing, fists clenched at her sides, she said, "I did what I thought was right, John. Sam said he would take care of me. Of you."

John wheeled back to face her. "He took care of me, all right. He beat and bullied me, and you stood by. You let him. How could you let him? How could you, *Mother?*"

The plea in his voice got to Debra. Her cool mask slipped. She stepped forward, her hands outstretched. "John . . . Johnny, I'm . . ." The hand she lifted to her temple trembled. "It was me Sam wanted to hurt. Because I married your father. It wasn't you. It was never you—"

"But I'm the one he beat!" John roared. "How did that hurt you?"

"You were my son," Debra exclaimed. "You were mine and Johnny's son. Don't you see? By hurting you, Sam *was* hurting me."

"Then why did you stay?" Spring demanded, unable to sit still in the face of such twisted reasoning. "You should have taken John and gone."

"You don't understand," Debra insisted. "I tried to make Sam happy. I tried to have a family with him. I kept thinking it would get better, that he would forget about Johnny or least think I had forgotten him."

She turned pleading eyes to her son once again. "I tried to give him a son of his own. I knew that would make a difference. I miscarried again and again. And then I had Logan—"

"And Sam just hated me more," John muttered.

Debra closed her eyes, swaying on her feet. When she looked up again, her pretty face was drawn and pale. Quietly, she said, "I wish it had been different, John."

It was no apology. However, Spring suspected it was as close as Debra could get.

The woman left without another word, snatching her coat and purse from the back of a chair and slamming the door behind her.

John stayed where he was. Motionless.

A log fell in the fireplace.

A bell on the tree jingled as Basil slipped from his hiding place. He crossed the room and rubbed his whiskers against the leg of John's black jeans.

It seemed to Spring that both man and cat turned to her with equally accusatory eyes.

"What was the point of this?" John asked, his voice low and furious.

Spring clasped her hands together. "I wanted you to face her, put her on the spot, demand some answers. This conversation was long overdue."

"And what purpose did it serve?"

"You always wondered why Sam hated you so much. I think that's a little clearer."

"But it doesn't change anything that happened."

She stepped forward. "Of course it doesn't. Nothing can change how he treated you or how Debra allowed it to happen. But surely knowing more about this can give you some peace."

"Peace?" John repeated. "You think knowing all of this gives me peace about my past?"

"It's a start, John, a—"

"This was for you. You set this whole thing up for yourself."

She scowled, confused by his accusation.

John came closer. "You think you can mend my family. You pushed me toward Logan. Now you're trying to smooth things between me and Debra. You want me to believe there can be a magic circle in that house of Sam Nelson's."

"That's not true," Spring denied. "I know you can never forgive Debra. I don't expect that."

"What you expect is that I'll have all these warm, nice thoughts about what my family could have been. You think that's going to make me want a family of my own."

Spring swallowed hard, shocked to realize he had seen her intentions even clearer than she had seen them herself. She had started out trying to bring some healing to the scars of John's past. But, unconsciously, perhaps she had also wanted to change him, make him adapt to the changes that had occurred in her since she had begun to want a child. She wanted, fiercely, to make them fit as they had at the beginning of their marriage.

She reached out and took John's hand. "Things could have been different. Your father and Debra started out on the right track. They loved each other. You came out of that love."

"That doesn't change how it ended up. That doesn't make me want to take a chance on bringing a child into this world."

"Children aren't chances. They're gifts."

"Like I was a gift?" Turning from her, John spied the photo album she had dropped earlier. He picked it up and rifled through the pages to the last snapshot of him laughing into his real father's face. He held it up. "You look at that, Spring. Look at that, then remember how it turned out. Remember how Fate smacked me and him for a loop."

"But you would never make the choices Debra made," Spring protested. "I would never make those choices."

"And if we were both gone? What would happen to our child then?"

"My family—"

"Might fail," John shouted. "They just might fail, Spring. For all their good intentions and all their love, if you and I were gone, our child could fall through the cracks. Like I did. Like Logan has.

How can you doubt that, knowing me? How can you think otherwise, seeing what you see through your work?"

Spring's eyes widened. "Is that the real reason you don't want a child? Because you might die and leave him? That's crazy. You can't live like that. You can't—"

"Yes, I can." John jabbed his finger at the picture of his father. "I bet this man didn't think he was going to die at twenty-two. I bet he didn't dream he wouldn't raise me. And if he had known what would happen . . ." John's voice broke. "If he could have seen what would happen, I'm sure he would have kept me from being born."

Spring started a protest that John wouldn't allow. He didn't want to hear any more. He was tired of talk. More than that, he was tired of the limbo the two of them had been living in.

He summed it up in blunt, harsh terms. "You want a child I won't give you, Spring. If that's what the marriage comes down to, then it's over. Those are my terms. Take them or leave them."

John couldn't give her a chance to answer. He knew, deep in his heart, what she would decide.

He couldn't hear that now. Not tonight. Not with the tragic, twisted story of his parents still whirling in his head. Spring was right to think John saw the possibilities of the family that might have been. He had lost so much.

And now he was losing Spring.

That knowledge sent him hurtling out into the cold, dark night.

In the middle of the next afternoon, Callie appeared at Spring's door. Her face was drawn, older somehow. She carried a basket of cinnamon muffins. And she sat for a long time on the sofa, just holding her baby girl as she cried her heart out.

Spring wanted a child. And she wanted John. But she couldn't have both. He had made that clear.

Their other problems could be solved, Spring said. They still loved each other. That love could bridge the gaps that years of marriage, maturing, and change had brought to them. But love alone couldn't fill her womb. That need was as old as time, as real as her tears, as powerful as the moon's pull on the tides. It left Spring with no choice.

"Give me a cure, Mama," Spring said, when her tears were spent. "Dandelion tea or an herbal salve."

"I wish that would help, Daughter." With hands that had been taught to work and heal and soothe, Callie stroked the blue-black hair she used to plait into braids when Spring was a child. She wished that somewhere in the medicine some called magic that she had a tonic to ease the pain her child was enduring.

Spring sighed and laid her head back on

Callie's shoulder. "You disappoint me, Mama. I thought you could fix everything."

"Me too, Spring darling. Me too."

Chapter Eighteen

White's Creek had never seemed uglier to John than it did on that leaden New Year's Eve afternoon.

The sky was gunmetal gray. Heavy. Threatening. The forecasters said freezing rain and sleet would move into the mountains late that night. John thought of the partygoers who would disregard that prediction and climb into cars, and shivered. He could feel the tragedies gathering in the damp, cold wind.

He should be on his way to Atlanta, ahead of the bad weather. In truth, he should have left two days ago. He had packed his clothes, his computer. He was ready to shake the last, lingering trace of this place from his heels.

He hated admitting he had waited for some word from Spring. He knew what she wanted. Her silence said everything. They could talk out the details through the lawyers.

He figured he should go out to say good-bye to Ned and Callie. He owed them that much. But no matter how many times he repeated that to himself, he couldn't get up off his lumpy motel bed and drive to the farm. He couldn't face looking into Ned's kind eyes or feeling Callie's warm embrace.

But one thing he had to face. He had to tell Logan good-bye.

Funny, how that twisted his gut. He didn't know if anything he had said or any of the time he had spent with his brother had really made any difference. But John knew it had changed him, made him feel a little less alone. He never expected to feel this way.

Before the day faded, John pulled himself up and drove to Debra's house. He remembered his first night back in town, when the fog had turned the landscape spooky. Today, that house just looked like what it was—a cold, and rather sterile, wealthy person's home. He parked behind Logan's car in the drive.

Inside, the place was aflutter. Flowers were being arranged. Champagne flutes unpacked. Funny hats and paper streamers set out. Debra was giving a party.

She looked like a girl, John thought, when she fluttered down the stairs. In a soft yellow robe, her makeup just right, her diamond earrings already in place, she was the debutante before the ball. Giddy and expectant. Happy as only she could be when the occasion was social, and she was the center of attention.

He wasn't surprised that she could act as if their

Sunday night conversation had never taken place. Confronting reality had always been beyond Debra's capabilities.

John was beyond caring about this woman. Sunday night's conversation had accomplished that for him. Spring had been right about his gaining at least that small measure of peace.

Now, John asked Debra, "Where's Logan?"

"Upstairs. In one of his moods. I think he had an argument with that girl he's seeing."

Her tone set John's teeth on edge. *"That girl* is Mollie Stevens. She's a very nice girl."

She brushed his rebuke aside with one perfectly manicured hand. "I know her name. She's been around. Like a little mouse. I don't think she's right for Logan."

"You should be thanking God he has a girl-friend instead of being in jail, playing fuck-me games for some big, horny bastard who's doing ten to twenty-five for grand theft."

Debra gasped, flushing beneath her makeup. "There's no need to talk to me that way, John. I know just what you think of me."

"So you admit that?" John demanded. "You admit to yourself that I despise you?"

There could have been a flash of regret in Debra's face. But her poise didn't slip as it had Sunday night. "I know your feelings and I accept them, but I'd like us to at least be civil if you're going to be staying here in town and spending time with Logan."

"That's just it—I'm leaving."

"With Spring?"

He didn't answer, turning toward the stairs instead. Logan stood halfway down, hands stuffed in the pockets of loose jeans, his face sober. "So you're going," he said.

"I came to say good-bye to you."

"Okay." Logan nodded, a muscle working in his jaw. "I'll be seeing you."

That wasn't enough. Not nearly enough. John thought they had gotten beyond this stiffness. He wanted more. As he had told Spring, his family would never hold the magic of hers, but he wasn't willing to just walk away from Logan.

"You can come and see me, you know," John told his brother, stepping forward. "You're welcome to come to Chicago. Anytime."

"Is Spring going with you?"

John shook his head, unwilling to attempt any sort of explanation.

That, at least, got a real response from Logan. "Jeez, man. You blew it, didn't you?"

"We've got problems we can't work out."

Logan just shook his head.

John held out a card. "This is my number. Call me anytime you want. Collect."

Behind him, Debra said, "Really, John. We can pay our phone bills, you know."

He jerked around, suddenly so sick of her that he couldn't stand it. "I know that, *Debra*. Paying the bills is the only thing you've ever concerned yourself with."

A maid who had come in from the living room stared at them with round, startled eyes.

With false sweetness, Debra asked him, pointedly, "Aren't you going, John?"

He turned back to Logan. He walked up the stairs and stuck his card in the pocket of the boy's shirt. Quietly, so Debra couldn't hear, John said, "You call me, all right? You tell me if it gets to be too much here. If you need me . . ." Leaving that hanging, he went down the stairs and out that familiar front door. For the last time.

John was at his car when he heard Logan call his name.

The boy came through the door like a tornado. He ran right up to John and tore up his card in his face.

"I don't need you," Logan shouted.

John wasn't about to argue with him now. He turned away. "I'm in the book if you do."

But Logan pulled him back. "When I needed you, you weren't here."

"What do you mean?"

Logan put his hands against John's chest and shoved. "You left me, you bastard! You left me here with them. With *him!*"

John stumbled back against his car, something in his chest giving way at the devastation in the boy's eyes. It had come at last—the confession Logan had been running from. John reached out, trying to catch his brother. All he could think is that he needed to put his arms around him and hold on.

Eluding him, Logan backpedaled. "Didn't you know what would happen? Didn't you figure out he'd turn on me, too?"

"But you were his boy, *his.*"

"That didn't matter." Tears were streaming down Logan's face. "Didn't you know it wouldn't matter?"

John had no chance to explain he had thought it mattered. Logan ran to his car. And was gone.

As the engine faded, John turned back to the house. Debra stood on the porch, her yellow robe rippling in the cold wind.

He strode up on the porch and took her by the shoulders. "How could you?" he whispered. "I know your excuse for what he did to me. But what about Logan? Why'd you stand for that?"

"I didn't know what to do," she said. "Sam kept promising he would change. I just kept hoping—"

"And living in his house and spending his money. That made it easy to look away, didn't it?"

"I've tried to make it right," she told him. "When Sam was gone, I tried to get Logan some help. I let him go to school here, like he wanted. I kept him out of trouble. I gave him the things he needed and wanted—"

"Yes, you gave him plenty," John cut in. "Everything but what a kid deserves. Everything but love and protection—"

"I did the best I could!" Debra shouted. "I did all I knew how to do for both of you."

Disgusted, John shoved her back into the door,

back against the house she had sold her sons to possess.

He had no time to listen to her excuses.

Logan was in trouble. John knew that deep in his gut. He had to find him.

Now.

John drove around for hours, sweeping up and down the same streets and out on country roads. He called Mollie. Callie and Ned. The sheriff's office. There was no sign of Logan.

At Debra's house, the party was in full swing, just as if her youngest son wasn't off somewhere, trying to run his fury out in a fast car on slick roads.

Finally, in desperation, John went to Spring.

She didn't want to let him in when she first answered the door. Then he told her what had happened. And she took him in.

Like always.

They sat in silence, waiting for the phone to ring, for someone to tell them Logan had been found and he was fine.

In the quiet gloom, sleet clicked against the windows.

John put his head in his hands. "Why didn't I see it before I left here, Spring? Sam was a brute. Why didn't I see he would hurt Logan?"

"For all the reasons you tried to tell him," she said gently. "You thought Sam hated *you*, just you."

"He just needed someone to control."

"Because he couldn't control your mother."

Standing abruptly, John stared at the phone. "Come on, damn it. Ring. Somebody find that kid."

"You're awfully concerned about a boy you didn't even want to see six weeks ago."

"I feel responsible for him."

"John, when you and I left here, we were really young. I don't think we could have seen what would happen to Logan."

"I know that. I wish I could change it, but I know I was just doing the best I could for myself by getting away, once and for all. What I blame myself for is today, for not stopping Logan."

"He wouldn't have let you."

"I should have handled this differently. I know Logan's a powder keg, always ready to explode. Debra said he and Mollie had a fight, and he was already upset. Then I come in to tell him I'm leaving . . ." John drew a deep breath. "I should have seen. I should have—"

The ringing telephone cut him off. He snatched up the receiver.

It was Mollie. She was terrified. "He called me, John. Logan called, and he sounded crazy."

"Do you know where he is?"

"He said he was going to Devil's Point."

"Oh, damn." Another shower of sleet tapped on the windows. In weather like this, the road up the mountain could become impassable in a hurry. "I'm going to get him," John told Mollie.

"I have to go with you."

It was easier to agree with her than to argue. With Spring, as well. John got her to call the sheriff and ask for some help while he found some rope and tools in the old garage out behind her house.

They got Mollie and started up Potter's Mountain.

Logan's car was in a deep ditch about a mile from the bridge below Devil's Point.

He wasn't in it.

Face stinging from the windblown ice pellets, John crawled up the embankment to where Mollie and Spring were huddled together beside the car.

When he shook his head, Mollie began to cry.

Spring drew her close. "Stop it now. We've got to keep our heads."

"I guess he's hiked up the trail to the Point," John told her. He toed the pavement beneath his sneaker. "I think the road's doing better, actually. It feels like the temperature's gone up a little." Even the ice crystals in the air were turning to rain. "We can drive to the bridge, and I'll go up the trail."

She agreed, and they got back in the car. But even with road conditions improving, it took almost half an hour to inch their way to the bridge.

Carefully, John pulled off in the road near the

trail entrance. He told Spring to leave the engine running with a window cracked for ventilation, in case the temperature dropped again and ice blocked the exhaust pipe. She and Mollie were to keep a look out for the sheriff's car that was supposed to be following them up the mountain.

"Mollie can stay here," Spring insisted. "I'm coming with you, John."

"That's crazy. Mollie could need you."

"The police will be here soon, I know. She'll be fine. You might need my help on that trail."

She won in the end. With the rope and the tools in hand, they started for the trail.

But on the wind came a scream that stopped them in their tracks. It came from the bridge.

From Logan.

He was silhouetted against the cloudy night sky. Halfway up the steel spires above the bridge. He was screaming something. John didn't try to figure it out before he ran forward, shouting the boy's name. He slipped and fell and kept going, until he reached the railing and started to climb.

"Don't, John," Spring called as she stumbled and slid her way down the road behind him. "Wait for the sheriff."

John ignored her. Upward he climbed, from the railing to one slippery steel beam to another, until he was just below Logan. The boy was standing on a girder, hands clutching a thick suspension wire. John had no idea how he had managed to get there. They weren't really that high. If John fell, he would land on the bridge. Hurt, probably, but not dead. If Logan slipped, however, he would probably tumble into the river.

"Go away," Logan shouted at John.

"I can't." Carefully, John tied his rope to the girder just above his head. He reached out his hand. "Come on, Logan. This rope will keep us from falling."

"But I want to fall."

"Jesus, Logan. Your father isn't worth this. Don't give him this satisfaction."

"This isn't for him. It's for me." One hand slipped, and the boy's feet churned, fighting for a purchase on the slick girder.

Grabbing for him, John's breath hitched painfully in his chest.

Somehow, Logan grabbed hold of the wire again and held on.

"Come to me," John ordered, putting his hand out again. Below them, he could hear Mollie and Spring yelling. The falls were roaring. The white water was gushing over rocks. But all that mattered, all he cared about right now, was that Logan put out his hand.

"I'm sorry," he shouted to the boy. "I'm sorry I left you here with Sam. I thought he loved you. I never knew he'd hurt you."

He could see Logan squeeze his eyes shut, his chest heave beneath the thin flannel shirt that was frozen to his body.

"That thing I threw over the falls last weekend," Logan yelled. "It was a trophy Dad gave me once. When I was little. He said it was just for being his boy. I remember, because the very next month, when I blew a baseball game for my team, was the first time he beat me up."

"I know," John shouted. "I know what he was like. But it's not your fault, Logan. It wasn't my fault, either. We've got to show him up now. We've got to survive. Give me your hand."

"But you never struck back."

"What?"

"You said you never hit him back. I did."

John's feet slipped on the girder. He fell to his knees and wrapped his arms around the beam, his stiff, cold fingers clinging to one end of the rope.

"I hit him," Logan screamed. "The night he died, I hit him back. He was slapping me, you know, the way he did. But then he grabbed his chest and fell and I . . . I watched him die. That's how I hit him. I could have called for help before I did, but I didn't want to. I wanted him to die. I'm glad he's dead. But I'm sorry, too. And I just want to die, too."

Mute with horror, John stared up into Logan's wind- and cold-ravaged face. What could he say? What would ever make this go away for Logan? John understood, all too well, the boy's wish to throw himself off this bridge. He might not have struck back, but in his heart, thousands of times, he had wished Sam dead.

With all the strength he possessed, John shouted up to Logan, "I'm glad he's dead. He deserved to die. But you don't." Rising to his feet again, he tied the rope around his waist and flung out his hand. "Now grab hold of me. This minute."

He didn't know what changed Logan's mind, persuaded him against a swan dive into the river.

But Logan put out his hand. John grabbed hold.

Together, they climbed down.

But even on solid ground, John couldn't let go of him. He wouldn't ever let go of his brother again.

John did not let go. All the way to the hospital, in the back of the emergency van that arrived on the scene before he could attempt a drive off the mountain, John held Logan's hand.

He stayed with him at the hospital. When a nurse tried to tell him to leave, when a doctor ordered him out, John refused. He wouldn't budge.

Until Debra appeared.

He met her at the door of the treatment room, before she could get near Logan.

"You stay away," John shouted at her. "You get away, and you stay away."

The busy emergency-room activity ceased, everyone staring at the angry, bedraggled man wrapped in a blanket, facing off against Debra Nelson in her fur jacket.

She flung up her head, crimson in her cheeks. "He's my son. You have no right—"

"It's you who have no rights," John insisted. "You come near him and I'll break your neck."

For a long time after, the emergency-room staff talked about how she crumpled. She spun for a moment, like a rudderless sailboat, looking from face to face to face before she rushed out the doors.

Back in the treatment room, where Logan was being treated for exposure and shock, the boy looked up at John with tears in his eyes. "You're all right, you know. You're all right."

Chapter Nineteen

∾ Pure, golden light rimmed the mountains surrounding White's Creek. The dawn was as clear as the night had been stormy. The last trace of ice glittered in the bare, January trees. Like jewels, Spring thought. Gems sent to decorate the New Year.

Uncommonly moved by the beauty outdoors, Spring turned from the long hospital window where she stood. Across the waiting room, Mollie sprawled along a cushioned bench, sleeping. Spring had tried to rest as well, but she couldn't get comfortable. She had settled for gazing out the window and watching the world come to life.

She was glad she hadn't missed the first streaks of light on this first day of the year. This morning was a fresh slate, a turned page, possibilities unlimited.

Leaning her shoulder against the window again, Spring envisioned the new start she wanted. She prayed for the wisdom to make it happen. She thought of light. Crystalline, perfect light. Like this dawn. Like the message she had once glimpsed in a park far away.

"Daughter?" Her father's quiet voice roused her. She straightened, blinking, as Ned smiled. "You were sleeping standing up, girl."

"I wasn't asleep." Her yawn called that claim into question.

Ned laughed out loud and pressed a cup in her hand. "Here's some blackberry tea. Your mother thought you could use it."

"Mama's here?"

"She went in to see Logan."

Spring took a sip of the sweet, hot liquid. "Logan's going to be fine. Physically, at least." Over her father's shoulder, she spied Callie coming down the hall.

"Logan's resting well," the older woman said as she reached Spring's side. "His color's good. He's breathing even and deep."

"And how about John?"

"He's sleeping, too." Callie chuckled. "Sitting up in a chair."

Spring frowned. "I wish he would lie down. He didn't want to leave Logan for a minute last night." She recounted the scene between John and Debra that had taken place in the emergency room.

Ned sucked in his breath. "I know why John made her leave. I would have, too."

"But Logan is her son," Callie murmured. "I'm sure she loves him."

"Mama," Spring protested. "This is Debra we're talking about."

Born optimist that she was, Callie insisted, "There might be some good that comes from all of this. Some healing."

"I just want her to stay away." Spring sighed. "John and Logan both need her to stay away. Maybe without her, we can become a family."

Callie gave Spring an intent look. "How are you?"

Spring took her mother's hand, squeezing her fingers hard. "I'm good. Really, really good."

Callie's eyes widened. A smile bright as the daybreak lit her face. She touched Spring's cheek. "You're shining inside."

Laughing, Spring kissed Callie's cheek and hugged Ned before she headed down the hall.

In the small room Logan had been assigned in the middle of the night, John was, indeed, sleeping in a straight chair. Spring glanced at John, then studied his brother. Logan looked so very young, his blond hair tousled, roses in his cheeks. Gazing at him now, it was hard to believe what could have happened, what *would* have happened if they hadn't found him up on that mountain.

She tiptoed around the bed and touched John on his arm. He came awake with a jerk, mumbling his brother's name.

"It's okay," she whispered. "Logan's doing fine."

John stretched, rubbed a hand over his pale, lined features, and glanced up at her. He looked about as green as the medical scrubs the hospital staff had given both of them to wear in place of last night's wet clothes.

"You should get out of here for a minute," Spring told him.

He shook his head. "What are you still doing here?"

"You didn't think I could leave, did you?"

"But there's nothing you can do."

Logan moaned and shifted in his sleep. John came out of the chair like a shot, but the boy didn't waken.

"Come here," Spring murmured, taking John by the hand.

"I'm not leaving."

"Just over here." She tugged him toward the window.

In the morning sunlight that poured through the glass, she put her arms around him. This was what she had wanted to do ever since he and Logan had come off that bridge last night.

His hesitation was brief, then he held on to her. *Hard.*

"He could have died," John whispered against her hair. "He wanted to die."

Spring drew back and framed his face with her hands. "But Logan didn't die, John. You didn't let him."

"He needs a lot of help."

"He'll get it," she promised. *"We'll* make sure he gets exactly what he needs."

Her words made no impression at first. Then John took a ragged breath. "Spring?"

She pressed her lips to his. This was the beginning she had visualized as dawn broke over the mountains.

He drew out of her arms, questions brimming in his eyes.

"I'm here for you," she answered. "I want to be with you forever. On your terms."

"But Spring, I know what you want—"

"I don't want anything more than I want you. We've come through so much. We grew up together. We have magic together. How can we let that go?"

"I don't want to let you go," he said, fiercely. "But I want to be fair, Spring. I want you to have what you need. You say that's a child."

"I need you." The simple words said all she felt.

This knowledge had begun growing in her when she watched John struggle with Logan on that bridge. She had sorted out her emotions during a long night of soul-searching.

She explained them to John, "I've told you again and again that you can learn from your parents' mistakes. I've learned from them, too. Love like we've got doesn't come along very often. I'm not letting it go. I don't want to be a woman like your mother, who threw away what was most precious to her."

"You could never be like Debra." Bitterness darkened John's tone.

Spring lifted her hand to his cheek. "Who knows what I would become without you?"

"I'm not planning to let you find out." John put his arms around her again.

She laughed up at him, content as she hadn't been for a long, long time. "So when do we leave?" she asked.

"Leave?"

"Aren't we going home to Chicago?"

John shook his head. "I don't think so. This is home."

"You don't want to live in a town with your mother."

"And you don't want to live out of sight of these mountains."

"But John—"

He silenced her with a kiss.

In the open doorway, Callie smiled, delighted at the tender scene playing out between John and Spring.

Ned stepped up beside her, eyes widening. He leaned close and whispered, "Callie, did you put something in that tea?"

Her eyes twinkled. "I just sweetened it with prayer, my darlin'. Simple prayer."

Epilogue

～ The small silver car pulled away from the curb.

Hands in his pockets, John walked out into the street, watching the car. He resisted the urge to call out or motion for the driver to turn around.

The thought was no sooner in his head than the brake lights flashed on. Logan leaned out the driver's side window. He waved. One last time.

"See you soon," John called, despite the lump in his throat.

With a final salute, Logan drove away.

John watched until he turned the corner.

A long journey felt at an end.

It was late summer in White's Creek. The trees were full and heavy. Bees buzzed over the zinnias Callie had planted by the front walk. Over a year and a half had passed since that awful New Year's Eve up near Devil's Point. After getting his high-school diploma only a year late, Logan was going to college.

The help John had secured for his brother had gone a long way toward helping Logan heal. And going through that painful process with him, John had put to rest some demons of his own.

Sam Nelson was buried. Dead to him, completely.

Last month, on Decoration Day at the Methodist cemetery, John put flowers on his father's grave. Johnny Clayton's grave.

As for Debra, Logan had decided about this time last year that he wanted to see his mother on occasion. John stayed away. Debra had made that easier by moving to Gainesville a few months back. As she had explained to Logan, she liked being near her friends and the club, and she could run the businesses Sam had left her just as well from there. Logan seemed able to accept Debra for what she was. John had just let it go. Let her go.

Debra's shortcomings no longer mattered. John had a full life. A real family. A book on the best-seller lists. A newly remodeled home on this quiet, tree-shaded street.

He gazed with satisfaction at the freshly painted white cottage. The sunlight glinted off the windows of the attic study and master bedroom that Ned had helped John complete last fall.

From the deep front porch, Spring called out, "Are you sure you don't want to chase Logan's car to the city limits?"

John came slowly up the front walk and joined her. "Logan will be okay. He knows we're here. He has his head together."

"And Mollie's waiting for him at school. She left yesterday."

Logan and Mollie were close. But just friends now. John guessed not every first love worked out the way his and Spring's had.

Spring gazed at him in concern. "You sure you're okay? You look pretty sad."

"I'm going to miss having him around all the time. That hit me when we were loading his stuff." Secretly, he had been dreading this day for months. He had learned a lot from Logan.

"The house will seem empty. And quieter."

As if to dispute her claim, a cry erupted from the stroller at her side.

John laughed and bent to comfort their daughter. April was five months old, and she looked just like her mother and Callie. Black hair and silver-blue eyes. And a temper like nothing else.

"Now, now," he murmured, stroking her cheek. But she continued to cry.

"She wants you to pick her up," Spring said. "You've spoiled her rotten. You and Logan pick her up every time she whimpers."

"We do not."

Basil slunk over from the patch of sunlight where he had been sunbathing and lifted his paws to the side of the stroller. He looked from the crying child to John and back again, tail twitching.

Obliging that silent feline command, John rescued April. Her tears dried instantly, replaced by a wide, drooling smile.

Basil meowed and rubbed his face against John's leg.

Spring chuckled. "Who would have guessed you'd be such a doting daddy?"

He had taken to the role in ways he had certainly never expected. Helping Logan made the difference in John's feelings about having a child. The experience had given John true insight into what it took to support and care for someone else.

Debra and Sam had taught him everything not to do. Spring and Logan had showed him what he could do. By the time Spring became pregnant, he had been eager for this new adventure.

April had come into the world on a day late in the month for which they had named her. When the daisies were beginning to bloom out at the farm.

Holding her for the first time, John had known he would do anything it took to keep her well, happy, and safe. He supposed that was why he couldn't stand to hear her cry, even for a minute. Too soon, she would be walking, moving away, driving away as Logan had just done.

Spring put her arms around him and April. She had read his thoughts. "Logan's going to do just great. Stop worrying."

"I do know he'll be fine. Callie said so."

"And Mama's never wrong," Spring said.

April gurgled her agreement. As the only girl of her generation in Callie's family, she had exceptional powers of communication and comprehension, even at five months old.

"Let's go for a walk," Spring suggested. "It's a beautiful morning."

"Like most mornings with you."

She kissed him, then reached for the stroller. But John stopped her. "I'll carry April."

"She's getting pretty heavy."

"I don't mind."

Spring smiled and tucked her hand in the crook of his elbow as they set off down the street.

The next-door neighbors waved and came out to chat.

Mollie's brother, Larry, drove by and stopped to tell Spring all about his new girlfriend.

Around the corner, Willa Dean was sweeping her clean front porch, but she paused long enough to comment on the weather and offer a few tidbits of news. Dan Strickland was leaving for a big job in the state education department. Ebbie had told everyone she was retiring. And a Burger King was going in next to McDonald's.

It was another slow day in White's Creek.

And it suited John just fine.

Discover Contemporary Romances
at Their Sizzling Hot Best
from Avon Books

Avon Romances—
the best in exceptional authors
and unforgettable novels!

Avon Romantic Treasures

*Unforgettable, enthralling love stories,
sparkling with passion and adventure
from Romance's bestselling authors*

LADY OF WINTER *by Emma Merritt*
77985-4/$5.99 US/$7.99 Can

SILVER MOON SONG *by Genell Dellin*
78602-8/$5.99 US/$7.99 Can

FIRE HAWK'S BRIDE *by Judith E. French*
78745-8/$5.99 US/$7.99 Can

WANTED ACROSS TIME *by Eugenia Riley*
78909-4/$5.99 US/$7.99 Can

EVERYTHING AND THE MOON *by Julia Quinn*
78933-7/$5.99 US/$7.99 Can

BEAST *by Judith Ivory*
78644-3/$5.99 US/$7.99 Can

HIS FORBIDDEN TOUCH *by Shelley Thacker*
78120-4/$5.99 US/$7.99 Can

LYON'S GIFT *by Tanya Anne Crosby*
78571-4/$5.99 US/$7.99 Can

Buy these books at your local bookstore or use this coupon for ordering:

Mail to: Avon Books, Dept BP, Box 767, Rte 2, Dresden, TN 38225   F
Please send me the book(s) I have checked above.
My check or money order—no cash or CODs please—for $_____ is enclosed (please
add $1.50 per order to cover postage and handling—Canadian residents add 7% GST).
Charge my VISA/MC Acct#_____Exp Date_____
Minimum credit card order is two books or $7.50 (please add postage and handling
charge of $1.50 per order—Canadian residents add 7% GST). For faster service, call
1-800-762-0779. Prices and numbers are subject to change without notice. Please allow six to
eight weeks for delivery.

Name_____
Address_____
City_____State/Zip_____
Telephone No._____   RT 0397